Black Venom

Black Venom

Waves of Darkness Book 4

Tamara A. Lowery

Steele Rose Publishing

Black Venom

By

Tamara A. Lowery

1st Edition, Gypsy Shadow Publishing, November 2014 eBook, February 2015 print

2nd Edition, Tamara A. Lowery DBA Steele Rose Publishing, 2023

talowery.wordpress.com

Published in the United States of America

ISBN eBook 978-1-956849-07-3

ISBN print 978-1-956849-06-6

Black Venom

Table of Contents

Foreword, Acknowledgements, and Warnings________________vii

Dedication____ix

Once Upon a Tide…___________________________________1

Chapter 1____11

Chapter 2____25

Chapter 3____37

Chapter 4____61

Chapter 5____77

Chapter 6____91

Chapter 7____105

Chapter 8____121

Chapter 9____125

Chapter 10____129

Chapter 11____139

Chapter 12____143

Chapter 13____151

Chapter 14____157

Chapter 15____161

Chapter 16____167

Chapter 17____179

Chapter 18____187

Chapter 19 _______________________________________ 195

Chapter 20 _______________________________________ 199

Chapter 21 _______________________________________ 213

Chapter 22 _______________________________________ 219

Chapter 23 _______________________________________ 225

Chapter 24 _______________________________________ 231

Chapter 25 _______________________________________ 235

Chapter 26 _______________________________________ 243

Chapter 27 _______________________________________ 247

Chapter 28 _______________________________________ 255

Chapter 29 _______________________________________ 263

Chapter 30 _______________________________________ 273

Chapter 31 _______________________________________ 281

Chapter 32 _______________________________________ 287

Here Be Spoilers _______________________________________ 299

About the Author _______________________________________ 305

Foreword, Acknowledgements, and Warnings

Ahoy! Welcome back returning readers and welcome aboard new readers. When this book originally saw publication in 2014, I instigated a tradition of red-shirting in my stories. For those of you familiar with Star Trek: The Original Series and its fandom, you will recognize the term outside of the more common sports-related slang. A red shirt is a member of the away team who is almost certainly doomed to a horrible death in the TV show. In books, it means a character named for a real person is given a usually horrific literary death.

My first ever red shirts were Matthew Barnett, William Higgenbotham (aka Higgens), and Lisa M. A. Winters. Barnett was a coworker at the time and is now a supervisor. He also has the notoriety of being the only person I've red-shirted twice. He griped that I didn't give him a sex scene before I killed his character, so I will bring him back as a name-sake relative, give him his requested sex scene, and kill him again in Hunting the Dragon: Waves of Darkness Book 8, due for release in May 2025. Higgens was a coworker but is no longer with my employer. Ms. Winters was a contest winner whose name was drawn at Chattacon in January

2014, a literary SFF convention held every January in Chattanooga, TN. Her name was applied to a male character for the story's sake.

As stated in this segment in Silent Fathoms: Waves of Darkness Book 3, I am including synopses of all previous books in the series as part of the after matter I'm titling Here Be Spoilers. This is after seeing a reasonable complaint from a BookTuber I follow, Petrik Leo, about how many fantasy series do not include such a feature. The purpose of this is to allow returning readers a means of refreshing their memories of story events without having to re-read the books before stating on the latest one. This is especially useful for more voracious readers who follow several series at the same time.

Now for the usual warnings. My pirates are not nice people. Vampires are, by definition, serial killers. This book contains extreme graphic violence and implied violence. Slave trade is mentioned. For the phobic, there are multitudinous poisonous creatures including spiders, bees, wasps, scorpions, snakes, poison dart frogs, and jellyfish.

You have been warned.

Dedication

For Kim Canalli for her support and friendship— and free coffee.

Tamara A. Lowery

Once Upon a Tide...

Midsummer of 1761 found Vik Brandee and Hezekiah Grimm in a small ketch just off the southwest shore of Puerto Rico. They planned to wait for darkness before going ashore to meet their contact, which also involved a trek into the jungle. Meanwhile, they did their best to appear to be fishermen.

Vik showed Grimm how to use a cast net. "I can't believe you've never done this before, Hezekiah. You've been at sea longer than I have."

"Never had to, Vik." Grimm held the net like he'd been shown, or so he thought. "Usually had enough supplies to last the voyage. In port, I always had enough coin to get a good meal or found some wench willing to feed me for free."

"You have to hold the top edge in your mouth to keep it stretched out." Vik put his own net's edge in his mouth to show his second mate how. He held one side of the net in each hand with the draw rope's end wrapped around his wrist. Once he saw Grimm held the net correctly, he twisted to the side then snapped back the other way, releasing the net at the apex of the swing. The cast net spun out over the water in an almost perfect disc before it hit the surface. The stone weights around the edge quickly drew it under. He let it sink until the rope had no more slack, then gave a quick jerk on the rope to close the net before drawing it back up.

Grimm did his best to mimic his captain's cast. He felt gratified to see his own net sail out across the water in much the same fashion.

"Not bad. With some practice, you could be very good at this." Vik praised the older man.

"How did you learn to do this? More importantly, why?"

Vik lifted his net up onto the boat. There were only a couple of fish in it, neither an edible species. "Hmph, good thing we're not fishing for profit or food right now," he grunted in disgust. "I grew up in the salt marshes near Savannah. Learned how to cast a net as soon as I was big enough to hold one. Mother Celie's not a rich woman, and it's often cheaper and easier to catch fish or shrimp than to buy food."

"That makes sense. I grew up inland, but I took to the sea as soon as I saw her." Grimm began to pull his own net up. He gave a startled cry when the draw rope went taut and began to jerk from side to side. "Whoa! I've got a fighter, Vik! Strong one, too."

"Need some help?"

He shook his head. "No, I think I can handle it. It just caught me by surprise."

He wrestled with the net's draw rope. Slowly, he managed to bring up the net and whatever he had caught to the surface. Both men marveled at the large ray which thrashed about in the cast net.

Vik whistled. "No wonder you had such a fight. Look at the wingspan on that thing!"

The ray nearly filled the bottom of their ketch. It thrashed about wildly, which made removing the net somewhat difficult. The boat rocked so violently, it threatened to capsize.

"I think we're going to have to cut the net, Captain."

"Agreed; we need to get this thing off the boat before it sinks us."

Black Venom

Both men drew their knives and began to hack at the mesh of the net in an effort to free the ray. The terrified creature only knew it had to return to the water. The longer it remained in the air, the more frantic its thrashing became. Suffocating in the alien environment, it was a victim of instinct and panic.

Viktor let out a garbled scream when the ray's barbed sting stabbed through the muscle of his calf. Grimm reacted quickly and slashed down with his heavy knife to sever the barb from the animal.

The shock of the maiming caused the ray to seize up. This allowed Grimm enough time to lever it back over the side.

The boat gradually settled in the calm water. Grimm knelt to examine the damage his captain suffered. The spiny barb stuck out from both sides of the wound lodged in the muscle. Luckily, the bleeding didn't look too bad yet.

Vik sat covered in clammy sweat as shock threatened to make him pass out. Grimm stopped him when he reached for the severed end of the sting and shook his head. "We need to push it through, Vik. If you try to pull it out that way, the barbs will shred the flesh and poison you. Plus, it would hurt more."

"It can't hurt much more than this," Vik growled. "Do what you have to, Mr. Grimm."

Grimm wrapped some sailcloth around the barbed end to protect his hands. He grasped the sting firmly and yanked it on through the wound. This time, Viktor did pass out.

The young pirate woke not long after sunset. Pain like a firebrand raged in his leg. He looked down at it in the lamplight and saw the limb already swollen to twice its natural girth from knee to ankle.

Grimm noticed he'd awakened and handed him a flask of rum. "Here, this should help deaden the leg a bit. I cleaned it out as best I could before stitching it up."

Vik took the bottle and frowned at the lightness of it. "We brought more rum than this."

"Aye. Figured the rum was better than seawater for that leg. Didn't look like any of the stinger broke off in ye, so it should heal clean."

"Thank you, Hezekiah. I'd hate to lose the limb. I'm rather attached to it," he said in an attempt to joke around the pain. "Where are we?"

"A couple of leagues up the river. We still have a half hour before the rendezvous. Do you think you'll be able to stand up for it, Captain?"

"I'm going to have to. Carmine is not to be trusted; especially if he thinks we are weak."

Grimm nodded his understanding. He'd never dealt with the man personally, but Carmine Fuentez had a reputation as someone who wouldn't hesitate to sell a man out, if there was a profit in it. He also had a reputation as a coward. If he thought a deal might come back to bite him, he would avoid it like the plague.

"Remind me again why we are even dealing with this bilge rat."

"Because he can get what we want more quickly than we can," Vik answered. "And he knows not to cross me."

Grimm laughed. "You can be a scary bastard. I'm surprised you didn't bring Rigger along."

"Couldn't; not and hope to seal the deal, anyway. Jim almost killed Carmine the last time we had dealings. Hell, I couldn't even tell him who we were dealing with this time."

"What did the rat do to anger the lad so?"

"I wasn't in the room at the time, and Jim won't talk about it. The hatred is strong enough that my first mate resents the very fact that Carmine still draws breath."

Grimm grunted. "Must have been pretty bad."

"Indeed."

After they grounded the ketch in a side shallow, Grimm helped Viktor out of the boat. The swelling in his leg had gone down some, but it still hurt and burned. They both agreed they needed to conclude their business quickly. The shadows would help hide the swelling.

Carmine had a large bonfire going. It burned so brightly; it blinded them to the dark jungle which surrounded them. This put both pirates immediately on the alert. For a man who didn't like to draw attention, Carmine seemed to be doing his best to be found by anyone curious about the blaze.

"Stay sharp, Mr. Grimm. This doesn't feel right."

"Aye, Captain, it doesn't."

Their contact soon showed himself along with a couple of burly men, presumably his bodyguards. "I see you didn't bring that brat with you this time."

Vik kept his voice and face neutral. "Considering how well you two get along, I thought it best."

"Who is this?" Carmine pointed at Grimm.

"My second mate."

The smuggler persisted. "I thought as much, Brandee, but I'd like to know his name. I want to know the people I'm dealing with."

"Will it make this deal go more quickly?" Vik sighed. Grimm noted his captain attempting to hide his growing irritation. Carmine was stalling, which was not a good sign. It meant either he didn't have the item, or this was a trap.

"It will."

"Fine. Carmine Fuentez, meet Hezekiah Grimm."

The smuggler visibly paled. "The Grimm Reaper. I'd heard rumors he was sailing with you."

It came as no surprise that Grimm's reputation frightened the smuggler more than Viktor's did. The second mate had been pirating longer than the pirate captain. Plus, Hezekiah was nearly thirty, an age few pirates lived to see, whereas Viktor was only twenty-two.

The information made Carmine nervous enough to spring his trap prematurely. "They're here! Take them now!"

Vik and Grimm immediately bolted for the darkness of the jungle. They'd purposely hung back from the fire, just in case something like this happened. Much cursing followed them as their would-be captors changed course to pursue them. The two pirates knew they'd been lucky to pick a spot that hadn't been closed in yet, but they also knew their luck might not hold out.

"Split!" Vik ordered as they ran. Grimm veered off away from him.

Black Venom

The younger pirate's luck soon ran out, however. His wounded leg betrayed him; some of the stitches popped loose, and the wound tore wider due to his exertion. The leg collapsed under him. His pursuers were on him in seconds and tossed a snare net over him to prevent him from fighting back.

One of them cudgeled him, and he lost consciousness.

Grimm managed to elude the hunters chasing him. Only two followed him. The rest went after Brandee. He knew when they captured his captain. He heard the shout of the young man's pursuers.

Once sure his own pursuers left off the chase, he circled back to the meeting point and hid in the shadows. He did this for two reasons: One, Vik Brandee had more than earned his loyalty. Even though younger than him by several years, Brandee proved the best pirate captain Grimm ever served under. Two, the hunters probably had someone watching their boat in the hopes of catching him as well. It's what he would do in their situation.

Grimm kept his guard up to ensure no one crept up on him, and watched the encampment. Six men accompanied Carmine. Clearly, he'd underestimated the two pirates. If not for Brandee's injury, they wouldn't have caught him. Grimm listened to the pirate hunters and quickly formed a plan.

Grimm had been right. They'd left one man to watch the ketch. Grimm slipped into the water several yards upstream from the boat. He blackened his face with river mud so he wouldn't be easily seen in the water. Just as he figured, the guard watched the jungle, not the river. He climbed into the boat silently and crept toward the man.

The hapless pirate hunter never even saw the blade that slit his throat.

Grimm stripped the body of weapons and valuables, then hid to the side of the path. "Hurry!" he shouted. "I've got him!"

Soon, two more hunters ran crashing through the jungle. They stopped short at the sight of their partner's body. It was all the distraction Grimm needed. He skewered one and shot the other in the head before either could react. He quickly retreated to the shadows and made his way back to the encampment. He knew the gunshot would draw the others.

Once he returned to the campfire, where they held Vik, he saw all but Carmine gone to help at the boat. He also saw Vik's eyes glitter between his lashes as he feigned unconsciousness. His captain's captors had made the mistake of tying his hands in front of him.

Carmine smiled down cruelly at his captive. He muttered to himself as he grabbed Vik's trousers by the waistband and pulled them to his knees. "I'd hoped for a shot at that whelp you call first mate, but you're still young enough and pretty enough to suit my tastes."

He dropped his own trou and started working himself erect, his attention focused solely on his victim's ass.

Slowly enough to not draw attention, Vik eased his hands up to his head. He managed to slip out the knife he always kept at the nape of his neck, hidden under his hair, unnoticed.

Grimm deliberately entered the clearing on the other side of his captain from their betrayer.

"Carmine."

The fool still thought Vik was out of it and started to step over him. He began to raise his weapon, but never got it leveled. Brandee stabbed upward and caught him in the inner thigh close to the groin. Carmine let out a strangled scream when Brandee twisted the blade to slice open the femoral artery.

Grimm moved quickly to them and kicked the weapon out of the dying man's hand. He then buried his own blade under Carmine's ribs.

The traitorous smuggler collapsed. Blood burbled from his mouth and nose and spurted from his leg—in time with his slowing heartbeat. As the flow slowed, his eyes glazed. Within minutes, he lay dead.

Meanwhile, Grimm helped his captain get free of his bonds. Brandee quickly pulled his trousers back up but had trouble standing. The bandages on his wound looked dark, soaked through with fresh blood from the torn stitches.

"Do you think you can walk?"

"Aye. It hurts, but it still works. I just won't be able to run or move fast," Vik replied. "We need to get into the jungle before they come back."

Grimm nodded. "There are only four left. I killed three by the boat."

"I like those odds."

By morning, the remaining hunters lay dead and unburied. The two pirates sailed their ketch, making plans to acquire what they'd thought to get from Carmine. It ended up costing much less, since they found a place to just steal it.

The real hold up on their return to the ship was finding a decent physician to treat Vik's leg wound. The infection reached the point that Vik feared he might lose the leg after all.

Grimm didn't really trust physicians in general. He'd seen too many good sailors butchered by them.

Only three days from the nearest port, the fever took Viktor. Grimm knew his captain's life hung in the balance, but he had favorable winds to speed them to the one person who might be able to save both Vik's leg and his life.

Mother Celie always seemed to know when her adopted son would visit. Grimm wasn't a superstitious man, but even he had to admit there was something uncanny about the old woman who'd raised Vik Brandee.

"You got him here just in time, Hezekiah." She frowned at Vik's swollen leg as she spoke. "Now shoo. Go swap lies with old Billy Black. This boy is going to need a month to heal enough to travel again."

He obeyed but made a point to come check on his captain's progress every day. Finally, the old swamp witch declared the boy healthy, she was sick of the sight of both of them, and wanted them out of her hut.

They eventually made it back to their ship. As agreed, Grimm never discussed where they had been or what had happened; nor did Viktor.

Chapter 1

Fourteen years later, the *Incubus* lay in port at Havana. They'd come in the night before and started taking on supplies at first light. Mr. Grimm used his connections in the port to speed the process up and get a good deal.

Viktor felt grateful that his last encounter with Hells Breath Island and Uncle Zeke resulted in the mysterious, travelling island depositing the ship back in the Caribbean. Hell's Breath manifested shortly after Vik finished dealing with *Tia* Rosalia, the third Sister of Power he'd found, on the Pacific coast of Mexico. The encounter saved the pirate considerable time travelling around South America. He very much appreciated anything that expedited his quest for the Sisters. Although no one seemed able to tell him how much time he had left, he knew he must find all seven Sisters before the curse which made him a living vampire overwhelmed and destroyed him.

What he didn't appreciate was getting saddled with finding a home for his son. Zeke gave him the option of taking the boy to Mother Celie, Viktor's own foster mother, or to Granny Gloribeau, the second Sister he'd found and the only one that hadn't tried to kill or enslave him. Viktor had to admit they were the only ones powerful enough to manage the child's wild magic, let alone someone he trusted enough to hand the boy over to.

Viktor went into the port with Jon-Jon to hunt. The giant second mate proved useful for getting the victims back to the ship quickly and quietly. Vik would have preferred the siren aid him in the hunt, but she insisted on remaining aboard.

Belladonna was entirely too obsessed with his son for his liking. The toddler was a new hybrid he had got on a mermaid named Alyssa. Unlike other mers, the boy could take human form, much like a siren. He also had his father's raven black hair and green eyes, which made him unique among the fair-haired merfolk.

Belle refused to leave the ship or let the boy out of her sight. Vik didn't worry she might eat the boy, even though the merfolk were the siren's favorite food above human or shark. If she did, it would enslave her even more to the vampire. That fear, however, was not what kept his son off her menu. The child's latent magic had bewitched the siren. His mother was dead, and he wanted a new one. Any female who came in contact with him would fall in love with him until he found the one he wanted, unless she was powerful enough to override his spell.

Viktor met up with Grimm at the Crescent Inn. His first mate and Manuel, the owner of the establishment, awaited him at his regular table. A bottle of the Crescent's finest rum and four glasses sat on the table between them. Both pirates knew the Crescent was a safe haven, as well as the best source for information in Havana.

The innkeeper looked tired and old, a dramatic change from the last time they'd seen him, somewhere around a year previously. The Crescent seemed much less busy than usual.

"You look worried, old friend," Vik observed as he sat down.

"*Si*," Manuel confirmed. He glanced around furtively before he spoke further, an action which instantly put both pirates on alert.

"Things are going *mal* here. There are eyes and ears that do not belong. People are afraid. A few have disappeared. It is very bad for business. The Governor has even stopped using Valarie's services."

Vik frowned. "This sounds serious. What happened to cause this misfortune?"

Manuel spoke low to avoid being overheard. "There is a new pirate hunter in these waters. He is British Navy, and he hunts Viktor Brandewyne. If you see the *Capitan*, warn him to avoid Havana. The port is being watched." They noted that he carefully had avoided identifying Vik. It told them he suspected a spy among the other patrons present.

"Captain Brandee has never feared a pirate hunter, especially a British one," Grimm scoffed.

"This pirate hunter is different, and he claims to have the sister to Brandee's ship."

Vik pushed back from the table and nodded at Grimm to do the same. As he stood, he placed a pouch of coins on the table. The pouch quickly disappeared into Manuel's apron. "*Gracias, amigo.* We would stay longer, but my cargo has to be delivered before it spoils. If we see Captain Brandewyne, we'll pass the news along," Vik thanked him.

"Aye," Grimm added, "and we'll keep an eye out for this pirate hunter. Do you have a name for him?"

Manuel nodded. "*Si,* his name is Commodore Critchfield."

The two pirates made straight for the dock, but they did not hurry. Both knew that sneaking, circuitous routes after Viktor's declaration of needing to deliver cargo would draw the very kind of attention they wished to avoid; so would rushing back to the ship.

Only someone who knew them well would have recognized their subtle, silent communication and vigilance. Each knew the other's signals and what they meant. They'd spotted the man who slipped out of the Crescent after them. He wasn't nearly as subtle as he thought himself.

As they strolled along, they made conversation as if nothing was amiss. "Expected Mr. Jon to come with you," Grimm commented.

"I sent him on ahead with the new recruits."

"How many? I want to make sure we took on enough supplies."

"Twenty."

Grimm grunted. "May need to get some more rations. Why so many?"

"I don't want to impose on Jeorge. I don't plan on being there any longer than it takes to make my delivery to Glory."

His first mate nodded then turned aside to an alley. "I'll catch up in a bit. Need to hit the head." He flipped Vik a little salute, letting him know it was time to take out their shadow.

As Grimm stepped into the alley, Viktor continued on toward the docks. The man who had followed them from the Crescent Inn had to make a choice of which one to follow.

The shadow continued to follow Viktor, possibly to discover what ship he was on. It meant the man left his back open to Grimm. Vik thought the hunter felt sure he would blend in with the rest of the foot traffic on the streets. He obviously was unaware that the two pirates knew they were being followed.

Black Venom

Grimm made a show of relieving himself, partially hidden by some barrels. What he really held in his hand was his long knife. The act was in case the interloper glanced at him in passing or if he should come down the alley.

He saw the man go by. After counting to ten, he exited the alley and made his way through the crowd. He saw Viktor stop and look over some produce on a vendor's cart.

Grimm didn't give the man time to try to melt into the background. He draped one arm around his target's shoulders and pressed the point of his knife into his ribs, just enough to get his attention.

"There you are." He grinned as if he'd met an old friend. "We'd been wondering where you'd gotten to, man. Captain, look who decided to join us."

Viktor turned glowing emerald eyes to their new captive. He smiled. "Thank you for joining us, sir. Please, accompany us back to our ship. I've some fine brandy in my cabin. We can discuss business."

"I'd be glad to," the man choked out.

Back aboard the *Incubus*, they took their captive to Viktor's cabin. Jon-Jon already had his "recruits" locked in the special larder hold. Including the captain, the crew boasted seven vampires, which made it necessary to keep blood stock on hand. To stretch the supply of blood out over long voyages, they bled their victims into casks to create a 50/50 mixture of blood and rum or whatever spirits were available. The alcohol kept the blood from congealing.

"Mr. Grimm, have Mr. Jon and Mr. Murph start processing the blood stock for my cadre." Viktor's order tacitly dismissed his first mate and clued their captive in on who he was dealing with. For pure malice, the vampire released his hold on the man's will.

"Mr. Grimm?" The man blanched. "If he's the Grimm Reaper, then you must be—."

"Viktor Brandewyne, at your service." He gave a mock bow. "Oh, and Mr. Grimm?"

"Aye, Captain?"

"If the supplies are laden in, tell Mr. Bland to have the lads cast off and make sail."

"Aye." Grimm left to carry out his orders, chuckling at the look of horror on their prisoner's face.

To his credit, the man hadn't soiled himself at the revelation of who his captors were. Still, he reeked of fear and sour sweat. "What are you going to do with me, Captain Brandewyne?"

"You show some respect. I like that." Vik nodded his approval. "First, I am going to ask your name, sir."

"Cabrio Ortez."

"Would you like some brandy?" He continued to treat the man more like a guest than a prisoner.

Rather than calm Cabrio, this treatment made him even more nervous. Stories about Bloody Vik Brandee made it well known that the pirate was at his deadliest when he was calm and polite.

"*Si, gracias*." He took the glass with a shaky hand unwilling to provoke his captor. He took a sip and said, "This is a fine vintage. You honor me."

Viktor watched his prey carefully. The man was terrified of him. The brandy only dulled the fear a little. He'd thought he might have to take the man's will again if he wanted straight answers out of him.

He'd try asking, first. "Why were you following us?"

Cabrio feigned surprise. "I wasn't following you, Captain Brandewyne."

Viktor stared at him, still not using his powers. "Really."

The pirate's tone of voice garnered the desired effect. The captive took a gulp of the brandy and coughed from the after burn. His eyes darted around the cabin nervously. Viktor could see he was foolishly going to try for the door, and he was going to let him.

To unknowing eyes, Viktor appeared to be unarmed. Tales about the throwing knife kept in a sheath at the nape of his neck did not exist. The only people who'd witnessed that knife in use were dead, part of the crew, or afraid to even whisper about it.

It wasn't Vik's plan to use the blade, however. Instead, he used his speed to place himself between his prey and the door a split second before he could reach it.

Cabrio stumbled backward and fell to the deck in shock.

"I will ask again." Viktor loomed over him. "Why were you following us?"

"I did not know who you were, I swear," Cabrio stammered. "I only overheard you talking about the hunter looking for you. A generous reward has been offered just for information about Bloody Vik Brandee. You sounded like you had some."

The vampire laughed, genuinely amused. The sight of his fangs sent a shock of terror through the prisoner.

"You were right, man. I do have information, more than anyone else in the world, as a matter of fact, about Bloody Vik Brandee. The most important bit at the moment is that he's very Hungry."

The man's scream could be heard through half the ship.

Jon-Jon got an unpleasant greeting from Belladonna when he knocked at her cabin door. "What do you want?" She hissed and added, "Keep your voice low. The baby is sleeping."

"Cap'n said to bring this down to you." He got right to the point and hooked a thumb toward the headless body he'd laid at her door.

The siren barely glanced at the offering. "I'm not hungry. Go away." Before he could say anything further, she shut the door. He heard the bolt slide into place.

"Fine, be that way." He hefted the body onto his shoulder and headed topside to throw it overboard.

Needless to say, the second mate's report both irritated and worried Viktor. He hoped Belladonna wouldn't hinder their progress with foul weather or becalm the ship.

He really needed to get his son to a safe haven away from her as soon as possible. He needed to start his hunt for the next Sister of Power, which meant he needed Belladonna undistracted. Without her visions, he might as well sail around aimlessly with no hope of surviving his curse.

The relatively short voyage to New Orleans passed without incident, something Viktor felt grateful for. Gloribeau had been the second of the three Sisters of Power he'd found so far in his quest to free himself from the curse that had made him a living vampire. He still had three more to find. The seventh Sister was the one who'd cursed him.

Considering the nature of the Sisters of Power, he knew dealing with Glory would be time-consuming. A price, usually some task or side quest, had to be met to gain their cooperation, and he was about to ask her to take on his son as ward.

He decided to give the crew shore leave. As far as he knew, New Orleans was still a safe port.

He set out for Angel and Celine's along with Grimm, Jon-Jon, Zach Brumble, Belladonna, and the child. Viktor figured Celine was the best connection for arranging a meeting with Glory. He sincerely hoped the Sister would not make herself difficult to reach. He knew better than to enter her bayous unbidden.

Angelique nearly knocked him down, running to him, when they entered Celine Thibideaux' street-level shop in the Quarter. The rooms above it made up the brothel the two women ran.

"Viktor!" The blonde madam hugged him fiercely then stepped back and slapped him hard. "You bastard! Every night you torment me with dreams, yet you wait months to return to me!"

Celine remained a little more reserved, although she aimed a condescending smirk at her business partner. Just a little over a year previously, they had been bitter rivals in the sex trade of New Orleans. Their partnership was born of a deal Viktor had made with Jeorge, leader of the city's vampires, to guarantee their protection.

As his link to Gloribeau, he needed Celine safe. The living vampire had fed on the older woman, Angelique, effectively making her his slave. When she died, she would become one of his vampires unless someone beheaded her body or cut out her heart.

The Creole madam felt grateful she would not suffer such a fate. Her service to Gloribeau made her life blood sacrosanct. She knew Viktor would not risk angering the Sister of Power.

"She has been going on and on about your return, Captain Brandewyne, for over a month," Celine said. "Please, take her upstairs and fuck her so she will stop driving me insane!"

Grimm raised an eyebrow and smirked, while Viktor willed Angel to be still and silent. She still managed a small whimper and watched her master with pleading eyes.

The first mate asked, "Is the partnership not working out, lass?"

"Oh, business has been very profitable," Celine answered. "But for weeks now, she has been moping for the Captain. It has affected her performance, and her exclusive customers have started to notice. I do not want to lose their business."

"Speaking of business," Viktor said, getting right to the point, "I need to arrange a meeting with Gloribeau."

She only took a moment to process his abrupt request. She quickly capitalized on it. "If you will deal with Angel's needs, I will see what I can do. She is not expecting you, or, at least, has not sent me word. Why do you need to see her?"

"Belle."

Reluctantly, the siren stepped forward carrying a blanket-wrapped bundle. The uncharacteristic behavior caught Celine's attention more than the bundle, until it moved.

"What is that?"

"My son," Viktor answered.

She immediately clutched the talisman she kept in her pocket and eyed the siren warily. "By you?"

Belladonna shook her head. "No, his mother was a mermaid." She turned to the vampire and pled, "Viktor, please, don't do this! Let me keep him. I can protect him. I know I can."

Celine backed away. "She's bewitched." Her voice held both fear and awe. "How did I not sense his power when you brought him in?"

The siren gently brushed a strand of hair from the toddler's face. "He's asleep now. Don't wake him."

"Yes, don't," Vik agreed. "He is why I need to see Glory. He wants a mother, and her power is probably the only thing potent enough to manage him. I cannot keep him with me. A ship is no place for a small child. He can't stay here, either. It is too close to the sea, and I'd wager all of your girls would fall in love with him."

Celine smiled doubtfully. "There is nothing wrong with love, Captain Brandee."

"You say that now. If I am a distraction to Angel, my son would be even more so to every female here. Think about it, Madam Thibideaux. He is powerful enough to make a siren besotted with him. Her natural instinct should be to feed on him, not nurture him. The merfolk are her favorite prey."

She absorbed that information. Finally, she responded. "I shall send Timon to the rendezvous point with a message for Gloribeau. Be aware, she will answer when she sees fit, if ever. In the meantime, you can all go up. Penelope will get you settled in and find a place to keep the child for now."

Viktor bowed and kissed her hand, which raised a rare blush to her cheeks. "*Merci beaucoup,* Celine. I shall see to it that Angelique is sufficiently sated to resume servicing her customers without distraction. And who knows, perhaps you could use some attention as well?" The last was added with a leer.

"Ha! You are a temptation, but I must stay here to tend my shop for now."

Grimm had to ask. "What happened to René?"

Her face darkened a bit. "After he recovered, he refused to run any more errands for Gloribeau. He wouldn't even touch any of my girls for several weeks. About four months ago, he put out to sea."

"Hmph." He grunted, as Vik took Angel toward the back stairs. "He chose a hard life. Jon-Jon, why don't you take Mr. Brumble and fetch us some beignets? I want some food before wenching, and I need to get Belladonna and the boy settled in before he wakes up."

"Did you say Brumble?" The madam stopped them before they could get out the door.

Zach nodded. "Yes, my name is Zachary Brumble."

"Do you have a brother named Thomas?"

"Yes." He was on his guard now. Her tone boded ill.

"Do not use your name in this port, *m'sieur*. It will only bring trouble to you and to my house. The Lord Mayor has offered a large reward for information or capture of the man he believes to be Thomas Brumble."

"Why?"

"He thought his daughter had eloped with him, but he has not had word from her since her disappearance last year. Nor does the father of her kidnapper admit any knowledge of her or the trade agreement used to gain entry to the mayoral manor."

Jon-Jon saw the color rise in Zach's face and laid a hand on the man's shoulder. "The Cap'n did what he had to do. Now come along. I'll tell you about it when we get back from Marie's with the beignets. Wouldn't be wise to discuss it in public."

Zach didn't look happy about it, but he held his tongue and left with the second mate.

Chapter 2

That night, as an exhausted Angelique slept it off, Viktor sat and smoked. He was pleased that she held over the habit of keeping good tobacco and cigars on hand for her clients. It had been one of the signatures of her brothel before the former bishop ordered it burned down.

She whimpered in her sleep. He noticed and wondered if her tie to him was strong enough for his thoughts to influence her dreams. He deliberately thought of the fire and used his memories to add sounds and scents to the images in his mind.

Her whimpering increased to an unspoken sound of protest. She began to shake her head and mumbled, "No."

He remembered that some of her employees had perished in the blaze.

"No! Leila! Marietta!" she cried out.

Viktor blinked in surprise. He hadn't expected the experiment to work. He saw that Angel now sobbed in her sleep and decided to try to make her dreams more pleasant. He felt no remorse for the nightmare, but he saw no need to be cruel. She'd done nothing to earn his cruelty. Rather she unwittingly helped him discover a new ability.

He concentrated on what he would do to seduce her if given the luxury of not having to worry about time. It didn't hurt that things which took long stretches of time to perform took only moments to think of.

Gratifyingly, her sobbing ceased. He suppressed a chuckle for fear of waking her, as he watched her body begin to writhe in pleasure. He reveled in the sounds and scent she emitted as orgasm after orgasm took her. He'd always enjoyed watching a woman sleep, but this was new and exciting.

Eventually, he had mercy and left her dreams which let her lapse into a deeper, more restful sleep.

"Thank you, Angel," he whispered and laid a gentle kiss on her cheek.

Across town, Melanie went to Jeorge, the leader of the New Orleans vampires.

"I did not summon you, child. What do you want?" the seeming teenaged boy asked.

"Forgive me, my lord. My master has returned to port."

He smiled. "Thank you, child, but my day watchers have already informed me that the *Incubus* made port today. I am sure your sire will pay his respects in due time. I imagine he is indulging himself in some carnal pleasures after his stretch at sea."

She nodded confirmation, her eyes bright with echoed passion. She had not fed yet, or she would have blushed. "He has, my lord, but that is not all."

"Oh?" Jeorge could sense something had her both frightened and excited.

"*Oui,* he has discovered an ability to control his pet's dreams."

"He can control the siren's dreams?" He sat up, acutely interested.

"No." She shook her head. "I meant his human pet, the blonde whore."

"Ah." He relaxed. "It is a bit early for that gift to develop, but then he is an exceptionally unusual vampire. We shall have to experiment soon to see if you develop as quickly as he does."

She smiled. "I would like that, my lord."

Aboard the *Incubus*, Viktor's cadre of vampires caught a hint of his meddling with Angelique's dreams. Their general reaction was bawdy enjoyment. Only Thomas Brumble seemed a bit embarrassed. He wasn't a virgin, but his experiences in no way matched the images his captain was projecting. Thomas had never heard of nor dreamt possible some of the things Viktor imagined doing with and to the New Orleans madam.

He did have enough sense to keep that to himself. Sailors, especially pirates, could tease a man mercilessly. Being undead didn't change that.

Celine knocked at Viktor's door before sunrise. When he answered, she brought in a tray with two breakfasts.

"Thank you, pet, but you might want to take Angel's back to the kitchen to keep it warm. I don't think she'll be getting up any time soon," he said as she set the tray down.

Celine immediately went over to the bed where her business partner lay in a tangle of sheets. Vik watched her breathe a sigh of relief once she confirmed the woman was still breathing and no blood stained the bedding.

He had to laugh. "Did you think I'd turned her?"

"I had feared so for a moment," she admitted with a nervous laugh of her own.

In a split second he stood beside her and pulled her into his arms. He had to fight his Hunger for a moment as the sudden fear in her scent spurred the predator in him.

"Don't worry, pet. You are safe from that particular appetite." His voice was a seductive purr. "Your servitude to Glory makes you too valuable to risk damaging you. Besides, if I had turned Angelique last night I would have to deal with Jeorge. I wouldn't have taken her with me."

"You may still have to deal with him during this visit. He is very old, and he would take it as an insult if you did not at least pay him a formal visit while you are in port."

"And how would you know so much about vampires now?"

"A few months ago, Gloribeau foresaw that something would cause trouble among the city's vampires; something connected to you somehow," she explained.

"Wonderful." He growled irritably and released her.

She stepped away from him, surprised at her own reluctance. He definitely exuded a compelling aura about him. It took her a moment to realize that the reluctance was not entirely her own. Her mistress was attracted to him, as well.

Just as that revelation hit, the Sister of Power took possession of Celine's body.

"Hello, Captain Brandewyne." Gloribeau's voice spoke through her servant's form.

"Gloribeau?"

She/they nodded. *"You have brought something you want me to safe keep; I have been told."*

"My son, yes."

Her/their expression betrayed no emotion. *"Bring the child to me today. I will decide. If I agree, I will then name my price."*

Before he could respond, her presence returned to its source. Celine collapsed to the floor, unconscious. He knelt and gently scooped her up, then placed her on the bed next to Angel.

Belle finally roused to the sound of loud knocking and the baby's hungry cries. She felt exhausted and ravenous. She was also a little disoriented by the steadiness of the floor beneath her. She realized she wasn't in her cabin, but it took a few moments for her memory to clear.

The toddler saw that she was awake and began to scream irritably. Viktor forced his way into the room and shattered her wards in the process. Belladonna cried out and clutched her head as the pain of her spells breaking struck her full force. "Ow!"

"What have you done to my son?" he demanded.

"Nothing, yet. If you'll hand me that flask of milk, I'll feed him." Her response sounded tired. "He's hungry."

"Oh." Viktor blinked, relieved that it was only that and a bit bewildered by his own burst of protectiveness. He'd seen a few of his offspring on occasion, but he'd never really felt any kind of connection to them other than the "I made that" sense of male pride. In fact, his most common reaction was one of annoyance with their mothers for being foolish enough to think that bearing his brats entitled them to something from him.

"Why did you have the door warded?" he asked.

She considered saying, "To keep you out," but felt too tired for the argument that would've led to. "To help hide his presence. I know Celine has the entire house warded, but the fewer supernatural beings that are aware of his power the better."

As she fed the child, and quiet returned, Viktor leaned against the vanity and crossed his arms. "He has bewitched you, pet. Even I feel uncharacteristically protective toward him. I suspect he would be safe from attack."

"From females, perhaps, but I fear someone like Jeorge would only view him as a potential meal." She sighed. "You sired him, so you are naturally connected with his power, whether you like it or not. You can't help but protect him. Other males will not be so friendly toward him."

He gave her a hard look. "Why not?"

"Rarity isn't the only reason there are so few mermen. They are very territorial creatures during their relatively brief life spans. The only time two mermen encounter each other and don't try to kill each other is if one sired the other. Even then, there would be a chance the mature offspring would try to kill the older merman. They don't like to share their harems."

"Interesting. Then it is a good decision to leave him with Glory, if she will take him."

Belladonna nodded. "It's why I haven't fought harder to keep him. You will eventually have to retrieve him once he matures and teach him combat. As powerful as he is, magic will still only go so far in protecting him from an intelligent attacker or predator. The one true advantage he has over other mermen is his ability to take human form. He can get out of the water to escape, if necessary."

As an afterthought, she asked, "Why do you think Glory might not accept him?"

"She just possessed Celine and told me she would decide once she's seen the child. Then there is the matter of her price, should she agree."

She sighed. "There is always a price. I imagine you'll want to take him this morning."

He nodded. "How soon can you be ready?"

"Once I've finished feeding and cleaning him, *you* can take him. I am not going. I need to hunt, and even if I didn't, I would not risk entering Glory's bayous and becoming human; not for you or your son."

He kept his relief hidden. He'd secretly dreaded having to separate the siren from the child. This made it easier. It made him feel better that she also seemed to be looking out for her own welfare once again.

"Very well."

Bundling up the child and the few accessories necessary for his care didn't take long, although Vik was mildly surprised that the baby goods bundle was almost as large as the child. It was becoming clear to him that babies were a lot of work and rather expensive.

The launch dock used to send supplies out to Gloribeau had been rebuilt. Only Viktor, Grimm and the child went in search of Glory. Jon-Jon and Zach stayed in the city to keep an eye on the crew.

Within perhaps two hours of entering the swamps, they reached the supply dock. The Sister was being very cooperative. Rather than presenting them with a maze, the ancient cypress trees seemed to funnel the little skiff directly to her dwelling.

She did not meet them at the little hammock island, however. Viktor got out and held the boat while Grimm tied it to the dock, then handed the boy up to him. The child immediately began to squirm and whine.

"Hush," he ordered his son. Amazingly, the child obeyed, looking up at him with big eyes.

Once ashore, they headed for the catwalk leading to Glory's house. Rather than try to climb up one-handed while carrying the boy, Viktor flew the short distance. The child cooed, laughed and clapped his chubby little hands in delight.

"Oh, you liked that, did you?" He smiled at his son. He was rewarded with a toothless grin and an enthusiastic squeal.

"Rambunctious little bugger." Grimm chuckled as he climbed up onto the catwalk.

Glory stood outside her front door when they finally arrived at her stilt house. Her face remained devoid of emotion as she watched them approach. Only a nod showed that she acknowledged their presence.

"Set the child down." Her voice was neutral and betrayed nothing of her thoughts.

Viktor tolerated her speaking to him that way. He had a good idea of her true power and didn't want to alienate her. He feared it would be much harder to separate the child from the siren if he had to take him to Celie instead.

Silently, he set the boy down. Confused, the child looked back and forth between them.

"How old is he?"

"Just under a year, I am told."

"He looks older, more like three, except for his lack of teeth."

"His dam was a mermaid. I don't know if that has anything to do with his rapid maturing or not."

She looked at the boy a little more sharply. "It does. It also explains the amount of raw power rolling off him. Can he walk?"

Viktor shrugged. "He can stand. I haven't seen him walk. Belle has been tending to him."

Glory focused all her attention on the sitting child. "Robert."

Immediately, the child looked at her, alert, as if he recognized the name.

"Robert, stand up and come here."

To the men's amazement, the boy obeyed. His walking was unsteady, but he wore a look of determination. He stumbled once and almost fell. Viktor started to reach to steady the child before he caught himself and stopped. Grimm noticed but wisely kept silent.

Finally, the child reached Gloribeau. He stood on tiptoe and reached up, signaling he wanted to be picked up. When she didn't, he tugged on her skirt and whined.

"No, Robert." She shook her head. "You can walk. You do not need to be carried."

He whined louder.

"I said no."

Viktor had a flashback to childhood and hearing that same response from Mother Celie in about the same tone of voice. Robert sat down and pouted, but he didn't keep trying to get her to pick him up.

"He's definitely your whelp." Grimm chuckled.

"Aye, that is much how I was at that size."

Gloribeau stared at the vampire for a while before she spoke. "Why did you bring him to me? I know Zeke told you Celie would be acceptable, too."

He knew better than to ask how she knew that. Instead, he gave her a straight answer. "You were closer and better positioned to deal with him than Celie."

"And what brought you to that conclusion?"

"He is my son. Already I can see much of myself in him, and his magic is very strong. He was able to enthrall Belladonna, whose natural inclination should have been to view him as food, given his species."

She nodded. "Go on."

"I don't know who is stronger, you or Celie, but your magic is tied to the bayous and fresh water. It nearly turned Belle human. Robert…." He tried out the new name and found it felt right. "…is a creature of the sea. Celie lives in the salt marshes, too close to his native habitat. He doesn't need to be near that until he is old enough and skilled enough to defend himself."

Glory smiled. "You answered well, Viktor Brandewyne. If you had only chosen me over Celie because of convenience, I might have refused to take the boy. But I will take him. Hezekiah Grimm, please take Robert inside and get him settled in. Viktor, walk with me. We will discuss my price."

Grimm shrugged and walked over to the sitting child. "Come along, Robert. Granny wants us to go inside." He held a hand out to the boy.

Robert looked back and forth between the three adults, an unsure expression on his face. Glory gave a small smile and a nod. He burbled, then used Grimm's leg to pull himself into a standing position before he took the pirate's hand. There was no mistaking, even with his toddler's body language, that he allowed the man to lead him into the stilt house. He had definitely inherited his sire's arrogance.

Gloribeau laughed, a musical sound. "He is like a miniature version of you. I've a feeling I may not look on you so kindly when next we meet, Viktor Brandewyne. Now, let's walk."

"Lead the way."

She led him down the back catwalk, but its course had been changed. It no longer led to the little hammock where they had killed Tulimanchulo and restored Glory's youth to her. Instead, it seemed to have doubled in length, ending at another stilt house.

"Come in, Viktor." Her voice took on a seductive timbre.

He scented the air before he passed through the door. He had a feeling he knew what her price would be, and he wanted to make sure there were no spells to entrap him.

"Don't you trust me?" she asked with a laugh.

"Let's just say your Sisters have taught me caution."

"Then use your senses and know I speak without deceit. I am the oldest and strongest of my kind. I have no need or desire to ensorcel you, Viktor Brandewyne. From this moment on, you are free to come and go as you will in my bayou. I will not attempt to trap you, hold you against your will, or enslave you."

He felt the power behind her words. On some deep level, he knew she was now bound by them and no longer had the ability to break her oath.

He entered the house with a confident, lustful smile on his lips. "Now, name your price, Gloribeau."

In answer, she dropped her dress to the floor.

Chapter 3

"You are going to have to deal with the vampires before you leave port," Glory told him the next day as they dressed.

"So I have been told." Viktor sounded less than happy about it.

She chuckled at him. "You should have listened to me when I told you to avoid them."

"I would have had to deal with them eventually." He shrugged. "I've a feeling Jeorge would have sought me out."

Glory agreed. "Yes, he is a persistent creature and very protective of what he considers his territory. He will be curious about what you were doing last night. We released an amazing amount of energy." She stretched and shivered as her body remembered the pleasure.

"Yes, we did." He grinned and pulled her to him for a kiss. He held her tight enough that she could feel he was ready to go another round.

Laughing, she pushed him back some. "Captain Brandewyne, you are truly insatiable."

"Mm-hm." He moved in closer and nuzzled her neck.

"No."

He pulled back, puzzled. Her body language and vocal tone, even her scent, grew frigid, the change drastic and abrupt.

She explained. "You have met and surpassed my price, Viktor Brandewyne. If I were to entertain you further, you would not want to leave, and I would have broken my vow."

He could see, just for a moment, the regret in her eyes. Part of him wanted to stay. The power was almost as addictive as blood. But he knew she was right. He couldn't stay.

He turned and finished dressing with a sigh, careful not to look at her. "I hope Jeorge will understand that my visit to him must be short. I would like to sail with the tide tonight."

"It is wise of you to be brief with him. I would also caution you to make no mention of Robert at all. If they only think you brought me some trinket of power, they will leave it alone. If they learn of the boy's existence, they will be drawn to seek him out," she said in warning.

He nodded. "I have been careful to block any images or thoughts of him from Melanie. Jeorge has been using her to spy on me; something I intend to bring a halt to this evening."

Viktor couldn't suppress a smile as the toddler ran to him and hugged his leg when they returned to the main stilt house. He reached down and ruffled the boy's hair.

"I have to go now, Robert. You mind Gloribeau." He gently disengaged the child from his leg and turned him toward the Sister. Robert went to her outstretched hand and took it, turning to look back at the two men.

"Is the boat ready, Mr. Grimm?"

"Aye, Captain."

They turned to leave. Robert raised his free hand and waved. "Ba-bye, Da."

Viktor whirled to stare at the child. Until that moment, the boy had not spoken, only burbled, laughed or cried. For a split second, he forgot to shield. In that split second, he knew he was being watched and that Jeorge now knew about his son.

He immediately slammed the connection shut with a blast of hot rage at his young vampire. From the look on her face, he could tell Glory knew, too.

"I had hoped to avoid dealing with them, but I can keep them away from the child. No creature enters my bayou without my leave and survives," she said with a sigh.

Once back in New Orleans, Viktor tried to sense where Belladonna was. He got a fleeting image of ships' hulls and knew she was hunting the harbor. He sent a thought at her that he would be in port at least until high tide that night, possibly longer. He had no idea how long it would take to deal with the vampires.

The siren let him know she would join him before nightfall. There was a familiar sting to her mental presence that let him know she was not happy with him. He imagined she knew what had taken place with Glory.

He chose to ignore her jealousy.

Celine gave him an unhappy look when he and Grimm returned to the shop. "A message was delivered for you today."

"It's from Jeorge, isn't it," he stated. She nodded confirmation.

"I'm not surprised. He's probably curious about what happened in the swamp."

"He is not the only one," she grumbled. "I think the entire city felt that, judging by the panic and chaos that ran rampant in the streets last night. What did you do?"

"I merely met the price set by your mistress." His tone remained unapologetic. His body language let her know she would get no more answer than that out of him. It also implied how dangerous it would be to continue questioning him about it.

Wisely, Celine left it alone and just handed him the sealed message. He could see it remained untampered with or read.

He broke the wax seal, opened the folded parchment, and read the message. His only response to the content was to grunt, crumple the parchment up and stuff it in his pocket.

This guaranteed he would be stuck in port at least one more day. He was beginning to not like New Orleans. Every time he went there, it seemed harder and harder to get away. That was a dangerous enough situation to be in with a price on his head; not knowing how much time he had to find the other Sisters of Power only made it worse.

"Lazarus, come forth." He summoned the creature that had once been his first mate, Jim Rigger.

Obediently, a huge black cat appeared, seeming to coalesce out of mist. "Mrow."

Viktor fished out the crumpled summons, for that was basically what it was, and held it in the flat of his upturned palm. "Mr. Grimm has gone to prepare the ship to sail. Take this to him. He'll know what it is."

Lazarus morphed into his raven form and flew out with the note.

Satisfied that Grimm would see to it the crew knew they wouldn't be sailing that night; Viktor turned his attention to the

Creole madam. His expression remained unreadable as he gazed at her. He could feel her magic on the air, the taste of it like a watered-down version of Gloribeau's. There was no way Celine could deny her tie to the Sister.

She returned his stare but carefully avoided meeting his gaze directly. She already knew from past experience that she wasn't immune to his power. His silence and unwavering stare made her nervous enough to finger the talisman she always kept in her pocket. She wanted to just flee the room, but she knew it would be a bad move in the presence of a predator.

Finally, he spoke. "Call one of the girls down to watch the shop for you."

"Why?" She risked a glance at his face. In that moment, he had crossed the space between them.

"Why do you think?" He leaned down and kissed her.

Viktor left Celine sleeping and exhausted in her bed and got dressed. For a human, she was one of the most skilled lovers he'd had. However, even though her magic was closely tied to Glory's, the experience had felt bland in comparison.

The Sister of Power had been right. If they'd had each other one more time, he would not have willingly left her bed.

He pulled his boots on and decided to go find a tavern and a meal. One thing he had to admit was that the cooks and chefs of New Orleans knew how to feed a man well. He hadn't had solid food in two days, and he didn't want to risk losing control of his Hunger later that night.

Jeorge had invited him to join him on a hunt. The wording had been just shy of a command to join him, however. Viktor never had taken orders very well. Only a select handful of beings would he tolerate such treatment from. Jeorge was not on that list.

The only reason he didn't just ignore the summons and sail with the tide as he'd originally planned was that he needed to keep the peace with the local vampires. New Orleans was too important a port to him for many different reasons. He couldn't afford to avoid it for the rest of his piratical career.

Belladonna caught up to him just as he located a tavern he wanted to try out. He'd noticed the place on previous visits to the city but never gone in. Mouth-watering aromas came from the dining hall. Another scent began to override them.

Viktor could smell the siren's jealousy. It rolled off her in acrid waves. He sighed to himself and braced to weather the storm and hopefully calm it. His first goal was to prevent her from making a scene. He needed this food.

"Ah, Belle, you're just in time." He smiled as he greeted her. "I was about to get some food. Join me. We can talk about what has happened and what we need to prepare for."

She returned his smile, but he saw the venom behind it. "Yes, we definitely need to talk about what happened last night." Her voice was a cold as the waters of the abyss.

They went in and found a table. Both were dressed a little rougher than the other patrons, but they had no trouble getting a waiter. The young man took their order and treated them courteously. It probably saved his life.

Black Venom

Despite the good service and pleasant demeanor of the waiter, Viktor found him irritating. The looks the man gave both of them coupled with his scent let the vampire and siren know he wouldn't mind a dalliance and wasn't particular about which one it was with.

Although the signals irritated Viktor, they soothed the siren. Belladonna found the human's attention to both of them amusing. "He would make a nice dessert." She teased Viktor after the waiter had delivered their meal and gone to wait another table.

"We don't have time for that, pet." He set to eating. "Try that tartar and see if you like it."

She poked at the raw beef and sniffed it before she put a bite in her mouth. Her motions were deliberate and slow, since she was unused to eating with utensils. She'd been surprised to learn that some humans would eat raw flesh.

After the initial bite, she poked the rest around and only nibbled along. She wasn't really hungry. Earlier that day at least five sailors stood too close to the railings of their ships. It took almost no effort for her to propel herself out of the water to snatch them over the side.

She made each kill swift, not in the mood to play with her food.

After a while, Viktor noticed she wasn't eating. "Something wrong with your food, pet?"

Belle shrugged. "It is all right, I guess. I'm not really hungry right now. This meat is old. I prefer a fresh kill."

He grunted and went back to his meal.

"So, how was she?" Belle kept her face deceptively bland when the question made him look up.

He made it plain he wasn't going to rush the mouthful he had just to answer her. When he finally swallowed and wiped his mouth, he said, "She was the best I've ever had, and I hope I can forget that one day."

She blinked. It wasn't exactly the answer she had expected. "Why would you want to forget?"

"I enjoy sex. I had Celine today and found the experience almost boring. Keep in mind that Celine is one of the best at what she does."

Belle sat back and let a slow malicious smile spread across her face. "The magic, no, the level of magic makes a big difference, doesn't it?"

He narrowed his eyes at her. "You speak as though you know from experience, pet."

She reached over and patted his arm condescendingly. "Don't worry, you'll get used to humans again — eventually."

He grabbed her wrist before she could react. Turning her hand palm-up, he kissed it; a gentle brush of lips. Then he traced a circle on her palm with the tip of his tongue. He deliberately channeled some of his power into the action. Looking up at her while he did it, he saw her eyelids flutter as she responded to the magic rush.

She snatched her hand away from him and held it close to her body as if it were burnt. "You bastard," she hissed low.

Viktor sat back with a smirk and went back to eating.

Belladonna hugged herself as if she were cold. "If that had been a physical explosion instead of a magical one last night, you and Glory would have set off a tidal wave big enough to drown this city.

Every human with any sensitivity to magic at all nearly went mad on the rush of power."

"Celine did mention something about that. Jeorge and his vampires felt it, too. There was a summons to hunt with him tonight left for me at Celine's and Angel's."

She sat up straight. "A summons? Are you going to obey it?"

"Not out of any fear or respect for him, but I do have business with Jeorge. He used Melanie to spy on me. Robert caught me off guard with something he did. Now Jeorge knows about the boy, which will force Glory to defend him."

"I will force feed my blood to any vampire that dares touch that child!"

He smiled. "I feel the same way about him, pet, but I doubt that will be necessary. If Gloribeau doesn't want someone in her bayous, they won't survive long enough to reach her or the boy."

Belle sat back, still agitated. "I'm coming on this hunt with you."

He nodded. "Actually, I had planned on it."

They arrived at the designated meeting place at dusk. Of course, their host for the hunt had not arrived yet. They didn't expect Jeorge to show up until full dark.

The siren made no apologies for letting her irritation show when several hours passed by without any sign of him. Vik felt equally irritated but determined to not let it show in any way. He had the feeling this was a test by the older vampire and that they were being watched.

"Peace, pet," he said as she paced in front of him.

"Where is he?" she growled.

"Watching us, I imagine. Now be still." The calm in his voice masked his own irritation at the petty delay.

Sighing, she obeyed. She knew he was right about Jeorge. Several vampires lingered nearby but out of sight; their scent unmistakable to her. She just wondered why he was testing them. Like Viktor, she wanted to put this port behind them, although for different reasons than his.

Not a full minute after she settled down, Jeorge and his entourage made their appearance.

"Ah, *mes amis*, I see you made it." He greeted the pirate and siren. "My apologies for our tardiness. It seems there is always someone who forgets a scarf or watch or some other trinket and has to go back for it." He made it sound as if they had been getting ready for some *soiree,* rather than to hunt for prey.

On closer inspection, Viktor saw that the local vampires had indeed dressed for a party. "You should have let me know we would be attending a special occasion, Jeorge." He made the chide sound amiable. "We would have dressed more appropriately."

The erstwhile teen waved a hand in dismissal. "You will fit in just fine, Captain Brandewyne, and the *mademoiselle* will provide the perfect distraction for our prey, regardless of how she is dressed."

Belle bowed her head slightly and gave him a tight-lipped, not entirely friendly smile. "So, where exactly did you propose to hunt tonight?" she asked.

His smile managed to be both amiable and wickedly evil at the same time. "The Lord Mayor is holding a reception for the new governor. From all reports it may be a somber affair. I thought a reunion with his daughter might cheer the old fool up."

☠

At Jeorge's arrangement, carriages arrived to transport everyone to the reception. He reasoned that walking to the gate meant a chance of being denied entry. Flying in would definitely raise the alarm. He invited Viktor and Belladonna to ride with him. Melanie also occupied the carriage. The young vampire presented as a beautifully decked out corpse, dead to the world.

The siren kept her face neutral as Viktor leaned forward to examine the girl. Acting on an instinct he'd never realized he had, he held his palm just above her body. First, he held it over her face then over her heart.

Gently, he took her limp hand and whispered, "Melanie."

With a jerk, she opened her eyes. Then, she screamed.

"Peace, girl," her maker said. She fell instantly silent, her eyes locked on his.

"Good." He nodded then turned to Jeorge. "A truce between us. If you will not use her to spy on me, I will not use her to spy on you."

The vampire nodded. "Agreed. I am impressed you learned that skill so early. You are still young to our world. It will be interesting to learn if your daughter enjoys the same rate of progress."

Mentally, Viktor sent a warning to Melanie. *"Show no reaction to this contact, pet. For your sake, pray you do not develop your powers as quickly as I have. Jeorge strikes me as the type who would see it as a threat, which could lead him to cut your existence short. I protect what is mine, but I am rarely in port for long."*

Aloud, he addressed his host. "Thank you for inviting us to the hunt, Jeorge. Hopefully, there will be no trouble getting through the gates."

"Oh, no trouble at all. I arranged for a wealthy, but remote, planter to include us in his entourage. I am afraid he might not be wealthy enough to be invited back in the future, however."

"And why is that?" Viktor asked, mildly curious. Belle merely sat back and watched the vampires. She had no interest in the politics of human society.

Jeorge smiled and feigned innocence. "A mysterious disease has been decimating his servants."

"Yes, I can see how that would affect his profits. Yet somehow, I get the feeling that the man won't be too worried about it much longer." Vik gave a knowing leer.

His host laughed. "He hasn't worried about it for a couple of months now. In fact, he hasn't worried about anything at all. Ah, we have arrived."

All four carriages were permitted to pass the gates. The drivers handed over the engraved invitation and the letters proclaiming the number of the entourage. The blinds remained drawn and hid the passengers from view.

When their carriage arrived at the mansion door, the footman got down and opened the compartment. Jeorge got out first and turned to offer a hand to Belladonna. This left Viktor to escort Melanie in. Their entrance had the effect Jeorge had planned on. The mayor's daughter had last been seen in the pirate's company a little over a year before.

To their credit, the servants resisted the impulse to gush about their former mistress' return, but it was only with a visible effort. The *maître d'* quietly approached them about how they should be introduced upon entering the ballroom.

"Welcome home, madam." He smiled. "Your father has been worried sick since you eloped. He will be relieved to see you are safe and sound. I do not know what his greeting will be for you, *m'sieur*. Shall I introduce you as *Monsieur* and *Madame* Brumble?"

Viktor shook his head. He felt recklessly bold this evening; an after effect of his time with Gloribeau. "No, for Thomas Brumble is not my true name. It is merely the name of a man I killed. Also, Melanie is not my wife."

The man frowned. "Then how shall I introduce you? And what do you mean she is not your wife?"

Before the man could say more, Viktor's eyes flared with emerald fire. His victim didn't even have time to squeak. "I meant exactly what I said. She is not my wife, nor any other man's wife. You will introduce her first by her proper name. You will introduce me by my given name and my title; Viktor Brandewyne, Captain."

"Oui, m'sieur." He led them through the door to announce them to the room. Belladonna, Jeorge, and his other vampires already mingled among the guests. They'd entered first, wanting to watch the guests and host's reactions to the entrance.

The mayor, standing with the new governor and his wife had grown deathly quiet at the sight of his daughter on the arm of the man who had taken her away from him. "Melanie," he breathed.

"Lovely young woman; do you know her, Louis?" the governor's wife asked. "Her escort looks to be quite the rogue."

"She is my daughter," he answered. "I haven't seen her in over a year, and that is the bastard who stole her away."

"Presenting *Mademoiselle* Melanie duChamp and Captain Viktor Brandewyne."

A hush fell over the ballroom at the mention of the infamous pirate's name. Viktor watched Louis duChamp carefully to see what he would do. Since the new governor stood next to him, Vik watched him as well. He wanted to be ready in case any guards were set upon him. It was an old habit he'd had since he was human. He hadn't survived as long as he had as a pirate by allowing himself to be blindsided.

When neither man signaled for help, Vik smirked at them and led Melanie into the room. They both could hear what was being said about them. Even though a path opened through the crowd for them, they took their time making their way to the receiving line.

"I remember you saying that Thomas Brumble of Brumble and Sons Shipping eloped with your daughter," Governor Rouget mentioned.

Louis grew pale over the revelation of the man's true identity. "When I met him, he introduced himself as such. Now I know why the old man refused to honor the trade agreement I thought his son and I had worked out. He said his son was dead."

"*Mon Dieu!*" *Madame* Rouget exclaimed. "Do you mean to say this man murdered the young man and used his name to gain access to your daughter?"

"I fear so. What amazes me is that he brought her back." His voice held uncertainty.

The pair in question reached them. Jeorge and Belladonna moved to stand with the two vampires. They separated and Jeorge stood next to Melanie, while Belladonna flanked Viktor.

Even though the pirate's return of the mayor's daughter caused a stir in the room, nearly every male eye, and a few female ones, followed Belladonna. Wearing only a man's shirt and breeches, the siren exuded raw sexuality. The reception guests held the opinion that this was the most interesting social event they had ever attended.

They had no idea of how deadly interesting it would become for some of them.

"You have some gall showing your face here, *m'sieur*," Louis fairly growled. "Melanie, child, I hope he hasn't mistreated you. Come over here."

"No, Father." She did not move from between her sire and her master.

"What do you mean, 'no'?"

"No, he has not mistreated me, and no, I will not return home."

Louis grasped his daughter's hand with a pleading look in his eyes. "Melanie, child, you needn't fear I would cast you out for being despoiled by a pirate. Such a fate is hardly something you could prevent by yourself."

"Despoiled?" She laughed and looked to both Viktor and Jeorge for approval before she continued. "Shall I tell him the truth?"

"Feel free." Jeorge nodded.

Viktor added, "I don't care what you tell him about it."

She smiled sweetly and met her father's gaze. At the moment, she had no plans to use her powers on him. "Yes, Captain Brandewyne did despoil me, as you so delicately put it. However, I feel no shame or remorse for it. It was the most glorious experience of my life, right up to the moment he took my life and gave me a new one."

"I don't understand. I know it seems like your life is different after the event, but you are still my Melanie." He shook his head.

"No, you don't understand, Father." She finally allowed her fangs to show. "He literally murdered me, then gave me a new life. Now, I am with Jeorge."

"Jeorge?" Louis shook his head, completely confused and currently oblivious to the fact he was hosting a reception or even who it was for.

"*Moi.*" The vampire in question smiled. He took the mayor's mind and ensured that the man would only remember what he wanted him to. "I would have asked you for her, but I feared you would deny me. Therefore, I contracted with Captain Brandewyne to procure Melanie and bring her to me."

Viktor didn't bother to correct him on a few points. If Jeorge wanted to tell his own version of the events surrounding the girl's abduction, that was his business.

Louis furrowed his brow. "Forgive me, *m'sieur*, but what do you want with my daughter?"

"I needed an excuse to be here tonight. I very much wish to discuss some business with our new governor." He turned to face the Rougets.

"How is that possible? Louis said the girl has been missing for over a year. I did not even know about my posting here at that time," Governor Rouget said.

Jeorge smiled and turned his full charm on the man. "I have connections, Governor. Shall we retire to the gardens to discuss it in private?" He turned back to Viktor. "Captain, why don't you and the lovely Belladonna select some companions for the evening? Come along, Governor, and bring *Madame* Rouget with you. This greatly concerns her, as well."

They left, headed toward the garden. Melanie led her father off toward his study, leaving the remaining guests to the mercy of the pirate, the siren, and the other vampires.

Vik and Belle observed for a while, noting the discreet manner in which Jeorge's vampires hunted. To an uninformed observer it would only appear that a few guests were pairing off and slipping out of the party to find some more private trysting place.

Viktor debated not hunting at all. Everyone at the party now knew who he was. If he made a kill, they would know what he was, as well. Still, it might cause trouble with Jeorge if he didn't at least make a show of eating, so to speak.

Mentally, he spoke to Belle. *"I'm glad I ate earlier. There are too many witnesses here."*

"I agree," she replied through their link. *"I fed well in the harbor. Perhaps if you just use your knife. You can have a drink without leaving a potential vampire for Jeorge to use against you."*

"And how do I explain the knife wound?"

"There won't be so much as a scar after I heal the wound, and you can give your meal a false memory." The siren smiled up at him with deceptive innocence.

He returned the smile with a roguishly wicked grin. "Well, the question now is which one," he said aloud. Turning to scan the crowd, he smirked. "I don't think finding a willing partner will be a problem for either of us."

Nearly every male openly eyed Belladonna. A few women gave Viktor the same treatment. Even more cast furtive flirtatious glances at the pirate.

Belle chuckled. "They all seek the thrill, but do not take the danger seriously."

"That is why they are prey," he whispered.

Vik carried his unconscious victim to a secluded garden seat. He stopped himself before he took too much blood. Belle quickly healed the knife wound to prevent any further blood loss. Once the vampire laid the woman on the bench, he set about arranging her body.

"What are you doing?" the siren asked.

As he cut the lacings of the woman's bodice which allowed her breasts to spill out, he replied, "The memory of a ravishing that never actually happened will seem more real if it looks like it did."

"I understand that; I just don't understand why you don't go ahead and ravish her. It's not like you, Viktor." Lifting the woman's skirts and spreading her legs wide, he made a face, then stood back to check his work. Not quite satisfied with his posing, he reached down and placed her hand over her exposed folds.

"There, if nothing else that will muffle the odor." He turned to the siren. "One, I don't want to spend that much time here. Two, she is diseased, going by the scent and taste of her blood."

"*Oui*, she is," an unknown male voice chuckled. Its owner soon came into view. "The widow duBois has gone through at least four husbands, already. Apparently, she is immune to the disease she carries. Her husbands were not, though."

"Who are you?" Viktor demanded.

"Guillaum." He bowed. "Jeorge sent me to give you the message he will receive you at his home tomorrow evening to discuss matters of business."

Vik growled irritably. "I had hoped to conclude our business tonight and be out of port at the next high tide."

"My apologies, Captain Brandewyne. My master—." Vik thought he detected a touch of distaste in Guillaum's tone at the use of Jeorge's title. "—wishes for me to act as your companion while you are in the city. He will be busy with the new governor for the remainder of the evening."

The pirate and the siren both looked at the vampire. Belladonna spoke first.

"At least he's not trying to be sneaky about it this time."

"Actually, he was." Guillaum shrugged. "But I'm a bit more familiar with the Captain's reputation than he is. I doubt I would be able to just insinuate myself into your company without drawing suspicion."

"Hardly," Vik said. "Still, I suppose we are stuck with each other. If Jeorge will not be available tonight, I'm going to hunt one of the lower wards. I want to get the taste of the widow duBois, did you say, out of my mouth. Some healthy Creole should do the trick and be less conspicuous."

Before she could protest, he grabbed Belle about the waist and launched into the sky. Guillaum quickly flew behind them.

"What are you thinking by letting him tag along?" she asked through their link.

"He would have followed anyway, pet. I've a feeling there is no love lost between him and Jeorge. It was plain to me that he doesn't like the man."

"And how could you tell?"

"I know seafaring men just as well as you know mermaids. Those who ply the waves have been my prey since I was a lad. I know a potential mutineer when I see one, and before this night is over, I will know how to use him to my advantage. Jeorge will learn that information about Bloody Vik Brandee comes with a price."

Viktor found that he actually liked Guillaum, and the other vampire appeared to like him. The siren remained suspicious, but that was part of her job.

Still, Vik remained cautious without appearing to. He'd played this game before. As a pirate, he knew becoming too chummy before really knowing a man could lead to a hangman's noose. He learned far more from the vampire sent to spy on him than Guillaum learned from him.

Finally, the vampire left them before the dawn could catch him.

Viktor returned to Celine and Angel's to meet up with his mates.

"The sooner we're out of this port, the better, Vik," Grimm said over a shot of whiskey.

"Aye, Hezekiah, I agree. I don't intend to be put off by Jeorge this evening. I'm not particularly happy with the position he put me in last night."

"What about this Guillaum?"

Viktor sighed. "He would have been better suited to the deck of a ship than tied to this port and Jeorge."

"You like him; I can tell."

"Aye, but I don't trust him."

"You don't trust anybody, Vik." Grimm laughed.

"The man has not been getting on well with his master. We're not that different; neither of us like following another's command. I'm not sure if Jeorge was hoping I'd be willing to take Guillaum on as a crewmate, or if he wanted me to dispose of him."

"I would advise against taking him aboard." Grimm sat up. "He couldn't be controlled like the others, given whose and what he is."

Vik lit a cigar and sat back. "Oh, I have no intention of doing that. Besides the fact he belongs to Jeorge, we are too much alike to be on the same ship, as I already said. If I kill him, I'm sure Jeorge will insist I provide a replacement. I really don't want to invest that much time and energy here. I just want to make sure the bastard doesn't try for Robert."

Viktor and Belladonna arrived at Jeorge's house just after sunset. The pirate wanted to make sure he caught the vampire in, before he found some other excuse to put him off. It irritated him having to deal with him at all.

A servant answered the door promptly. It was a different human than the one he'd seen the last time he'd been there. He gave the lad his and Belle's names.

"*Oui*, the master has been expecting you, *m'sieur*. Please, follow me."

The young man led them to a small library. Jeorge sat at a desk with a large book in front of him. Viktor admired the wealth of collected writings which surrounded him. Some of the titles he recognized. Some of the older, but obviously well-cared for, books boasted titles in languages he could not read.

A part of him wanted to stay and pour over the volumes. The culture of his native Savannah encouraged a love of reading in all the city's citizens, regardless of social standing or class. Viktor had been no exception to that.

The siren who approached the stacks with enthusiasm, however; a fact which surprised Viktor and amused Jeorge.

"By the Abyss! I thought these were lost forever!" She hovered near some cylinders.

"What are they?" Vik asked, curious despite himself.

"Ancient papyri, if the contents are as original as their containers."

"Oh, they are." Jeorge smiled. "Do you know where they are from?" His expression said he already knew the answer; he just wanted to know if she did.

"They are part of the collection from the Library of Alexandria, thought to have been lost in the fire. How did you come by them?" she asked.

"They were part of my maker's collection," he answered. "I am curious to know how you recognized them so easily."

Belladonna smiled. "I regularly visited that library as a child. When your prey is sentient, it helps to study how their minds work."

"Indeed." Jeorge laughed.

Viktor decided to steer the conversation back to the subject he wished to discuss. "I appreciate a good book myself, but we did not come here to discuss literature and philosophy."

"No, nor was it my intention to distract you or the siren with my library," Jeorge said. 'When you arrived in my city, you did not seek me out. I feel slighted, Captain. Pray, tell why you felt the need to do so?"

Belladonna became instantly alert and watched for any sign from her master. She knew Viktor well enough to know it wouldn't take much for this to turn violently ugly. She hoped they wouldn't have to fight their way out.

"You already know the answer, since you had Melanie spying on me." His voice was calm and polite, a bad sign by the siren's reckoning. "I am a pirate, sir. I owe allegiance to no one, and I come and go as I will. My business is my own. But since you already know, I brought my son to foster with a friend. The deck of a ship is no place for a child."

"How old is the lad? You should have brought him by. I would have liked to meet him."

Belle growled. She didn't bother to hide her true teeth.

"You'll have to forgive Belladonna. She is uncharacteristically protective of the boy. She rescued him from the one who killed his mother. He's not quite a year old."

Jeorge raised an eyebrow. "I had heard of new vampires still being able to sire children, but usually only within the first month or so. You surprise me, Captain Brandewyne. I meant no offence or harm to the child, siren. It is just my curiosity. I have existed long enough that anything truly new is a rare treat."

He stood and gave them a bow. Viktor returned it but kept his head up to signify he was not showing submission. Belladonna stood defiant.

"Thank you for satisfying my curiosity. Please, do not be a stranger when next you visit my city. I am about to break fast, if you would care to join me."

"Thank you, but no." Viktor politely refused. "I have already been a-port too long. I would like to catch the high tide."

"Of course, I understand. *Bon voyage, mon ami*; until next time."

Chapter 4

Unbeknownst to Samantha, Captain Bainbridge posted a message to Tobias Brumble to let the man know the progress of his daughter's quest to rescue or ransom her brothers. He carefully omitted the coordinates of the slave camp they had liberated or of where they were going to search next. He knew the old man would send ships to fetch Sam home. Tobias might sacrifice his sons to save his own neck, but his daughter was his heart.

Gregory, one of the children they rescued, now an orphan, refused to stay in Santo Domingo with the others. He clung to Sam with something between adoration and desperation. He was fiercely protective of her and she of him.

Bainbridge didn't protest the boy's remaining with the crew. He saw the boy as an emotional anchor for Samantha. Gregory gave her something to focus on besides her obsession to find Brandee and try to rescue her brothers. He would also give her someone to care for when Bainbridge's suspicions about the Brumble boys' fates were confirmed. He honestly believed neither Thomas nor Zachary was still alive. But he knew it futile to try to convince Sam of it.

They finally arrived near the Archipelago de los Roques. None of the ring of islands looked to be occupied. The largest had very lush jungle, but the lookouts spotted no smoke to indicate a settlement. The thickness of the vegetation looked impenetrable beyond the beach. The heights appeared to glitter and glint in the sunlight. From a distance, the phenomenon looked like gold covering the landscape.

"Probably a trick of the light on the rocks," Bainbridge said when Sam noted it. "I've seen similar effects before around the Isle of Youth off the western tip of Cuba. If it really was gold, the Spanish would have plundered it years ago."

"I hadn't thought of that," she ceded. "It makes sense."

"Mr. Durham!"

"Aye, Captain?"

"Tack around the other side of the archipelago but take it slow. I want soundings taken every five minutes. These waters are shallow, and I don't want to run aground like that derelict we saw yesterday."

"Aye-aye."

Sam frowned at the islands. "What if there is no settlement? Do you think that foul creature lied to us?"

"It's possible. He may have feared retribution," Bainbridge said. "Brandee has a ruthless reputation of dealing with those he believes have betrayed him. He is also noted for hunting down any who hunt him rather than run or hide from them."

"Good. That should make it easier to find him once word gets out that we are looking for him."

He kept his thoughts on that silent, and Samantha ignored the look he gave her. He knew it was an argument he would never win. She was obstinate.

Instead, he suggested, "There is the possibility that Brandee merely had a rendezvous set up here to exchange goods rather than put in at a village or port. If we don't see any signs of habitation, there is a small port not far from here. We can ask around there."

"Very well."

The islands yielded no sign at all that a human had ever set foot there. Not so much as a rotted boat along the shore could be seen. Given the relative proximity of the mainland and the fact that the large lagoon was probably rife with fish, Bainbridge found it odd. Even the crew was spooked by it. Several swore they felt like they were being watched.

Bainbridge decided to spend a couple of extra days sailing to the nearest small port even though it was little more than a fishing village. If nothing else, one of the fishermen may have seen the pirate's ship. It was a distinct vessel, and much larger than the usual merchant ship seen in these waters.

If they had, it would give him a better idea of the time frame they were dealing with.

They were unable to get any leads on the *Incubus* in the village. None of the fishermen or local sailors could recall seeing a ship of that size or description. They were able to tell them something about the "golden isle," however.

"It is haunted, *señor*," the barkeep at the dockside tavern told Captain Bainbridge. "The island is cursed. Anyone foolish enough to seek out the gold has never returned. It has been so for more than two years."

"Two years?" Sam asked.

"*Si*. That is when the gold first began to appear. The jungle was not so thick then, and men from the village had been going there twice a year to fish the lagoon. All was as it had always been during the first trip, but when they returned a few months later, the jungle had grown dense, like a living wall around the island. On the heights, the first glimmers of gold began to appear."

The barkeep continued, "A few were curious and pulled their boats up on the beach. All was well until they neared the jungle's edge. The vines came alive like snakes and writhed out to grab the men. Three were dragged into the jungle, screaming. Then the screaming stopped. A fourth fisherman hung suspended in the vines. The vines ripped him apart before the very eyes of the fishermen still in the lagoon. Then they grew around the severed parts until the man's remains disappeared."

"A few tendrils whipped and writhed, waving toward the water. The remaining fishermen quickly paddled back out of the lagoon."

"To this day, no man from this village will venture near the place. It is cursed and inhabited by evil spirits. You were wise not to put ashore there."

Bainbridge thanked the man and gave him some coins. He and Samantha exchanged doubtful looks once they returned to the streets.

The doubt remained but grew tinged with worry and suspicion when they got similar or identical tales elsewhere in the village. The consistency of the stories spoke of a truth to them, but that it was the work of evil spirits was questionable.

"What do you think really happened, Captain?" Sam asked when they were back aboard the *Shining Star*.

"It confirms that some pirates have used the place, even if it wasn't Brandee." He grunted. "They probably set booby traps and may have even left a few men hidden on the island for the sole purpose of frightening the locals away from the place."

"But what about the fact that no one has claimed to see the ship?"

"A ship that size would have plenty of small boats. If they were going to go to that much trouble to keep people away, they wouldn't want a ship as recognizable as the *Incubus* to be seen."

"Are we going to check out the island?"

Bainbridge nodded. "Definitely. We have an idea of what traps to look out for. I doubt that any pirates stay there year-round. We will take precautions and go ashore with a large number, just in case there is a pirate or two still lurking about."

Sam thought about it for a few minutes then suggested, "Perhaps we should go at night like we did at the slaver's. The moon is waxing and will give enough light for us to see by until the jungle grows too dark."

"Excellent idea. Now, get some rest, Miss Brumble."

"I will."

They found a couple of places in the ring of islands deep enough to allow the *Shining Star* to sail into the lagoon. They had to use the small boats to approach the shore, though. The merchant ship rode too deep in the water to pass the shoals.

They chose a wide stretch of beach to land on. Bainbridge picked it, not out of fear of some supposed curse, but because of the slight chance pirates or smugglers might be hidden on the island. He wished the moon wasn't so bright, but they needed the light to see enough to navigate.

A shadow in the moonlight remained harder to target than a lit torch, at least.

They pulled the boats far enough up on the sand to keep them from floating back out into the lagoon on the tide. Bainbridge, Sam and the eight men chosen to go with them then made their way up the beach. They kept cautious and silent as shadows. After a while they found an opening in the jungle wall and followed the old path beyond it.

The going was slow. The path was narrow, and the Captain wouldn't allow a light yet. The gloom beneath the canopy felt nearly suffocating.

The sensation of being watched intensified as they made their way further inland. The path seemed to meander to and fro until it became impossible to keep track of their direction. They were still on the track and still in the jungle at sunup. Within an hour, the humidity became unbearable. Everyone in the landing party was soaked to the skin with sweat.

Samantha noticed that the jungle appeared denser on the right side of the path, as if it were trying to hide something.

"That's silly," she told herself. "Plants and trees just grow where they're planted."

"What was that, Sam?" Bainbridge asked.

She jumped a little at the sound of his voice. "I didn't realize I'd spoken aloud, Captain. It seems like the trees are trying to hide something to our right. Out of the corner of my eye they don't look that dense there, but when I turn to look directly, they seem to close in so that I can't see more than three feet."

"Still, they can't be moving," she added. "It must be a trick of the heat. Trees grow where they're planted."

"Aye, they do." He mulled it over. "Most of this jungle looks to be new growth, however. Very few of the trees are large-boled. They may have been planted to hide something."

"Seems like an awful lot of trouble to go to for a bunch of pirates."

"Perhaps, but Brandee is no ordinary pirate."

"No, I suppose not."

"Mr. Durham," Bainbridge called.

"Aye, Cap'n?"

"I think it is time to put the machetes to use. I want to see what is to our right."

"Aye, Cap'n. All right, you heard the man, lads. Let's see if we can't cut our way out."

What had looked like thick jungle gave way surprisingly easy before the machete onslaught. Durham was the only one who had to use a blade. About twenty feet in, they broke through to another path. To the left was the gloom of the jungle. To the right, the way grew lighter.

The group headed to the right, eager for sunlight and fresh air. Since he was already in the lead, Durham led the way. Rounding a curve, he saw the jungle end. It took his eyes a few moments to adjust to the brightness. The sunlight reflecting off of what appeared to be gold coated vines dazzled their eyes, nearly blinding them.

When he realized the gold was real, he gave a cry of joy and rushed forward. Within seconds, his joy turned to pain and terror. Bainbridge, Sam and the rest of their party rounded the corner just in time to see the vines snake out and engulf Mr. Durham.

So shocked were they by the sight of the writhing vines and the rapid desiccation of their mate, they didn't notice the green jungle creepers wrapping around their legs and arms until they were hoisted into the trees by them.

Struggling only caused the vines to tighten. They soon found themselves disarmed. Then the creepers began to transfer them from tree to tree. They were transported through the jungle until they came to a clearing with a single woven hut in it.

The creepers did not release them; rather the plants held them suspended spread eagle at the edge of the clearing. They watched the hut apprehensively, the air rank with fear.

After a few minutes, two women and a child emerged from the hut; one old woman who looked well past child-bearing age and growing withered, a younger woman in the bloom of youth and pronouncedly pregnant helping the older woman walk, and the child, a toddler with ebony hair, looked at them with huge dark emerald green eyes.

Samantha couldn't help but think she was the prettiest little girl she'd ever seen.

The child looked directly at her, blinked then looked up at her mother. "Mami, did *Madre* cry on her hair?"

The woman smiled at the child. "No *bonita*. She must come from a place where people have yellow hair instead of brown or black."

"I do not care where they came from," the old woman interrupted. "I only care that they leave as soon as possible."

She turned to face the prisoners. "Who are you? Why are you here?"

Black Venom

Sam answered before the captain could. "Release us, and we will tell you."

In response, a vine wrapped around her throat and began to slowly constrict. The old woman smiled maliciously. "Tell me, and I will release you. Do not, and you will die here and now. Either way, I will be rid of you."

"We offered you no violence, madam!" Bainbridge protested.

"Liar! You come on my island unbidden! You slash through my children! You try to steal my *Lacrimas de Oros*!"

All the vines began to tighten, stretching the prisoners' limbs until the tension threatened to rip them apart. Sam's face, already red, started to turn purple as the vine around her throat cut off blood and air. If it pulled any more, it would sever her spine and eventually pull her head off. Only she emitted no screams of pain, because she couldn't.

"Enough!" Bainbridge managed to gasp through the pain. "We are from the merchant ship *Shining Star*. We came here seeking word of the whereabouts of the pirate Bloody Vik Brandee."

The younger, pregnant woman waved her hand and spoke a single word in a language none of them recognized. Immediately, the vines lowered them back to the ground. Sam crumpled in a near-lifeless heap.

The two women began to argue in Spanish, the older one clearly not happy.

"You little fool! If they have any connection to him, they are trouble to us. Why did you release them?" she hissed.

The younger woman remained calm and answered her tutor. *"I want to hear why they seek him, Madre. I have kept one vine on each, in case they try to cause harm."*

The old woman started to raise her own hand. Before she could begin uttering any sort of incantation, the younger woman got right in her face.

"I will not let you kill them, Dorada. I want to hear what they have to say. If you hadn't toyed with them on the pathway, they wouldn't have used the machetes."

"I am Madre." Dorada slapped her. *"You would do well to remember that, Paella. They saw the gold vines. One was foolish enough to touch them and paid the price."*

"Si. I am aware of that. What do you expect when they don't know what they're dealing with? They would never have found that path if you had allowed them to go to the village." Paella's voice took on a hostile tone. *"Do not forget that I bear the Mermaid's Tear. Once my son is born and the ceremony completed, your power will pass to me. Then I will be Madre."*

The old woman seemed to shrink in on herself. *"Who taught you to be so cruel, Paella?"*

"You did, Madre."

While they argued, the toddler wandered over to the unconscious woman. Bainbridge tried to get to Sam, but the vine on his ankle prevented it. With no blade to cut it off, he was helpless to aid his charge.

The little girl squatted next to her head and patted her hair. *"Bonita."*

Sam started breathing again but did not wake up. The child frowned and looked at the vine on the woman's ankle. Pointing at it, she said, *"Mal!"*

Instantly, the vine retreated.

The child hugged Sam around the neck and demanded, *"Bonita,* wake up!"

The demand was loud enough to draw her mother's attention. "Victoria! Come here!"

The child ignored her, smiling triumphantly at the blonde woman's response. Samantha's eyes flashed open but held no fear. She smiled back at the girl.

"Hello, Victoria. That's a pretty name. My name is Samantha," she managed to croak out and raised a hand to the angry welt on her throat.

"Hola, Samantha." She struggled a bit with the unfamiliar name. "I like your hair."

"Gracias." Sam smiled at the child, then continued in perfect Spanish, *"You have very pretty eyes."*

The child's face lit up. *"You speak my language! Mami says I look like my Papi, but I have never met him. I am named after him."*

"Your father is named Viktor?"

"Si. Abuela says he is a bad man, but Mami says she loves him and misses him."

"How old are you, Victoria?"

"This many." She held up two fingers and added, *"But I'll be this many at harvest."* She held up a third finger.

Sam looked over at Bainbridge. She tried to keep her disappointment hidden but was unable to keep the sadness out of her eyes. "The timing is all wrong, Captain. We knew the lead was old; but I had hoped it wasn't that old."

"Victoria Auna! Come here this instant!" Paella barked at her daughter.

The girl recognized the tone of her mother's demand and knew it promised a spanking if she disobeyed. "*Si, Mami.*" She hung her head and quickly returned to her mother's side. Taking her hand, she turned her huge green eyes up and asked, *"Can we let them go, Mami? Sa-man-ta seems nice, and I don't think they meant to hurt Abuela's plants."*

"For now, we will allow her to be free; but we do not yet know why she came here. I do not trust men, not even Papi…."

"Especially not him," Dorada muttered.

Paella ignored her and continued in English, "So we will hear what they have to say, then decide."

Having already gained a tiny bit of confidence from them, Sam took the initiative and tried to explain their unwelcome presence. "We were warned to stay away from this island, but I had to come here."

"Why?" Dorada interrupted sharply.

"We had heard that the pirate, Viktor Brandewyne, had been here and we are looking for more recent news of his whereabouts."

Paella looked at her suspiciously. Her voice held an undertone of jealousy when she asked, "Why do you seek him out? Are you pirate hunters? Are you his lover?"

"What? No!" Sam had not expected that reaction from the other woman. "No, he has taken my brothers captive. My father has turned his back on them, but I want to try to ransom them, if they are still alive."

Bainbridge shot her a look of pity and surprise, but she ignored it. It cost her to admit that Zach and Thomas might be dead, a very real possibility that she had stubbornly refused to accept until now.

Paella calmed as her fears were allayed. "Oh. What are their names and when were they taken?"

"Zachary and Thomas Brumble. They were taken separately, not quite two years ago."

Paella shook her head and said, "Then I cannot help you. The last time I saw Viktor was months before our daughter was born. He could be anywhere by now."

Sam gave her a sad smile. "She is the most beautiful child I've ever seen. It is sad that her father hasn't even tried to visit you and provide for the two of you. I hope that your husband is a good father to her."

Before Paella could reply, Dorada cackled. "Sad, you say? Hardly. He is evil. They are better off without him. As far as I'm concerned, men are only good for two things: labor and siring children."

Several of the men bristled at the statement, but Bainbridge motioned for them to hold their tongues. They were still held by the vines. Until they were free and clear of this island, they were in danger.

"You make men sound like less than slaves; merely things to be used," Sam said with a disbelieving laugh.

"Most of them are," Paella said. "But they can be protectors and partners, as well." She ignored her mentor's sour look. "However, such a partnership is something I cannot allow myself to indulge in.

My duty as the future *Madre* is to breed with only the strongest, most clever, and most potent men. My son will not be as powerful as my daughter. None of my future children will be as powerful as she. There is no man to match Viktor Brandewyne."

Samantha sensed the woman meant more than what her words said on the surface, but she wasn't sure what. She wasn't really that curious about it, either. She needed to gain the freedom of their party, so they could continue their search.

"When and if we find him, is there any message you wish me to pass along?" she asked.

"Tell him that I still love him, and that I forgive him for not taking me with him," Paella replied. She pointed to a path at the edge of the clearing. "Stay to the path. Do not try to cross through the jungle. You will find your weapons on the sand near your boats. Do not try to return to this clearing and never set foot on this island again. If any one of you varies from these instructions, you will all die in the golden vines."

Sam and Bainbridge both nodded their heads; the creeper vines released the men. The captain also bowed. "We understand and will abide by your rules, *Señorita*. Our deepest apologies for having troubled you."

Before they could turn to go, Paella held up her hand. "Samantha Brumble, I do not know if your brothers are still alive, but there are two things I can tell you about Captain Brandewyne that may not be general knowledge."

"Any information would be greatly appreciated, Paella."

"He sails with Hezekiah Grimm as his first mate. He also has a powerful sea witch, a siren known as Belladonna, on his crew. She is deadly and dangerous. Beware of her." She then added one more thing, "Before I forget there is a third thing you should know.

Viktor is no longer human. He has become a creature of darkness that feeds on human blood. But unlike others of his kind, he can walk about in daylight."

"Forgive me, *Señorita*, but why do you say that he is some unholy creature of superstition?" Bainbridge asked.

"You have encountered our vines, yet still doubt the existence of magic?" She laughed. She lifted her skirt to show them the old fang scars on her inner thigh, looked pointedly at Sam, and said, "I know what he is, because he has fed on me."

"Captain, it is time for us to leave this place," Sam said, visibly blanching. The scars mirrored the ones she had discovered on her own thigh after the dreams she'd had months ago of being seduced.

"Agreed. Remember, lads, stick to the path and don't turn back," he replied.

Safely back aboard the ship and out of the lagoon, Sam met with the captain in his cabin. "I apologize for seeming to usurp your authority back there, Captain," she said.

Bainbridge gave her a wry smile. "I'm glad you did, Sam. Given the temperament of that pair, I probably would have gotten us all killed. They didn't have a very high opinion of males."

"No, they did not," she agreed. After a few moments, she noticed he was giving her an appraising look. "What?"

"You have the makings of a good sea captain. Your instincts are good, and you don't hesitate to step forward to take command of a situation," he stated. "You are a good navigator, as well. You kept a potentially fatal situation from getting out of hand."

She raised an eyebrow. "My father would have said that I was foolish, impetuous, and that we survived that encounter through pure luck."

"That's probably right." He chuckled. "I doubt his phrasing would have been that delicate, though."

"No, probably not." She laughed a bit. "Well, where should we go now? This lead was fruitless and cost us a man," she said, sobering.

"It wasn't entirely fruitless. We'll set course for Havana. Someone there may have fresher news of Brandee."

"Why do you say that?"

"If he truly is sailing with the Grimm Reaper again, and what we learned from the slavers and here seem to indicate that he is, then they have been there. It's the Reaper's favorite base of operation."

"It's worth trying," she sighed. "I just wonder if anyone will be willing to tell us anything."

"We'll find out."

Chapter 5

News of a British naval patrol waylaying and searching ships as they left the delta kept the *Incubus* in port for a week longer than Viktor would have liked.

Thankfully, Jeorge didn't trouble him anymore, although he had to tolerate Guillaum's presence every night. He found himself genuinely liking the vampire. He remained careful to only discuss things of importance during daylight hours, however, within the warded confines of Celine and Angel's brothel.

Viktor also kept wary for daytime spies. Partially an old habit used to avoid pirate hunters, he now applied it to Jeorge's minions, too. Apparently, Jeorge had realized the futility of sending humans to keep tabs on him, though. With his heightened senses, he would have picked up quickly on any shadows.

He did enjoy one bright moment from having to endure Guillaum. The vampire had learned from others in Jeorge's kiss that the blockade had set up because word had gotten out about Viktor's attendance at the reception for Governor Rouget. When Vik asked why the Lord Mayor hadn't sent the city guard to ferret him out, Guillaum told him that Jeorge had his vampires cloud the memories of the mayor and governor. As far as Louis du Champ knew, his daughter was still missing and had been taken by Thomas Brumble, not Viktor Brandewyne. However, although Jeorge originally thought neither the mayor nor any of his surviving guests or servants had any memory of the pair at the reception, his vampires must have missed someone, hence the rumors.

Although he never admitted it aloud, Viktor felt like kicking himself for revealing his true name in such a high-profile venue. It had been foolishly brash and quite unlike his usual caution. He supposed he should thank Jeorge for his intervention at some point.

Belladonna had taken once again to avoiding extended periods in his presence. He suspected it had to do with his tryst with Gloribeau. He knew the siren felt jealousy over that incident. He also knew it made her more frightened of what would happen if she and he were to give in to their mutual lust. She already chafed at being permanently bound to his will. He knew she didn't want the bonds to tighten even more.

The inactivity really began to gnaw on him. He couldn't shake the feeling that it was growing dangerous for him to remain in New Orleans. He needed to get out to the open sea.

He still had four Sisters of Power to find or deal with if he wanted to stand a chance of surviving the curse Mamaan Juma had put on him. Already, he could feel his Hunger growing strong. He knew if he took too long to complete his quest, the Hunger would take him over. He also knew that regardless of how much he fed, he would waste away and starve to death.

He would rather drink the siren's blood than allow that to happen. At least then his death would be quick.

"Lazarus, come forth." He summoned the creature that had once been Jim Rigger.

Obediently, the large black cat emerged from the shadows. No passerby noticed the creature coalesce. No one even knew Viktor was there. The rooftops of the city were not in a direction most people looked.

"Hello old friend." He smiled at the cat. "I need you to find this naval blockade that is keeping us pinned down here."

Black Venom

"Mrow."

The cat appeared to dissolve into an inky mist. Quickly, the mist resolidified, and a raven stood where the cat had been. With a brief caw, the bird took flight headed toward Pontchartrain and the passage through the delta to the Gulf.

Viktor sat back and leaned against the chimney. He closed his eyes and concentrated on Lazarus, which allowed him to see through the creature's eyes.

Finally, they spotted the blockade, two British Navy ships positioned themselves at the narrowest part of the channel. The *Incubus* could squeeze past them, but she would have to do so slowly to avoid scraping hulls.

Neither warship was large. They were only sloops; the pirate ship, on the other hand, had been built to be a class one ship-of-the-line. Viktor was willing to wager that the sister ship he had recently learned of was the only other vessel in all of the Gulf or Caribbean to rival his craft.

As he directed Lazarus to snoop about the two warships, he pondered how best to get rid of them. With her copper clad hull, the *Incubus* could just ram them out of the way. However, that would draw the wrong kind of attention, and the wreckage would block the channel.

He was about to fly directly there when he remembered something Jim Rigger had told him over half a year ago. His former first mate had discovered how to briefly regain his human form and found the Brumbles' sister out looking for her brothers. As Lazarus, Jim had bitten his paw and bled into the drink of the captain of her vessel, a trick Vik used to keep his own crew in line.

The upshot was that the experiment had worked. Jim had remained uninterrupted while he had his way with the lass.

Viktor smiled to himself and projected the image to Lazarus of what he wanted the creature to do. He stood and stretched, confident that Lazarus would get both British captains to head out to sea.

He went to hunt before he set the second phase of his plan into motion.

Belladonna jumped when she sensed the summons. Her first instinct was to shut down the link she shared with the vampire. She learned some time ago it was best not to do so, however.

Her apprehension eased when she sensed he was in a good humor. She headed back to the port to see what he wanted.

She found Viktor ensconced in his favorite chair in Celine's parlor. He radiated confidence that verged on smugness.

"I've a job for you, pet."

She crossed her arms and leaned against the door jamb. "You say that as if it were something I would enjoy."

"Oh, I think you will. The two Navy sloops that have been keeping us here are currently en route to Havana. They carry a combined compliment of eighty men. I do not want them to reach their destination."

Belle raised an eyebrow. "Am I free to dispose of them any way I see fit?"

He thought about it, then steepled his fingers in front of him with his elbows on the chair's armrests, his smile decidedly predatory.

"Not quite. I want the ships left intact and adrift. As for the crews, however, I hope you have a good appetite."

"Eighty men?" She grinned, displaying her needle-like true teeth. "A mere snack."

He laughed. "Come now, pet; I've seen you devour far less than that and be satisfied."

"That was just for physical nourishment. You need to remember, Viktor, that I personally devoured the entire previous crew of your ship. She sailed with a full complement of five hundred men."

"In one feeding?" He sounded skeptical.

She nodded. "In one feeding. Have you never wondered how I can eat even one human without my belly distending to the point of bursting?"

"It had honestly never occurred to me," he admitted. "Now that I think about it, I experience the same effect when I've had several kills in one night. Where does all the blood, or in your case, flesh go?"

"Pure energy and magic," she answered. "The more we feed, the more our power grows. It is part of our magical nature. That is why we can go without for long periods between large feeds, if necessary. Such binging habits are ill-advised on a regular basis, however. Otherwise, our appetites would get out of control. Then one of two things would happen: we would either deplete our resources, or we would draw the kind of hunters who know exactly how to destroy us."

"I will heed your warning, pet. Enjoy your hunt." He dismissed her.

The siren turned with a smile and left the room.

☠

Belle hadn't been gone half an hour when Jon-Jon bounced into the room. Viktor fought not to smile. The sight of the nearly seven-foot-tall man dancing from foot to foot in excitement was very comical.

"What has you so excited, Mr. Jon? Or do you just need to use the head?"

The burly pirate ignored his captain's jibe and answered, "Good news, Cap'n. Word all along the waterfront is that the blockaders have pulled out."

"As a matter of fact, I already knew. I arranged it. I believe you have further news, though. The blockade lifting is hardly worth this level of excitement."

"Aye, Cap'n. A couple of days ago, I heard talk of a fat prize sailing out of Vera Cruz headed for Seville. She's rumored to be taking the northern route through the Gulf and the Straits."

"Why didn't you mention this before?"

Jon-Jon rubbed the back of his neck and looked down, as if he didn't want to make eye contact with his captain. "Didn't see the point in it, Cap'n, what with being pinned in by that blockade. But the tide'll be high in a few hours. Most of the lads have had their things ready for a few days."

"Very well, Jon-Jon. Round them up and get them aboard. I'll fetch Mr. Grimm."

"Aye, Cap'n. What about Belle?"

Viktor smirked. "She is on an errand. I've no doubt of her ability to find us once she's finished."

☠

Knowing they still had a couple of hours until high tide, Viktor chose not to interrupt his first mate's pleasure. Instead, he decided to take up the hall seat outside the room Grimm and one of the girls were using.

After a while, he lit up a cigar and smiled. He had to admit, for a man just over forty, Hezekiah Grimm had impressive stamina with the wenches.

When an hour passed without any sign of a break, Viktor decided to take action. Still seated, he reached to the side and rapped on the door. "Mr. Grimm! Finish up and gather your gear!"

"Dammit!" The epithet came through the door slightly muffled. Grimm called out, "Aye, Captain!" slightly louder.

A few minutes later, Mr. Grimm emerged from the room. He had a sea bag slung over his shoulder. Spotting the shortened cigar Viktor was enjoying, he asked, "You wouldn't happen to have another one of those? I'm out of pipe tobacco."

"Here." Vik pulled out another stogie with a chuckle. "We'll step into the tobacconist's on the way to the ship. Wouldn't do for us to run into Zeke without smoke for him."

"No, it wouldn't," Grimm agreed. "He's probably still testy about the boy."

"Aye." Vik peered into the room to see who had been keeping his first mate occupied. "Hullo, Angel. Thought that sounded like you. Here, split this with Celine. I don't know when we'll next be in this port."

He tossed a hefty bag of coins onto the bed. The blonde madam stopped in the middle of cleaning herself to pick up the bag and test its weight.

"*Merci beaucoup*! I will let her know you have sailed, *mon amor*."

The two pirates turned and left.

Viktor filled Grimm in as they exited the smoke shop later, headed toward the waterfront.

"Do you really think Angelique will split that with Celine? That was quite a hefty purse, Vik," Grimm stated.

"She has no choice but to obey me, Hezekiah. She'll share. Jon-Jon should have the crew rounded up and aboard by the time we reach the ship."

They walked on in silence for a bit; then Grimm asked, "Where is Belladonna?"

"Following the two British sloops that had been blocking the channel. Once they're far enough away, she is going to dispose of their crews."

"Seems a shame to waste the boats and supplies."

"Someone will find them, eventually. We've a larger prize to go after."

Grimm raised an eyebrow. "Sounds like you're sending someone a message, Vik."

"I am." He nodded. "Lazarus discovered they'd been sent here to scout me out. Apparently, this Commodore Critchfield is determined to hunt me down. He has dispersed spies to all the major ports around the Caribbean and Gulf."

"Stubborn man." Grimm whistled. "As long as we were gone from these waters with that business with Rosalia, you'd think he'd have given up by now."

"I've a feeling the Commodore is just as tenacious as we are, Hezekiah."

Belladonna caught up with the *Incubus* just west of the Keys not long after the ship finished taking her prize.

Jon-Jon's earned an extra share for providing correct information. The vessel they pirated turned out to be a treasure ship, a rare catch. Since the Spanish lost control of the western waters almost a century ago, very few treasure ships sailed anymore. The so-called golden age of piracy in the 1600s took its toll on the Spanish Crown's coffers.

This prize carried gold ingots and coins, some silver ingots, a few emeralds and rubies, and several small casks of semi-precious stones. Amazingly, she only boasted a small escort with her consisting of three gunboats. One cut and run as soon as the *Incubus'* crew unmasked her guns. The other two remained and fought.

They might have gotten away after sunset with any other pirate. The second the day star sank beneath the waves, Viktor loosed his cadre of vampires on the escort boats.

He dealt with the treasure ship himself. He wanted that crew intact. The battle cost him a few men, so he planned to recruit replacements from among his captives.

When Belladonna arrived, headless bodies littered the water around the three vessels. It was Viktor's way of preventing any extra vampires. His cadre of six was more than enough to keep fed.

The siren made short work of cleaning up the leftovers before she boarded the pirate vessel. This feeding compounded with the one she'd just come from had her powers at peak. The result was that, despite Viktor's control over his crew, they all felt drawn to her.

The vampire immediately sensed this and summoned her over to the treasure ship. In a good mood from the feeding, she didn't try to fight the summons, even though she sensed his irritation with her.

Belle felt gratified to see her sexual aura had an effect even on Viktor. His irritation quickly turned to angry lust.

He strode over to her, grasped her arms, and launched into the sky with her, leaving Grimm to finish dealing with the prisoners. He flew the siren high enough that the lights of the ships looked like stars below them. He took some satisfaction that she clung to him, unable to hide her fear at being so far out of her element.

"You dare try to manipulate me or my crew? I thought you knew better than that, Belladonna." His tone wasn't friendly.

"I have fed well, Viktor," she answered. "It's been so long since my powers have been this full that my control over them is not as good as it should be. I didn't deliberately try to exert any magical dominance. Now please, take us back down." Her words came rapidly, another sign of her fear.

It wasn't an apology, but from her, it was close enough. Viktor could smell her fear and the truth in her voice. She still exuded raw sexuality though, so he wasn't about to risk returning to the *Incubus*.

He scanned about as he decreased their altitude. He spotted an uninhabited key and took them there.

Once on solid ground, he clasped her to him roughly. His kiss was not gentle. The siren had managed to clamp down on her glamour, but her fear kept his lust fired.

Belle endured the kiss. She wanted to return it, but she thought Viktor might interpret it as a deliberate play to use her powers on him. She whimpered with the effort to not respond.

He growled, grasped her hair, and forced her head back to bare her throat. His kisses trailed from her mouth to just above her pulse point.

She went very still as she realized the true danger of the situation. They stood close enough to the water that she could drag herself to it to heal if he tore her throat out. But she knew he wouldn't survive the encounter. A single drop of her blood was enough to kill the vampire instantly.

Viktor picked up on the sudden tension and realized what he had been about to do. In a split second, he put several yards between them.

"That was too close, pet."

"I know. If your Hunger is getting this out of control, we need to get back on course."

He nodded. "Indeed. Have you had any visions to give us a starting point?"

"No, I haven't had any visions, even with all the recent feeding or the renewal of my powers. I am afraid that particular power will require sacrifice on your part. One of the prisoners should do."

"Hezekiah won't like it," he said. "We'd planned on recruiting them to replace the lads that didn't survive this battle. However, I value my life and this quest above even his life or the ship and crew."

He held a hand out to her. It puzzled him that she just looked at it and shook her head. "Come on, Belle. We have to get back to the ship."

"I'll swim. I don't like flying, and I don't trust your control right now."

He saw the merit to her argument. He nodded and launched back into the air without her.

Back aboard the *Incubus*, the vampire landed and went in search of his first mate. He found Mr. Grimm in the infirmary, conferring with Matthew Coffin, the ship's surgeon.

Dr. Coffin, or "Stitches" as he was sometimes called, was fitting Sniff with an eye patch.

Viktor took in the situation quickly. "How did it happen?"

"A splinter hit him in the eye during the battle," the doctor answered. "If it had gone any deeper, it would have pierced his brain pan and killed him." He held up the offending piece of wood almost as long as a marlin spike.

"Damn, man! You're going to keep losing parts until you're nothing but a stump!"

Sniff laughed. Well into a bottle of rum, for medicinal purposes, he felt no pain. The hairless, toothless, noseless, legless, and now one-eyed rigging rat grabbed his crotch and cackled. "As long as the most important parts stay attached, Cap'n, I don't care."

"You and that damn whale dick of yours." Grimm laughed then turned his attention to Viktor. "You wanted to see me, Captain?"

"Aye. What has been done with the prisoners?"

"I had them put in the larder hold for now," Grimm answered. "They haven't been given any of the special rum yet. Its running low and I didn't see the point in wasting it on men we might not keep."

Vik slapped him on the shoulder. "Good man. Let's go pick one out to give to Belle."

Grimm followed him but frowned. "After the feed she's already had and what she nearly did to the crew, I hardly think she deserves a reward."

"The Hunger is trying to take me, Hezekiah. I need her to have a vision."

They continued on to the hold where the prisoners were being kept without further comment.

Chapter 6

Mere minutes after the siren took her victim off, Viktor knew something had gone horribly wrong. He was hit with a wave of pain and terror strong enough to nearly knock him down.

"Captain?" Grimm noticed the effect but didn't know the cause.

"She's in trouble," was the only answer Viktor gave. The next moment, the vampire was off the ship.

The vision hit Belladonna just as the last glimmer of life left the body of the man Viktor gave her. It caught her off guard coming so early. She was used to being nearly through with her meal before gaining a vision.

This time, however, she became instantly aware of the Sister of Power they had to find. She knew in a heartbeat the woman's name and location — and power base.

Unfortunately, the suddenness of the vision didn't allow her time to shield. She found herself now the focus of the Sister's power and attention.

She had time to scream; then everything went black.

Viktor spotted her floating face down. He also saw several sharks cautiously closing in on her. Even before he could reach her a small mako darted in and hit the uneaten body of her victim.

Despite the risk to himself, he dove into the water to get a good grip on the siren. He managed to grasp her around the waist and lifted her out of the water, grunting with the effort.

In her true form, she presented a considerably heavier and much more unwieldy burden. Her tail threw off the balance for him.

As soon as they cleared the water, the sharks closed in on the corpse.

By the time they made it back to the ship, Belladonna had returned to human form. Viktor felt very grateful for that. When she had her shark tail, her skin exuded a layer of some kind of mucous. He'd encountered it on fish all his life, so it hadn't surprised him, but it made her hard to keep a grasp on.

It worried him that she remained unconscious. He saw no marks on her. He wracked his brain in an effort to think of what could have done this to her.

Without being bidden, Grimm followed him as he carried her to his cabin. Even Lazarus manifested and trotted along beside them. After Viktor laid her on the bed, the cat leapt up and curled up at her side.

"What happened to her, Vik?" Grimm asked.

"I don't know." He shook his head. "I sensed she was in great pain and terrified. She was unconscious when I found her. There's not a mark on her, though."

Black Venom

Lazarus sniffed at the siren. He stood back up, reared up on Viktor and started to paw at the lighter of two silver chains the vampire always wore.

The heavier chain held the silver vial used to collect magic from the Sisters. The lighter chain held a milky white crystal. It had been given to him by Mother Celie, who had called it a "key." He had used it to summon Hell's Breath Island for the first time. In his travels since then he'd learned it had other uses and properties, as well, and that its proper name was the Elder's Stone.

"I should have thought of that. Thank you, my friend," Vik said to the cat. He fished the crystal out and held it near the siren. It flared with light.

Belladonna's breathing, previously labored, evened out. Slowly, the glow faded until the crystal returned to normal. The siren sighed, her eyelids fluttered, and she settled into normal sleep.

Grimm quickly deduced what had happened. "If this Sister has that much power, we've got our work cut out for us, Vik."

"Aye, Hezekiah. I've a feeling I'm going to need the Elder's Stone quite a lot with this one. It's the one sure guard against their magic. She's already sent the message she's not friendly."

"Is Belle going to be alright?"

"I think so. Lazarus, stay here with her. When she wakes, come let me know."

"Mreeah."

The siren woke with a start. Instinctively, she drew in a breath to scream as she remembered the magical attack. It came out as "oomph." The cat picked that moment to jump from the shelf to her stomach to the table.

This both irritated and relieved her. It gave her time to realize she was back on the ship. She knew Viktor wouldn't have appreciated it if she had screamed. That would have destroyed the minds of any humans within hearing distance.

A moment later, she realized she was in his cabin, not hers. The scent should have told her, but she was still mildly in shock. She picked up the pillow and pressed her face into it, inhaling deeply. Oddly, she found Viktor's scent comforting. She chuckled to herself. The pirate captain was just as deadly of a predator as she, definitely not someone who should make anyone feel safe.

His scent and her own thoughts distracted her so much she never heard him enter the cabin.

Vik raised an eyebrow at the sight of Belle nuzzling his pillow. He approached her as he watched. It spoke of how much she had not recovered yet that he could do so unnoticed. He sat down next to her and gently took the pillow from her grasp.

She jumped nervously, fear showing in her eyes for a split second.

"Easy, pet." He stroked her hair in an effort to soothe her. "You are safe here. I have fed well, and my Hunger is under control. The question is how are you? Did I get to you in time, or did her attack do permanent damage?"

Rather than shy away as he half expected her to, she tucked up against his side and huddled in on herself.

"Did you feel it, too? I've never encountered anything like her before, Viktor. Gloribeau may be more powerful, but this one is far more dangerous to me and more malevolent."

"No, pet." He tucked an arm around her since she seemed to need to feel comforted and protected. "I did not feel her attack, only your fear and pain. I didn't suspect what had happened to you until I exposed the Elder's Stone. It flared so bright it hurt to look at. Only the magic of one of the Sisters can cause that kind of reaction outside of Hell's Breath."

"She caught me off guard. I've never had a vision that early in a feeding before. I think my magic called to hers." She looked up at him, worry and fear plain on her face. That she didn't try to hide it alarmed him more than anything she could have said. "I don't think I'm going to be much help to you in dealing with her directly."

"Are you that frightened, pet?"

She shook her head. "It's not just fear, Viktor. *Mere* Venoma Noir has domain over all creatures venomous, even me. She may even be able to use me against you, whether I will or no."

He continued to hold her and stroke her hair as he mulled the situation over. The loss of the siren's aid would be bad but not crippling, provided it was only with this Sister that he had this difficulty. Belle was too valuable to his quest for him to risk losing or crippling her over this Venoma Noir.

Still, there was one glimmer of hope to outwit the Sister on this. "The crystal restored you from her attack. If you were to wear it, perhaps you would be protected from her."

She looked at him, amazed. "You would really do that for me?"

"It seems the most practical course."

"I appreciate it, but it would not work, although the idea has some merit."

He frowned. "Could you explain that, pet?"

"Mother Celie gave the stone to you. I'd be willing to wager that she never used it for herself. I could wear it, but its magic has impressed to you. It won't work for anyone else. It would just be a pretty bit of crystal," she answered. "But we won't have too far inland to travel to get to her; so, if I stay close to you, I should be safe from her power."

Viktor quickly caught the implication of her statement. "You saw where she is?"

"Yes, the connection was very short, but she revealed herself with the same clarity and intensity as the focus of her attack. We need to set ashore on the mainland not far from the islands of Trinidad and Tobago."

He nodded but did not get up right away. Instead, he continued to hold her, brushing his fingertips against her cheek. He hadn't dressed her while she had been unconscious, and he now found himself very aware of her continued nudity.

He knew the attack had taken its toll on her magic and that she couldn't use her glamour on him at the moment. The look of apprehension in her eyes confirmed that. She felt good in his arms; soft and pliable. Her vulnerability made him both possessive and protective. He knew how rare it was for her to display any behavior that might make her appear weak.

"Viktor?"

Rather than answer, he leaned down to kiss her. His hand drifted lower from her cheek to toy with her breast. He used the pad of his thumb to tease the nipple to hardness. And still, he continued to kiss her.

Belle moaned at the gentleness of his touch. It was so different from the angry kiss earlier on the key. As much as she wanted this moment to last or to continue to its natural conclusion, she knew she couldn't.

"Viktor, we can't. I want to, but we can't afford to. Magic is in flux for both of us. It could be glorious, or it could all go horribly wrong."

He sighed. "It's always something with us, isn't it, pet? You're right. That is a risk neither of us can afford right now."

She hung her head, no more happy than he was, but grateful that he was handling it so well. "I'm sorry, Viktor. Hopefully, one day all the circumstances will be right."

"That, or we'll just decide consequences be damned."

Jeorge summoned a couple of his vampires to his house. He had Maurice make sure that Melanie was out hunting before he received the two he summoned. Despite his agreement with Viktor to not use her to spy on each other, he didn't trust her.

She'd played witness to his agreement not to investigate the child Viktor delivered to the swamp witch. Jeorge had encountered far too many instances over the centuries of vampires betraying their masters in favor of their makers, regardless of oaths.

"Chloe, Jerome, I have a task for you."

The pair knelt before him. "We are yours to command," the male said.

"A most unusual child was delivered to the old witch in the northern bayou not long ago. The boy is a hybrid of vampire and merfolk. Find out what you can about him. If possible, bring him here to me. On no account, however, are you to feed on or harm the child."

"Understood," the female said.

Chloe and Jerome found out quickly the task given them was not as easy or simple as it sounded. Flying over the bayou proved futile. The canopy meshed too thick for even their sharp eyes to penetrate. An attempt to listen for heartbeats proved equally fruitless. The song of the insects and frogs nearly deafened them, and too many creatures inhabited the area to make filtering out a specific heartbeat from the multitude possible.

Even an attempt to fly through the swamp proved difficult. The trees kept shifting, always forcing them to the east, away from the river.

Jerome started to get frustrated with this. He finally caught the scent of something human or human-like. He began using his super-human strength to rip a swath through the trees.

Chloe saw the logic of this action and, also on the scent, joined him in his efforts. For a time, they made little headway, but then it grew easier.

"The witch is weakening," Jerome declared. They just caught sight of the stilt house.

A split second later, a heavy oak limb dropped and caught him mid-back. The blow did not harm the vampire, but it knocked him off balance in his flight. Before he could correct, a cypress knee thrust upward and impaled him.

Black Venom

Chloe had been on similar hunts in the past, although she'd never gone up against as formidable a guardian before. She pressed on toward the goal rather than allow her partner's demise to distract her. She almost reached the cabin and prepared to alight on the catwalk.

Without warning, a fountain of swamp water sprang up under her. It didn't blast into her but split mere inches below her feet and formed a sphere around her.

"A pretty trick, but this will not stop me," she said as Gloribeau stepped out of the dwelling.

"Oh, I think it will," the Sister of Power countered. "This is my bayou. I have blessed these waters, and they are holy to me."

"Impossible. Only a priest can bless the waters."

Glory laughed at her. "How old are you, vampire?"

"Three hundred and eighty-five."

"And yet, you are still a child to me. I am the most ancient of my kind. Before even the ancestors of the now-banished tribes came to these lands and waters, I was here. Do you honestly believe that only Christians can deem things holy? It is a matter of faith. What is holy and how it came to be blessed varies from person to person and who or what they believe in."

"Bah! Pagans and witches are just as unclean as I am."

"Then touch the water and prove me wrong, vampire." Glory smiled serenely.

Chloe bared her fangs in a snarl. "Jeorge said not to harm or feed on the boy. He gave no such instructions for you, witch." She thrust her hand through the thin wall of the watery sphere.

With a shriek, she drew it back even more quickly, now nothing but a blackened, bony claw. Too late, she realized the true peril she faced.

As if to drive the point home even more, Glory allowed the sphere to shrink a small fraction in diameter. Chloe found herself forced to draw up her legs and still maintain her hover to keep from touching the water.

Gloribeau studied the situation for a while in calm silence.

Chloe glared back at the witch and felt fear begin to gnaw at her. The perfect calm of the witch unnerved the vampire. The magic appeared effortless. The witch didn't even look to be concentrating hard.

The vampire, on the other hand, had to concentrate harder and harder to stay within the center of the sphere the longer she hovered there. Although it didn't, the watery cage seemed to shrink even more around her.

"Say something!" she yelled. "What do you want from me? Why are you just staring at me?"

With a voice that betrayed no emotion but only curiosity, Glory answered, "Are you Jeorge's get?"

Puzzled as to why she would want to know that, the vampire answered, "He made me, yes. Why?"

"I have something to say to him. Contact him."

"I don't know what you are talking about."

A single drop of water fell inside the sphere. It caught her on the cheek and made her hiss in pain as it scalded to the bone.

"Contact him, now." Glory's tone implied she didn't really care how this played out; she had the air of a goddess confronted with an insect that fancied itself her equal.

Chloe felt a small surge of energy, as Jeorge opened a circuit between them. She found herself forced to fight to keep her body from opening up. Her master didn't understand why she cowered before the swamp witch. Once the joining completed, however, he understood fully.

"You have changed since the last time I saw you, Gloribeau." His voice came out of Chloe's throat.

"I have been restored, Jeorge. I am surprised at you, however. You know better than to send your people into my bayou without my leave."

"I am merely curious about the child that Viktor Brandewyne brought to you."

"You are more than curious, Jeorge. The boy's magic calls out to you and all of your kind. You sent two of your minions to take him. One has already fallen to the bayou. Now this one must pay the price, as well. You may watch or not as you please; but remember this, Jeorge. Robert Brandewyne is under my protection, and no one, not even his own father, enters my bayou unbidden."

"Master! Save me!" Chloe pled.

"I cannot save you, my child." His voice held great sorrow and regret. "Your life is the price for my foolishness and greed. I will stay with you until the end."

"No!" she keened.

Gloribeau's voice drew her attention. "How long has it been since you fed?"

"Last night."

"Mm-hm, so you will not be able to keep up your concentration for much longer, not that it matters."

"What do you mean '*not that it matters*'?"

In answer, Glory held her hands out to the side, palms up. She closed her eyes, tilted her head back and drew in a deep breath. She released it as a long sigh then smiled serenely.

"The sun will rise soon. I give you a choice, vampire. You can witness your last dawn and perish slowly, or you can merely stand straight and let the water end things quickly."

"Jeorge, please don't let her do this! Make her release me!"

He kept his silence, although she could still feel his presence.

The treetops above the sphere parted. Already, the stars were fading and the sky looked more blue than black. The fountain which supported the water sphere began to rise higher.

Chloe screamed and contorted around in her watery prison in a desperate effort to match altitude and still avoid contact. She wasn't entirely successful. By the time the sphere cleared the canopy, she had sizzling blackened spots all over her hands, feet, knees and elbows.

Once the prison stabilized, she ceased to struggle and huddled in on herself. She continued to scream, sob, and plead with her maker to free her from Glory's trap.

As the sun neared the horizon, Jeorge manifested as a transparent image outside the sphere.

"Chloe, look at me."

She had no choice but to obey. She reached her burnt claw out to him and begged. "Release me!"

The sun rose, and her body began to smoke. She emitted a keen, high-pitched wail.

"Stand up," he commanded.

Chloe straightened up and shattered the water sphere in the process. For an instant, the supporting column of water engulfed her. Then, it collapsed back into the swamp.

No sign of her remained. The vampire had been completely dissolved.

The apparition of Jeorge descended back to the bayou to face Gloribeau.

"You have made your point, Gloribeau. No more of my people shall come for the boy. If any vampires enter your bayou without your permission, they will not be mine — unless they have earned such punishment."

"So be it."

He faded from sight.

Chapter 7

The journey passed fairly uneventfully. The crew of the *Incubus* took no more prizes before they reached their destination. In the interest of time, however, Viktor and Grimm selected an uninhabited cay to hide the bulk of the cargo stolen from the treasure ship on. Viktor wanted to reach Venoma Noir as quickly as possible. The conversion of that many ingots and gemstones into less conspicuous coinage could take weeks to accomplish without getting caught.

Shortly before they made landfall, things began to grow difficult.

Belladonna went to Viktor's cabin and entered without knocking. He sat in the midst of a meeting with Grimm, Jon-Jon and Brumble. He knew she wouldn't interrupt without knocking unless she had a very good reason.

"What is wrong, Belle?"

She gave him her most sultry smile. "Nothing."

That proved enough warning to let him know something was very wrong. The siren's abnormal behavior put Viktor instantly on the alert.

Grimm picked up on his captain's subtle body language. He realized there was an unaccustomed tension in the vampire.

Jon-Jon and Brumble remained oblivious to the danger. Despite the control Vik held over all of his crew, the siren exercised her sexual glamour and soon enraptured the two unwary pirates.

Both the captain and the first mate felt it. Grimm visibly struggled not to go to her. Only Viktor seemed completely immune. The warmth that the Elder's Stone emitted kept him focused. Since Grimm sat closest to him in the room, he reckoned the crystal gave him partial protection, as well.

"What do you think you are doing, pet?"

She laughed; a bell-like sound. "What do you think I am doing, Viktor?" She pulled the hem of her shirt out of her breeches and untied the waistband to allow them to slide down and puddle around her feet.

Jon-Jon and Zach watched her with eager, hungry faces. It proved especially tempting to the young Brumble. He'd enjoyed her favors before.

Belladonna stepped out of the pants and sashayed around the table. The shirt hem reached her knees, keeping her most tantalizing bits hidden from view but not from imagination. Trailing a hand along the backs of their chairs as she passed around the table, she made sure they caught her scent.

The poor men practically salivated.

She stopped behind Grimm and rested a hand on each of his shoulders. He locked eyes with Viktor, using him as a mental anchor as she leaned over to let her hair drape around his face. Her touch was the most gentle of caresses and raised gooseflesh — and other things.

She smiled at the captain. "It would only take me a second to extend my talons. In less than a minute, I could take his head." In stark contrast to her words, her voice was at the most seductive he'd ever heard it. "You could feast on his blood, Viktor. I could feast on his flesh. Then, you could fuck me until we're both too sore to move."

Viktor saw the tortured look on Grimm's face. The man's scent reeked of lust and terror, with a hint of anger. With a sigh, he realized it would be a while before he could trust the two of them not to try to kill each other, provided everyone survived this encounter.

"Why waste time on an appetizer, pet?" He kept his tone nonchalant. "There's the bed. We can go straight to the main course."

The siren's eyes flashed amber. She grinned and said, "I like the way you think."

Grimm relaxed as she moved away from him without drawing blood. His captain's next order surprised him, however.

"All of you, out — now."

He wanted to argue against leaving Viktor alone to face the siren. He knew something was wrong with her and that she could easily turn on Vik. But he knew better than to argue with him.

Besides, someone had to herd Jon-Jon and Brumble out. The siren's spell almost completely overrode the vampire's control over his men. Grimm didn't think he'd have too much trouble getting Brumble out, since the man was already standing, eyes locked on Belle. Jon-Jon presented a bit of a problem, but he had a plan for how to get the burly, larger pirate on his feet and out the door. He just hoped it would work.

"Mr. Jon!"

Jon-Jon blinked as if just waking up and looked unsure of his surroundings. He looked about and spotted the first mate. "Aye, Mr. Grimm?"

"There's a small keg of gin I've been saving in my cabin. What say we leave the Captain to his pleasure?"

"Hmm?" It took a few moments for the key phrases to sink in. "Oh! Aye, Mr. Grimm! The gin sounds like an excellent idea."

"Good. Bring young Brumble along with you. The lad looks like he could use a shot to clear his head."

Obediently, Jon-Jon snagged Zach by the arm and dragged him along trailing out of the cabin behind the first mate.

They left just in time to Viktor's way of thinking. If any of them had stayed long enough to see Belladonna remove her shirt and sit back on the bed, he doubted they would have left willingly.

She posed on the bed with her legs open in invitation, to let him know exactly what she wanted. He couldn't help but smile. He liked the view. However, he recognized it for the trap it was. The scorching heat from the crystal inside his shirt confirmed that Venoma currently controlled his siren.

That seriously irritated him.

Still, he played along. He felt it best to get as close as possible before breaking the Sister's hold on the siren. It would be a gamble that he could free her before she attacked.

He walked over to the bed. He kept one foot on the deck and placed a knee between hers on the bed. Then, he leaned over her, which forced her to lean back on her elbows. The heat in his eyes, matching the heat in hers, was genuine. He truly wished he could just go ahead and take her. As long as the Sister controlled her, giving in to his lust bore too great a cost. He braced himself with one arm and leaned in even closer. He kissed her as if he would devour her from the mouth down. She returned the kiss with fervor and wrapped her legs around his waist. She pulled him to her and let him know with her body how badly she wanted him to bury himself in her.

She growled in frustration at the barrier his clothes presented. Viktor smiled to himself. He'd hoped for this reaction from her. He reached his free hand up as if to unlace his shirt front.

Too late, she realized what he truly intended on doing. Her talons bit deep into his back and came just shy of reaching his lungs. He had to use all his speed to fish out the Elder's Stone in time to stop her from slicing him open.

The moment he exposed the crystal, the siren screamed. Luckily, it was just an ordinary scream of fear and anger rather than the mind-shattering shriek she was capable of.

Belladonna tried desperately to get away. Viktor was having none of it, however. He collapsed his full weight on top of her and pinned her to the feather mattress. Although she had the strength, she did not have the leverage to dislodge him. The screams turned to cries of pain as the crystal was pinned between them.

Her continued struggles let him know Venoma Noir maintained a stubborn grasp on the siren. As Belladonna bucked under him, he opened the bond they shared cautiously. He didn't want to risk the Sister gaining control of him, as well, but he had to determine how strong her hold was.

It felt similar to the experience of looking through Lazarus' eye when he sent the creature in its raven form to spy things out, yet it was different. What he saw wasn't a literal physical image but more of a symbolic vision.

Mere Venoma Noir sat at the center of a web of power. Most of the strands were localized to her, but a few she'd flung far. She tugged on the strand connected to Belladonna. He saw where it frayed, the glow of the Elder's Stone sawing at it. But, just like spider web, it was not letting go. It would have to be washed off.

In that instant, he knew what he had to do. He bit his tongue, lacerating it severely on his fangs. He then forced a kiss on the siren before the wounds could close and heal. She screamed into his mouth as Venoma tried to force her away from him. He refused to break the kiss until she swallowed some of the blood.

The moment she swallowed, Belle regained control of herself. She began to return the kiss, feeding hungrily at his mouth. She knew it would bind her that much closer to the vampire, but she'd rather be enslaved to Viktor than to Venoma.

The men almost reached Grimm's cabin when they heard Belladonna scream. All three men turned to look at the closed door behind them. When the screams turned to cries of pain, Zach seemed to return to full awareness.

He started to head back toward the Captain's cabin. Grimm saw it and ordered, "Stand down, Mr. Brumble. The Captain is not to be disturbed."

"He's killing her!" Zach protested.

"Mr. Jon, restrain Mr. Brumble."

Jon-Jon obediently grabbed the younger, smaller man by the shoulders, his weight enough to keep the man in place. Since he'd been sailing with him longer, he'd had opportunity to see what happened to anyone foolish enough to barge in on Viktor. It didn't hurt that he'd already recovered from the siren's spell. Clearly, Zach had not.

"Let me go! Belle needs our help!" Zach yelled. "The Captain is killing her! Can't you hear, man?"

Grimm leveled a pistol at Zach's face. "Stand down, Mr. Brumble. I won't tell you again." The first mate's voice held just the faintest edge of anger. "After what the bitch just tried to do, I don't care what he does to her. You are a good navigator. I would hate to lose you, but I will not hesitate to pull this trigger."

Viktor broke the kiss first. He smiled smugly at Belladonna, stood up and offered her a hand. She took it and tried to pull him back to the bed.

He shook his head. "Not right now, pet. We have damage control to see to."

She pouted but got up. "Do I need to get dressed?"

"It would probably help." She quickly pulled the shirt back on but heard angry voices outside the cabin. She realized what Viktor was talking about. "I can grab the pants later," she said as she brushed past the vampire. "It sounds like your first mate and chief navigator are about to kill each other."

They exited the cabin to see Jon-Jon holding Zach, and Grimm threatening to shoot the navigator. The second mate had turned so that the mini ball wouldn't catch him if it made it through Zach's skull.

Viktor moved to stand beside his first mate so quickly it made the man jump. He lifted Grimm's gun hand by the wrist. "Thank you, but that won't be necessary, Hezekiah."

Zach still hadn't seen Belladonna.

"Why did you kill her?" he yelled at his captain.

"She is not dead and is relatively unharmed, Mr. Brumble. Calm yourself." Viktor's voice was calm, but he could feel that the siren's influence on his navigator was overriding his own. "Belle, please release him before one of us is forced to kill him."

"I can't."

"What do you mean, you can't?"

"I don't know how," she answered truthfully. "If I let them get this far gone, it's because I'm going to eat them."

"Damn." He frowned at the dilemma. Then an idea struck him. "Mr. Jon, force his mouth open."

As the second mate obeyed, Viktor bit his own wrist. Making sure it was bleeding freely; he forced it into Zach's mouth. Grimm ended up having to help hold him still. As soon as he swallowed, the siren's spell vanished.

Belle's legs collapsed under her when control over Brumble returned to the vampire.

Vik looked over his shoulder at her and asked, "Are you all right, pet?"

"Yes." She nodded and braced herself against the wall to stand back up. "I've just never felt the bond break before. It caught me off guard."

"You can release him now," Vik said to his mates.

Zach immediately wiped his mouth and began to wretch. Vik silently willed him to stop. He didn't want to risk the man throwing up the blood he had just swallowed.

"Mr. Grimm, I think I may join the three of you for some of that gin. Let's make sure Mr. Brumble gets a double shot. It will settle his stomach."

"You aren't coming back to your cabin?" Belle asked.

"Not right away, pet. We should make landfall before tomorrow evening, so there is much to tend to." He saw the look of uncertainty on her face. He turned back to her and gently caressed her cheek. "Go back to my cabin. I won't be very long. I want you to stay close to me, so Venoma can't try that again."

She savored the touch, gave him a sad smile, and went back to his cabin to wait on him.

When they made landfall, Viktor and Grimm decided to leave both Jon-Jon and Zach in charge of the ship and crew. In truth, Viktor wanted his second mate to keep an eye on their navigator. After the incident with the siren, he didn't want the man anywhere near her, nor did he fully trust him with the ship.

Viktor didn't like how subdued Belladonna seemed. It wasn't like her. He'd gotten used to her normal attitude of self-assurance and near rebelliousness. It had him hoping that whatever quest this Sister sent them on took them far enough away she wouldn't have an influence on the siren.

"I'm glad she's not far inland," Belle said as they started their trek into the jungle.

"Why is that, pet?"

"This close to her, it would be unwise to leave me with the ship; but the farther from the sea I get, the weaker I grow. I wish we could just kill her."

He understood her fear, but he shook his head. "That is something I can't afford to do, pet."

"I know." She didn't sound happy about it.

About an hour into their trek, the siren got very skittish. "Be on your guard," she warned. "She's about to launch an attack." The entire company went on the alert. Look about as they might, though, they could see no immediate threat. It wasn't until one of the men at the rear of their group collapsed that they realized the true nature of the menace.

"Barnett, what is it?" Grimm called to the man, as he turned to check on him. A crawling horror played out before the pirates as they all turned to look.

Barnett lay writhing on the ground, or so they thought. Then they realized he was already dead. A horde of venomous creatures crawled on and in his body, making it appear to writhe.

Knowing what to look for now, it didn't take them long to realize that they were completely surrounded. Every kind of spider, scorpion, and snake imaginable closed in on them.

The men quickly huddled together. Belle got so close to Viktor's back that only their clothes separated them. No one noticed that the creatures seemed to shy away from Grimm as he moved to stay with the group.

Black Venom

The pirates tacitly agreed no one would make an effort to retrieve Barnett's body. Everyone was more concerned with not ending up in the same state.

Viktor felt grateful that Belle stayed at his back rather than cling to his front or side. Still, the other crew members huddled close enough to make him feel crowded. He found it very irritating; an effect he felt sure Venoma wished to achieve.

The creatures advanced no further than just outside the edge of their group. The pirates huddled closer. Yet their tormentors did not close the circle smaller as if some invisible line they would not or could not cross had been drawn around the group.

"What are they waiting for?" one of the pirates, Higgins, asked. The man kept glancing at the horror that had been Barnett. He sweated profusely and stank of piss and fear.

The vampire narrowed his eyes. He realized the Sister was beginning to play mind games. She might still try to kill him, but not before she'd had her fun.

Something began to tickle his face. He looked up and saw that several spiders had spun webs between the branches overhead. Although the spiders didn't drop down on their heads, they'd dropped a multitude of silken threads to dangle down.

"Gah! They're on me!" Higgins screamed and batted at the webs. He only succeeded in making them stick to him.

Viktor clamped down with his will in an effort to keep the man calm and prevent the panic from spreading to the others. "It's only webs, man. The spiders can't touch you inside the circle."

His words fell on ears deafened by an unreasoning terror. Viktor could only keep the other men from bolting.

"Get them off! Get them off!" Higgins continued to bat at the webs and scrub at his face. He started to back up as if that would free him.

Grimm tried to reach for him but wasn't close enough. "Stay with the crew, Higgins!"

A few seconds later, Higgins backed into his death. The moment he set foot past the invisible barrier, the creatures swarmed him. He didn't even have time to scream. The creatures flowed up his legs and covered his body. They poured into his mouth, nose, and ears.

Viktor put a mini ball through the man's forehead to end the brief look of pain and terror in his eyes.

"What's that hum?" Belle cringed and held her ears. A loud buzzing started and rapidly grew louder. It soon reached deafening levels.

Before long, they didn't have to wonder what caused the sound. The sky above them grew dark, and an enormous swarm of wasps, hornets, and bees converged on them. However, just like the land bound creatures, the airborne pests found themselves blocked by an invisible boundary. The group of pirates stood in a bubble, the edges of which throbbed with crawling death.

The air grew close and hot. The bugs vibrated to put off heat.

Viktor decided he'd had enough. Even he started to sweat in the living oven they were trapped in. He reached into his shirt and pulled out the Elder's Stone. It flashed bright, temporarily blinding everyone. The surrounding creatures emitted a high-pitched squeal followed by an eerie silence.

Everyone's sight soon returned. The bubble expanded considerably, with the sky once again visible overhead. On the jungle floor lay the carcasses of all the creatures trapped by the explosive expansion of the protective barrier.

Black Venom

As one, the remaining flying insects rose in a cloud and headed toward the shore. They would reach the *Incubus* in a matter of minutes. Viktor sent one desperate thought to all of his crewmen through the blood link he had with them.

"Smudge Pots!"

"What?" Belle, who heard the thought as well, asked.

"The smoke will help keep the bugs away," he said.

He smiled grimly as Lazarus sent him an image back from the ship. The crew got the message and, more importantly, understood it. They managed to get the pots lit and smoking just before the swarm arrived. Some of the men were getting stung, but it was nothing like it would have been without the smoke.

Suddenly a new horror faced them. The bodies of Barnett and Higgins stood up with a lurching, unnatural movement. The very creatures that killed them held them erect like meaty puppets. The partially digested condition of the corpses only served to make the spectacle more grotesque.

A whispering, chittering sound came from them as Venoma used the creatures to try to speak to them.

"Turn back now and I may spare you."

"I think not, and I call you a liar, Venoma Noir," Viktor replied. "You would kill us all, if you could."

"Then you will have no crew left to return to, vampire. Yes, I know what you are and what you think you are. I do not believe you are the One, regardless of what the others think. Come to me, if you can. I will set you a task you cannot hope to finish. I will prove to those fools that you are not the One."

He held the glowing crystal toward the corpses of his men. The creatures animating them fled before its light, allowing them to collapse in lifeless heaps.

He turned to Belladonna and asked, "Which way is she?"

"Northwest."

"Keep up," he said to the others. "If you fall behind, you've seen what will happen to you."

The Elder's Stone kept the creatures away from them for the rest of the trek. The only place where they had some difficulty was while climbing a steep incline.

The trees grew close enough together to use them to help climb up the hill; but a recent rain made the ground and leaf litter slick and slimy. It cost them one more man before they reached the top.

Mr. Winters was in the middle of the group. As he reached for the small tree bole above him, his foot slipped off the one he had propped against. It threw him off balance and he hit the hillside flat on his face, knocking the wind out of him, and leaving him disoriented.

He started slipping down the slope. By the time he recovered his wits enough to try to scramble for a fresh purchase, he was no longer within reach of anything solid other than one of his crewmate's legs. The man he grabbed started to lose his grip from the sudden extra weight. Grimm reached out and grabbed Mr. Bland, before Winters could drag him downslope with him.

Winters once again lost his grip and suffered a swift slide into the nest of snakes and scorpions. He didn't even manage a scream.

"You all right, Mr. Bland?" Grimm asked.

"Aye." He looked down at the death he narrowly avoided. "Poor bugger. I told him not to wear that red shirt. It's bad luck."

They reached the hilltop without further incident.

Chapter 8

The hill sloped more gently on the other side, forming a sort of bowl in the landscape before climbing again. Plainly, the mountains rose very close to the sea in this area.

At the back of the bowl a rocky outcrop with a small crevasse in it stood out from the hillside. Doubtless, a cave lay beyond the opening. Frogs of every color and hue covered it like a living rainbow, hiding the black volcanic rock beneath. Vivid shades of red, blue, green, yellow, and orange bejeweled its surface.

Belladonna gazed in childlike wonder at the novel sight. "They're beautiful," she said and started to move toward them. "I didn't know you had anything like this on land. It reminds me of a reef."

"I wouldn't touch them, lass," Grimm said. At the same time, Viktor laid a hand on her shoulder to keep her close.

"Why?" she asked.

"Mr. Grimm is right, pet," Vik said softly. "If they belong to Venoma Noir, they must be poisonous."

"Aye," Grimm added. "I've heard tales of wild men and headhunters of the deep jungles that use frogs like these to make poison for their darts."

"I've heard of that, too," Mr. Bland said. "But I thought those tribes were further south, several days' sailing up the Amazon."

"Doesn't mean the frogs can't range to these mountains," Vik said. "The scorpions are what surprise me. The only places I ever heard or read of such large black scorpions existing were deserts, not jungles."

"They were a gift, Viktor Brandewyne." The female voice spoke from within the darkness of the cave entrance.

Viktor gave a shallow bow from the neck, but his eyes never left the dark slit in the frog-covered rock. "Greetings, Venoma Noir, Sister of Power. None here shall offer you harm. Come out where we can see you."

"Pretty words from a handsome man. Why don't you come in and get to know me better?" She replied with a seductive tone.

"I think not, Venoma." He raised a single eyebrow. "I don't believe I would fit through such a tiny door."

A disgruntled sound emanated from the darkness; then a small woman squirmed out of the crack in the rock. Her arms and legs, spindly appendages, looked out of place with her bloated abdomen. Her hair hung lank and black. Her skin, possibly dark once, now held a waxy grey hue due to years of hiding from the sun in the darkness of the jungle and her cave.

It struck Viktor that she resembled a giant spider. Carefully, he kept the disgust he felt from his face and voice. Loathsome and murderous as she was proving, he still needed her help.

"Well, you made it here." She dropped any pretense of being friendly or trying to seduce him. "Now I am bound to help you, provided you can meet my price."

"And what would that price be, *Mere* Venoma Noir?" he asked.

She gave him a sly smile. "I will give you a choice of two prices, Viktor Brandewyne." She looked him up and down then continued,

"I believe you *can* enter my cave. The entrance only appears to be too small. The rock is actually quite slick, and you could squeeze right through the one narrow spot. Beyond, it is cavernous. The first price I name is one night in my bed."

He appeared to consider it. The rock indeed appeared slippery, but only the slime of the poisonous frogs made it so. Also, he caught the faint but unmistakable scent of rotting flesh and old bones. A quick glance at the Sister confirmed his suspicion that she practiced cannibalism. Teeth filed to points and the malnourished look of someone who subsisted solely on meat provided all the proof he needed.

"And what is the other price you will accept?"

Venoma frowned for a moment. She'd suspected he might avoid the obvious trap. She trusted the more subtle one would succeed.

"There is an amulet I once had. I want it back," she told him. "I cannot tell you where to find it, but I can tell you who had it last and may still possess it."

Viktor gave her a skeptical look. He doubted it could be this easy. "Who would that be?"

"I am sure you've heard of him." She smiled, an unpleasant spectacle. "Quentin La Forte."

Among the group only Belladonna failed to recognize the name. All of the pirates had indeed heard of the man; a slaver with a reputation for ruthlessness to rival Vik's or Grimm's. Going up against him would be a risky proposition but safer and much more palatable than the first option Venoma offered.

"We have never crossed paths, but I am familiar with his reputation. You will forgive me if I opt for the latter. After all, I do enjoy a challenge." He smiled with a shallow mock bow.

She gave him a cold smile back. "Then you should love that you have a time limit in which to find him, procure the amulet, and return it to me. I give you exactly nine months."

"Before I accept the challenge, I request safe passage back to my ship for my crewmates and myself."

Venoma frowned. "I do not owe you that courtesy. Besides, I thought you enjoyed a challenge."

"To expect me to attempt this without valuable crew members is unreasonable; and I feel that you do owe me the courtesy. I lost three men to your defenses just to get to this point."

She glowered at him. He knew she had to concede in the end. He passed her obstacles to reach her. The magicks set in play by this accomplishment bound her from interfering with him performing the task she set him. He saw it irritated her to no end that he knew this fact.

"Very well, you may pass through my territory unharmed to whatever crew you have left. I call off my attack on your ship."

"Thank you." He gave a curt bow, grabbed Belladonna's arm, and led the way from the Sister's grotto.

Chapter 9

They made it safely back to the *Incubus*. As soon as they boarded, Vik gave the order to cast off. He wanted to put some distance between himself and Venoma Noir. The siren sang up a wind to speed their journey.

Once satisfied they were safely under weigh, he called a meeting. Grimm, Belle, Jon-Jon, Brumble, and Coffin all gathered in the Captain's cabin.

"Mister Coffin, what are our casualties?" Viktor demanded of the ship's doctor.

"We only lost one man while ye were ashore, Captain. Poor bugger was up in the rigging when the swarm hit."

"Stung to death?"

"No, Captain. He panicked and leapt to his death. One of the others let me know he'd been deathly afraid of wasps and bees." Coffin shook his head. "Everyone who was above deck got stung at least once; only a couple got sick from it."

"Aye," Jon-Jon said. "Murph swelled up like a puffer fish, and he only had three stingers in him. Some wet tobacco did the trick on getting the poison out, though."

"Good. So the smudge pots were set out in time."

"Aye, Captain." Brumble nodded. "It was odd how the swarm just dissipated. It was like they were called off."

"They were," Viktor confirmed. He changed the subject. "I want each of you to tell me what you know of the slaver Quentin La Forte, including his possible whereabouts and what ship he sails. I already know he has a reputation for ruthlessness."

Brumble visibly blanched. "La Forte, did you say?"

"Aye. He has something I need to retrieve."

"He's a nasty bastard. My family never dealt with him directly, but I've seen some of his cargo at market, and I've encountered sailors who were wise enough to leave his service. My father's viciousness towards his crew pales in comparison to the tales I've heard."

Vik raised an eyebrow. "What of his cargo. What condition were they in?"

"That's the surprising thing, Captain. The slaves were actually healthier looking than most, but his crew was not. He'll sacrifice a crew to bring in a healthy cargo. That way, he can demand a higher price for them."

Grimm grimaced. "Never cared much for the slaving business, myself. Don't mind selling off some prisoners if I'm close enough to a dealer to make it profitable; but the people I've dealt with or encountered that make it their livelihood are a breed unto themselves. The less time I have to spend around them, the better."

Vik chuckled. "They're not all as greasy as Delacroix, Mr. Grimm."

"No, some of them are worse. La Forte is one of the worst by reputation. He is rumored to use black magic, as well," Grimm replied. "I'd never put much stock in that rumor before, but now, I'm not so sure."

"Noted, Mr. Grimm. Can any of you give me any more information?"

Jon-Jon nodded. "Aye, Cap'n. Bastard sails the *Black Scorpion*. He's been through a couple of ships, but he kept the name for each one. Keeps her well-armed, too, by all accounts. Some say to protect his cargo, but others say he'll do a little private hunting if his slave wranglers can't provide him with enough cargo."

Viktor sat back and stroked his beard as he mulled over the information his mates gave him. He harbored no doubt it would be a challenge to complete the task within the time frame Venoma had given him. His mates waited patiently for his word.

Finally, he spoke. "Venoma Noir is wagering that La Forte will defeat me. I do not doubt that he has the amulet she wants back. I am, however, curious as to how it came to be in his possession."

"Why would that matter?" Grimm asked.

It was the siren who answered. "How he got it could give a clue to its properties. Some power-imbued objects have strict rules on how they can be handled or transferred from one person to another. If the Sister has infused any of her magic into it, then she would have had to have given it to him personally. If it is just an ordinary amulet not tied to any one person's magic, then he may have stolen it."

"Given the rumors he uses black magic," Vik said, "I'd bet she gave it to him. To what purpose, I do not pretend to know. Still, that is a problem for later. For now, we need to set a course. If La Forte works on the same schedule as most of the other African slavers, he should be headed to pick up a fresh cargo at this time of year."

Grimm and Brumble stood. "We'll chart out the best course from here to the west coast of Africa, Captain," the first mate said. He and the navigator headed to his cabin to look over the charts.

"As soon as we have a course, I need you to provide us with favorable winds, pet," Viktor told Belladonna. "I don't want to waste any more time than necessary in travel."

She smiled grimly. "I suggest you use your strongest sailcloth and have the riggers wear lifelines. The quicker I can put distance between that bitch and myself, the happier I will be."

As Jon-Jon headed for the door, he said, "I'll double check with Murph and Bland, but I believe our stores are more than enough for the crossing. We might need to take a prize or find a port once we get there, though. I'll alert the riggers to start checking the sails and lines."

"Good job, Mr. Jon."

Chapter 10

Commodore Critchfield sat in the stateroom of his cabins aboard the *HMS Quicksilver*. Once again, he decided to peruse the two versions of the letter and report from the Brumbles.

Knowing old Tobias was willing to sell out his own sons to save himself, even though they might be innocent, brought a mixed reaction. He understood and admired putting business first, but he knew he couldn't trust a man who would betray his own family.

And then there was the man's daughter. Critchfield gave a growling sigh and smiled to himself at the memory of that encounter. He seriously wondered if he would have stopped himself before things went too far had Bainbridge not intervened. She had felt and tasted so good. It had been so long since he'd bedded a woman. Samantha Brumble would have been far sweeter an experience than some tavern whore.

A knock at his door interrupted his reflection. "Enter," he said, quickly and easily composing himself.

One of his officers came in and came to attention. "Your pardon, Commodore," he said. "A mid-size merchantman is approaching and signaling that they wish to pull alongside to exchange news."

"What name is on the vessel and what flag does she fly?"

"She's the *Lorelei*. I'm not sure of the exact country, but the flag is a type used by some of the Black Sea ports."

"Hmm, it's not one of Brumble & Sons; not that any of his captains would be so foolish," he muttered.

"Commodore?"

"Nothing of importance." He waved his hand. "Signal them to come along. Probably just wanting to learn what pirates are in these waters or perhaps report one."

"Aye, sir."

About a half hour later another knock came at Critchfield's door. Given it arrived just after sunset, he thought it was the cabin boy with his supper. Instead, the same officer entered when bidden accompanied by a rather sickly-looking Joseph Turlington and an unknown man and woman.

Critchfield found the state of Turlington's health surprising, but the concern slipped to the back of his mind when he laid eyes on the woman. She exuded some indefinable quality which commanded attention.

Before he realized what he was doing, he found himself standing and coming around the table to greet her. He took her hand and bowed over it to kiss it, then introduced himself, "Commodore Nathan Critchfield at your service, madam. Welcome aboard the *Quicksilver*."

When she spoke, her voice held a rich, alto huskiness and an accent that marked her as originating from one of the Slavic countries of Eastern Europe. He found it mesmerizing.

"Thank you, Commodore. I am the Lady Carpathia. This gentleman is Captain Wormsloe."

An aristocrat, he thought. Aloud, he said, "Please, milady, Captain, be seated."

Once they had taken a seat, Critchfield ordered, "Mr. Turlington, I will take your report later. For now, report to the ship's surgeon. You don't look at all well."

After a glance at Carpathia, who nodded almost imperceptibly, Joseph saluted, said, "Aye, sir." He took one step back before performing an about face and exiting the cabin.

"Now, milady, what brings you to these waters?"

She looked him straight in the eye, smiled without the slightest hint of fangs, and said, "I am hunting Viktor Brandewyne."

"You are the second female I have encountered in the past year or so to be suffering from this madness, if you'll forgive my boldness, milady." Critchfield furrowed his brow and half-smiled, half-frowned. "May I ask why you seek this pirate?"

"I have been sent to kill him."

He laughed long at that. Tears streamed from his eyes by the time he managed to ask, "And how do you propose to do that? You may be an aristo, but you are still a woman, Lady Carpathia."

Before he knew what was happening, she stood at his back with a razor-edged dagger resting against the pulse in his throat.

"I am a skilled assassin, Commodore," she purred in his ear. "I am faster and stronger than my appearance belies. I make full use of my feminine charms to get close to my prey. I am very good at what I do."

Just as quickly, she returned to her seat, smiled serenely and slid the dagger slowly back into the sheath nestled between her breasts.

Critchfield felt shaken, mildly angry at being taken by surprise, and aroused by the creature seated before him. It took him a moment to realize Wormsloe was speaking. It was unlike him to be so distracted. He'd always prided himself on his ability to stay focused under any circumstances.

"Your pardon, Captain," he said as he regained his composure. "Could you repeat that? I am afraid I missed what you just said."

Wormsloe nodded. "Of course, Commodore. What brought us to this vessel was the returning of young Captain Turlington," he restated.

"Ah yes, Turlington." Critchfield thought it odd that he'd already forgotten about the man but didn't let it show. "How did he come to be aboard your vessel? I dispatched him months ago to have Brandee put back on the lists."

"Well, sir, when we found him, he was the last survivor aboard a sinking ship," Wormsloe replied. "A small band of pirates had slipped aboard under cover of darkness and murdered his small crew in their sleep. He must've awakened before they could cut his throat too, for he bore evidence of a struggle. He had a head wound and leg wound that cost him much blood. He managed to kill one of the blackguards, but they left him for dead."

Carpathia picked up the story. "I am afraid Joseph still has not fully recovered from the blow to his head. I have some medicinal skills, learned during the course of my trade, and was able to save his leg and his life. It was a few months before he could tell us exactly who he was and what he was doing there. Through him, we learned that you, too, seek Brandewyne. He told us he'd been given orders from Port Royal to warn any ships encountered about the pirate and the ship he sails."

Critchfield raised an eyebrow. "You refer to Captain Turlington by his Christian name."

She nodded. "At first it was the only thing he could remember, poor creature. As I said, it was some months before he remembered that he was a Captain of the Royal Navy or what his mission was."

"But what of these pirates, Captain Wormsloe; what became of them?" he asked.

"They were frightened off by our approach. We were not far from a small island. I imagine they were a rag-tag band that operated from there via dugouts or other small boats, attacking any small ship foolish enough to anchor there overnight. I have encountered such bands before, both in these waters and in the Orient. Sometimes, there are entire communities that make a living off such petty piracy. Unless you know what to look for, you'd never even know their lairs existed."

"Ah yes, I know what you mean, sir." Critchfield nodded. "They used to call them buccaneers in this part of the world, and they are harder to weed out than wharf rats."

He turned his attention back to Carpathia. "You say that Turlington did eventually remember his orders to warn all ships. So, he must have told you that Brandee's ship is of the same lines as the *Quicksilver*."

"He did. He said the ship was once known as the *War God* but has been reportedly renamed the *Incubus*. Also, he said it is the second most formidable warship in these waters, with this lovely vessel being the most formidable. No doubt, this is due to the superior discipline of her commander and crew." She smiled, flirting with him.

He reacted as she'd hoped, puffing up just a bit, but keeping that suspicious, predatory gleam in his eye. She sensed his strong-willed nature. He appreciated the flattery but recognized it as such, thus treating it with suspicion. This was a man not easily duped, who knew flattery was usually a prelude to the asking of a favor or an attempt to manipulate him.

She decided on the direct approach as the better tactic with the Commodore. As much as she enjoyed playing games with a worthy opponent, she knew it could prove too chancy on the outcome using that approach with this man. She had put too much work into her plan to possibly throw it away on a whim.

"Commodore, there is a matter that could be to our mutual benefit I wish to discuss with you," she said, her tone suddenly all business. "Captain Wormsloe is already privy to the matter; therefore, his presence will not be required. Besides, it is something best discussed in private."

Critchfield's smile bordered almost on a smirk. Her move was not entirely unexpected. "As you wish, milady. I merely ask your word that you will not attempt to assassinate me. After all, how do I know the pirates didn't hire you to do so under the guise of hunting the most notorious of their number?"

Her laughter sounded like tinkling crystal in sharp contrast to her husky alto speaking voice. "My dear Commodore, if that had been my plan, I would have already killed you and been on my way before anyone aboard was any the wiser. No, you are far more useful to me alive. Besides, I am sure your Navy would attempt to hunt me down for your murder, since I have openly come here, and my face and ship are now known."

"Point, milady."

Wormsloe stood and gave them both a bow. "Milady, Commodore, by your leave." He turned and left.

Carpathia gave Critchfield her full attention. In a voice too low to be overheard, she commanded, "Tell your cabin boy to leave us and go to some other part of the ship."

Paul, just arrived with the Commodore's meal, passed Wormsloe on his way out.

Never realizing it was not his own idea, he said, "Thank you, Paul. I won't need you for the rest of the evening. You can bed down with the powder monkeys tonight."

"Aye, sir," the lad replied as he set the tray of food down. He left the cabin in search of the other boys who served as powder monkeys for the gunnery crews. Within the hour, word would go through the ranks that the Commodore was entertaining a noblewoman and was not to be disturbed. What was made of that news was up to each individual.

Once the door shut behind the boy, Carpathia stood and removed her travel cloak. She draped it over the back of her chair.

He was willing to wager she wore a corset. Her waist looked pinched, and her breasts mounded up in defiance of gravity. She wore a bodice of the latest fashion, so low cut the delicate pink of her aureoles peeked out in contrast to the ivory white of her breasts.

He appreciated the view and saw how she could easily get past most men's guard. He determined not to be so careless.

"Forgive me, milady, but I would feel much more comfortable if you would disarm yourself."

Her laugh raised gooseflesh on him. "Of course, Commodore." She removed the dagger from her breast sheath and laid it on the table. She then reached up and removed two long steel pins from her hair, which allowed it to cascade down her back. She bent over and removed another dagger from an ankle sheath. She sat back up and smiled at him.

"Is that all of your weapons?"

"You may search my person for more, if you like," she said with a playfully challenging tone.

He gave her an answering leer. "I can be polite when needed, but you will find that I am no gentleman, milady. If you would please, stand and place your hands on the table."

She raised an eyebrow but humored him. Given the speed she'd exhibited earlier, she possibly could have killed him many times over without any weapons before he could even blink. She seemed to find his caution amusing.

He was very thorough in his search, even though he didn't actually reach inside any of her clothing. He half-expected her to protest the groping, especially when he took his time in choice areas.

No sooner had he straightened back up from leaning over her than she turned to him. She boosted herself up to sit on the table and gave him a sultry smile, her dark eyes half-lidded.

"You've done this before, Commodore. Tell me, while you were enjoying yourself, did you find any more weapons?"

He looked back at her with a predatory smile as he wondered how skilled she would be in bed. He'd never had a noblewoman. "As a matter of fact, I did. You have a long knife sheathed on the inside of your left thigh."

"Well then, you are just going to have to disarm me." She smiled at him.

He chuckled. "Oh, you'd like that, wouldn't you, milady?"

"Maybe even as much as you, Commodore." She leaned back and spread her knees as wide as her skirts would allow in blatant invitation.

He moved forward and started to lift her skirts. She remained passive and watched him with a decidedly wicked smile. Once he had the hem up to her knee, he smoothed the fabric up her thigh back to her hip to reveal the knife in its sheath strapped to her leg.

With his right hand, he unfastened the catch close to her knee that held the blade in its sheath. With his left, he steadied the other end of the sheath. His fingertips brushed against the short curls surrounding her moist center. Only briefly did he puzzle over the unnatural chill of her flesh.

When he slid the blade free, she leaned forward, forcing his fingers to partially enter her. She reached up and pulled him into a kiss. At the same time, he laid the edge of the blade against her throat.

Deliberately, she pressed her flesh against the razor edge, drawing a line of blood against the pale white of her skin. In a husky whisper, she said, "Taste me, Commodore."

He hesitated only a moment. It had been a long time since he'd encountered a woman that enjoyed pain. That had been a whore in Bergen. He didn't even pretend to be gentle as he ran his tongue along the shallow slice, trying to force the wound wider. At the same time, he rammed three fingers as deep as he could into her, then spread them as wide as her opening would allow.

Carpathia arched her back with a moan of pleasure, working her hips against his hand. She laughed, knowing he had walked right into her trap.

"And now, Nathan Critchfield, I want to discuss our mutual problem of Viktor Brandewyne."

Chapter 11

Carpathia returned to the *Lorelei* just before dawn and went straight to her cabin. The following evening, she met with Captain Wormsloe, the *Quicksilver* leagues behind them hours ago.

"You look entirely too pleased with yourself." Wormsloe grumped at her, the involvement of any kind of authorities less than pleasing to him. "Are you sure you can trust this man?"

"Of course not." She smiled, unworried. "I have his next in command completely in my thrall, however. If the Commodore tries to betray me, Captain Turlington can deal with him."

"I still don't think it was wise to clue him in on where to learn more about your kind. Westin knows who and what you are. He'll try to convince Critchfield to use that information against you and your pet," he argued. "You'd best hope the young fool doesn't give himself away to the hunter or the Commodore. Critchfield strikes me as very shrewd and not to be underestimated."

"Joseph has no memory of being bitten, and I have made sure his scars that aren't hidden by body hair have been obliterated and are indistinguishable from the stitched gash on his thigh." She saw the look of doubt in his eyes and added, "I realize it is a calculated risk I take with Nathan. He took some effort just to influence. His will is very strong. After all this business is finished, if he survives, I am seriously considering bringing him over to be one of my consorts. He could be infinitely useful, if he can be broken."

Wormsloe frowned. "That is a very doubtful 'if', milady."

She waved it off. "I can always destroy him if he proves unmanageable. Sending him to Amherst will gain him the knowledge he'll need to survive Brandewyne."

She gave Wormsloe an almost condescending smile. She knew what the man's chief worry was. "Nathan Critchfield has begun to feel his mortality. I have planted the seed of the possibility of immortality in his subconscious. Even if he decides not to hunt the pirate for my sake or for naval glory, the thought that Brandewyne might be able to grant him that will make him seek him out."

"How is that good? If he does find Brandee before we do, why would he kill him for us or herd him our way?"

"He won't kill him for us. That is my job. He will herd him toward us, though. I implied that he would need my help to either take the pirate down or force his cooperation. He does not know what I really am, but he has tasted enough of my blood that he will believe what I tell him without question."

"I still don't like it."

"You don't have to."

The orders to make ready to cross the Atlantic puzzled some of the junior officers. It hadn't been long enough to rotate home for a furlough. They soon learned an English port was not their destination. Rather, they were bound for the Dutch port of Amherst.

Still, no one complained. The prospect of getting some good European food was welcome news indeed. Most of the officers considered Colonial cuisine rustic and unrefined.

Critchfield left orders for his escort fleet to remain in the Caribbean and Colonial waters to patrol and keep the maritime peace. There had been growing rumblings of discontent up around Boston and the other northern harbor towns.

For the same reason, he had his navigators set a course that avoided all English ports. He didn't want to risk arriving to waiting orders for him to remain on the American side of the Atlantic. It would spoil his plans.

Normally, he didn't succumb to superstition; but something about the Lady Carpathia made him want to believe her. Why else would she need the wiles, silence, and speed of an accomplished assassin if not to hunt such dangerous predators.

He had heard bits of lore here and there in his travels about the blood-sucking living dead, though he'd never paid much attention to it before. He'd dismissed it as stories to frighten small children and fools. But she told him that Brandee had become one of these creatures. She even showed him old scars where she said one of the creatures attacked her when she'd been a child.

It gave her account veracity. It also meshed with the reports that Brumble's man, Bainbridge, had delivered about the attacks on the emerald-smuggling operation. It could even explain the alleged female pirate one of the survivors had described as some murderous, blood-sucking demon.

He hoped he would understand it better after he checked with the expert on the creatures Carpathia told him about. She assured him that it would give him an advantage in the tracking and capture of Brandee. The pirate-turned-vampire would not expect anyone in the Royal Navy to know his weaknesses.

He smiled to himself. How often did one get to mask vengeance as duty? He had been dispatched with the *Quicksilver* to put down the lingering pirate and smuggler presence around the Colonies, after all.

It would also give him an excuse to encounter Lady Carpathia again. She had been one of the most exciting women he had ever been with. He imagined that being aware of the possibility she might try to kill him only heightened the thrill.

For a brief moment, he wondered how accepting of her story he would have been if he hadn't already gotten the reports from Bainbridge or encountered Samantha Brumble. He thought Sam and Carpathia were the exceptions to normal female behavior, but he wouldn't make the mistake of underestimating a woman again. Some of them could obviously be quite devious, clever, intelligent, and, most importantly, deadly.

Chapter 12

Venoma Noir could still sense the siren's presence and magic; she just couldn't control the creature as long as the power of the Elder's Stone interfered.

She tested the strand of her web of power she had attached to Belladonna, delicately, of course. She didn't want to alert the siren or Brandewyne to the continued connection. It didn't prove difficult to discern that the siren aided the pirate with weather magic.

Venoma frowned. With favorable winds, the man stood a better chance of meeting the time limit she'd set him, provided he could find and defeat La Forte. However, if the prey knew of the predator's approach and intent....

She chuckled and reached out along a different strand of her web.

Quentin La Forte found himself tangled in a nightmarish web. It took him a few moments to realize his predicament. He fought the urge to struggle. He knew that would only draw *her*.

He felt a vibration along the web and looked up. At first, he thought a giant spider descended toward him; then he recognized it as Venoma. Her spindly arms and legs extended out from her bloated body. Stringy black hair framed her face. She saw his eyes open and grinned to reveal her sharp, filed teeth.

She continued head down along the web toward him. He cast about in desperation, looking for some place to escape to. He saw nothing but darkness, the web, and *her*.

"Hello, lover," Venoma purred and caressed his cheek. "Did you miss me?"

He shuddered at her touch, and she laughed. He glared at her. "What do you want, Venoma? Why do you haunt me now?"

She pouted at him. "Why Quentin, I just want what is mine. Soon, I will have my amulet back. I've sent a pirate to retrieve it."

He scowled at her in irritation. "You are still saying I stole that? You gave it to me, Venoma."

She lunged at him, but he did not flinch. He'd finally realized this was just a dream. She couldn't really touch him here. If she could, she would have done so long ago.

"You failed to meet my requirement! The amulet is forfeit! I will have it back, one way or another."

"And you think some common pirate can take it from me? How many times do we have to go through this, Venoma? It seems like every five years or so you send someone after me. Why should this time be any different? For that matter, why are you warning me this time?"

Venoma's grin grew even wider in demented glee. "My Sisters think this pirate is the One. He carries the blessing of the Elder; but the thing that gives him an advantage the others I've sent did not have is the fact he enslaved a sea siren. Even now, she sings him up a wind to speed him to you."

He saw a small figure connected to a very fine filament of web. At first, he thought it a human female; then the legs of the figure fused to form a shark-like tail.

"She is quite venomous, as well. Once the pirate has brought me my amulet, I may take her from him."

She left the thread from the siren figure close to his hand. The darkness grew, and the dream faded.

La Forte woke in a cold sweat, the dream still fresh in his mind. He hated that she could do that to him. He'd thought he was free and safe from her influence on the other side of the ocean from her.

Still, he knew Venoma did nothing without a reason. She deliberately warned him; something she had never done before. She showed him a potential weapon and hinted it could be turned from its current master.

That last, he felt, he must explore.

Viktor stood near the helm and looked out over the activity aboard his ship. Salt spray blew back over the bow as it cut through the water. A handful of the boys who served as powder monkeys to the gunnery crews busily spread sand over the wet decks. The riggers called out to each other from aloft, lifelines secured about their waists. The sails billowed, bellies full of wind, or flapped and snapped as the riggers adjusted them to better catch the wind. Timbers creaked and groaned, and ropes hummed and thrummed in the breeze.

He loved listening to the sounds of sea and ship. Some days he could almost feel content just to sail with no other worries in the world.

His thoughts turned to more visceral pleasures as the siren's song drifted back to him. Her notes shaped the wind and current to speed the ship across the ocean. Belladonna claimed she could see the wind; he had to take her word for it. He just knew that her weather magic had them making the crossing in about half the time it would normally take.

She turned from her perch on the bowsprit to look at him, as if aware of his scrutiny. Her sly smile awoke a familiar ache in his groin. She stood and stalked toward the aft of the ship and his cabin.

"Mr. Jon, hold this course."

"Aye, Cap'n," the second mate replied with a leer. "Y'can send her my way after she wears you out."

"You'll have a bit of a wait on that, Jon-Jon. However, I'm sure she'll be hungry by the time we're done," Vik joked back.

"That's all right. I wouldn't want to give her more'n she can handle." Jon-Jon's voice sounded a little shaky.

Viktor chuckled and headed down to the quarter deck. He and Belle had both wanted this for a long time, but they'd had to abstain for one reason or another at every opportunity. He saw no obstacle this time. He should have known better.

He'd not quite reached the hatch for the cabins, when Belle let out a strangled squeak and collapsed to the deck, unconscious. He staggered as he felt her presence go nearly silent.

Over the next three days, the winds died, and the sea current stilled. Whatever attack the siren had suffered had broken her spells, as well.

Until she regained consciousness, Viktor stayed by her side. Periodically, he sponged her body with sea brine. Dr. Coffin objected to that. He favored fresh water. Viktor pointed out that she was a sea creature and did not respond well to fresh water.

Meanwhile, Mr. Bland organized boat crews to tow the ship. On the advice of Mr. Grimm and Mr. Brumble, they took a northeasterly heading in the hopes of catching an eastward current. The winds remained sporadic and unreliable.

On the third day, Belladonna finally awoke. Viktor could see she was very weak and would need to feed soon. He instructed Anvil, the huge ship's smith and a former slave he'd liberated from an indigo plantation, to bring one of the remaining prisoners up from the larder hold. He ended up having to carve the victim up and hand feed the siren to restore her strength.

"Belle, what happened? It felt like you almost died." Viktor didn't try to hide the worry he felt. He'd almost lost her, and it truly frightened him.

"The bitch's reach is longer than I thought. That tasted of her power and hurt like hell," the siren responded.

He definitely didn't like the sound of that. "I should have extracted a promise from her to not interfere," he grumbled.

Belle laid a hand on his arm. "That one wouldn't have given you one. I've seen her mind towards you. She hates you; for that matter, she hates everyone; but you, she fears, as well. That makes her dangerous. Viktor, she wants you dead."

He gave her a grim smile. "Trust me, pet; my feelings toward her are mutual. I do not like that she can influence you and use you against me even from this distance."

"About that; this attack smacked of desperation. It also felt weak compared to her initial attack when I first sensed her. I think the distance from her and my proximity to the Elder's stone helped protect me."

"Belle, you dropped nearly lifeless and were unconscious for three days." He marveled at how she could take this threat so lightly.

"That was partially my own fault, Viktor." She looked away and flushed pink.

He frowned, confused by her embarrassment. He reached out and gently turned her face back to him. "How so, pet?"

"I sensed the magic and heard the command, 'Kill your master,' and I panicked. Rather than risk her taking me over again, I shut down into a sort of hibernation. It's much like how you can cause the vampires in your cadre to go dormant; and much like them, I come out of that state weak and ravenous."

He smiled, leaned over, and kissed her. When he pulled back, he said, "Your instincts are good, Belle. What you did was nothing to be ashamed of. I can see why that is a defense you'd prefer to avoid, however, since it leaves you vulnerable to a physical attack."

Her eyes flashed to their true amber gold at his words. "I hate her for that."

"Understandable." He chuckled in sympathy. No predator liked for their weaknesses to be revealed. "Do you feel restored enough to work a little weather magic? We've been towing the boat in the hopes of catching the Gulf Stream."

"That current will take you too far north," she said. She closed her eyes for a few minutes. He patiently waited for her to assess her current abilities. When she opened her eyes, they once again had taken on their human guise of sea grey.

"Yes, I can. I apologize for leaving the ship becalmed. I will require at least one more meal afterwards, though. Hopefully, hunting will be good once we reach African waters."

"Indeed. I'll alert Mr. Bland to call in his boat crews and have Anvil pick out the largest, healthiest man from my blood stock for you."

"Thank you."

The remainder of the crossing passed without incident.

Chapter 13

The captain of the packet ship *Jolene* decided to head south from the Straits of Gibraltar after leaving Calais. He felt the winds and weather would be more favorable than trying the northern crossing at that time of year.

North Atlantic storms were notorious for blowing ships off course and into icebergs or onto shoals. He didn't want to risk it. Besides, he stood to make a hefty bonus for safe delivery of one of his passengers. A rich Virginia planter awaited his young bride.

Brianna Belmont spent the first few days of the journey in her cabin. Her maid, Nicole, stayed with her, suffering from seasickness. It not only gave her an excuse to stay out of sight, it gave her time to think about her situation and what to do about it.

Only a few months earlier, she had learned of her impending marriage. Until learning this news, she'd naively thought her father was just being overprotective. He'd discouraged and run off any and all suitors who came to court her after she reached a marriageable age last summer.

It came as a painful shock to learn he had betrothed her to a foreign colonist to seal a business transaction; the arrangement made when she had been a small child. Even more horrifying, her future husband was a few years older than her father.

Now, she found herself torn from the land of her birth and from all her friends, bound for some wilderness in the Americas. Her only solace was a handful of books, mostly accounts of the world she was headed for, and the companionship of her maid.

Nicole was an orphan her family took in. Nicole and Brianna were close to the same age, and both had lost their mothers about the same time. Nicole's mother had been a widow. She'd never known her father.

As they grew up together, the two developed a strong resemblance to each other. They looked enough alike that ugly rumors they shared the same father spread among the less charitable of their village. They were closer than sisters, and Nicole refused to be parted from her mistress.

The lie came, unpremeditated, when the captain sent a boy to invite the *mademoiselle* to dine with him that first evening at sea. Barely opening the door to their cabin to answer it, Brianna said, "Give the Captain *ma'm'selle's* apologies, *sil vous plait*. My mistress suffers from *mal de mer*."

This planted the seed of an escape plan.

Over the next few days, as she nursed Nicole back to health, she discussed the plan with her. The girl proved more than happy to trade places. She only held a qualm over what would become of her mistress.

Brianna assured her she would be fine. All she wanted was her freedom and, perhaps, some adventure.

She had no idea how much adventure she was about to be thrust into.

Black Venom

The captain did not regret his decision to take the southern crossing until they were just north of the Cape Verde islands. A heavy fog bank loomed ahead of them as they approached the islands. Rather than sail into it, he decided to go ahead and make the westward turn and skirt the fog. It would not be hard to re-plot his course to allow for the early change.

By the time the lookout spotted the pirate sailing out of the fog, any hope of making a run for it no longer existed. The battle was brief and almost nonexistent. The *Jolene* only carried light arms. Cannon were heavy and made the ship's owner no profit.

After the vessel was taken, the pirate captain ordered the surviving crew and passengers herded onto the deck. Brianna and Nicole were the only females out of seven passengers on board. The crew was small, further evidence of the owner's miserliness. The packet's captain and a handful of riggers were the only casualties.

The pirate and his first mate addressed the prisoners. "I am James Bartlett; you may have heard of me. You sailors, name your skills. If you have an ability I can use, you can live. Those of you I can't use can feed the sharks."

He stepped over to the passengers, gave the men a cursory glance then stopped in front of the women. He openly leered at them. "Mr. Graff, did you find the passenger roster?"

"Aye, Cap'n." The first mate grinned. "There's plenty of ransom to be had with this lot. These fancy gentlemen might be worth a little, but one of these lasses is worth a small fortune."

"Oh?"

"Aye! The *mademoiselle* Belmont is the betrothed of one Percival Worthing, Esquire, of Virginia. The captain's log mentioned the promise of a hefty bonus for her safe delivery."

Bartlett gave a wicked chuckle. "I've heard of Master Worthing, Virginia tobacco planter, business holdings in the Colonies from Boston to Charleston, as well as some interests in England and France. If he's willing to pay a bonus for the safe delivery of his bride, he should pay a handsome ransom to receive her unsullied. Now, the question is which of you lovelies are the bride?"

Both held their silence and clung to each other. Nicole, still weak from being seasick, looked ready to faint. Brianna supported her more than clung to her. She glanced fearfully at the man.

"Mr. Graff, see if any of the rest of this lot can tell me which is the bride and which is the maid."

"Aye, Cap'n. All right, you scurvy bastards, the first one to tell me what I want to know can have a quarter of my share of the ransom," Graff announced to the packet's crew.

"Mighty generous of you," Bartlett commented.

One of the cabin boys spoke up. "I can tell you, but I want to join your crew, also."

"What's your name, lad?" Graff asked.

"Tom Shelton, sir. I was the captain's cabin boy. He was a fair man, but the man we worked for was a cheap bastard," he answered. He pointed and said, "That one on the left is Miss Belmont. Her maid there has been taking care of her the entire voyage. Seasick, she's been."

"Thank you, Mr. Shelton," Bartlett said without taking his eyes off the two women. "Mr. Graff, I'll leave you to secure the prisoners and sort through who we want to conscript. I'll see after *Mademoiselle* Belmont and her wench."

He reached for Nicole's arm. Brianna tried to step between them. "The boy is wrong. I am Brianna Belmont. Nicole is my maid. We switched places because I don't want to marry some old man I've never met!" she cried out.

"You expect me to believe that?" He backhanded her viciously. The blow stunned her. She dropped to the deck with a split lip. He grasped Nicole by the arm and jerked her to his side. "Shank, secure that lying wench."

"Aye, Cap'n," a grubby pirate replied. He hoisted Brianna back to her feet. She let out a grunt of pain when he held her against him with a tight squeeze around her waist and a bruising grip on her arm. "Can I have her first, Cap'n?"

"We'll see." Bartlett answered.

Nicole came out of her state of shock and tried to struggle against her captor. "No! Please! My mistress is not lying! My name is Nicole Robierre. I am only a maid."

Although his grip was firm, Bartlett was almost gentle with her. "Your fear is misplaced, *Mademoiselle* Belmont. I doubt your betrothed would pay ransom for you if you were sullied. No, my dear, you have my word that none of my crew shall assault your virtue, providing Mr. Worthing agrees to pay my price."

She cast panicked eyes toward her mistress. Brianna nodded and said, "Don't worry, mistress. I will be fine. I am just glad to know that you are safe."

Nicole shook her head. She didn't understand why Brianna chose to continue the charade. "But what of you?"

"Oh, we'll take good care of her, lass, won't we, lads?" Shank leered. Bawdy laughter from the other pirates answered him.

Nicole turned to the pirate captain. "Please, *m'sieur*, spare her. She has done nothing to deserve such a fate," she pled.

He laughed cruelly. "Your value for delivery intact is the only reason I won't let the lads have *you*. The girl is of no value to me for ransom, and the lads have been without a woman for some time."

Brianna stood as straight as she could within the pirate's grip. "I will be fine, mistress." Her voice was chilly. Nicole recognized the hardness in her mistress' eyes all too well. Growing up together, many a village boy had learned the hard way that provoking that look would earn them pain. It was a practice that had been a source of contention between Brianna and her father.

"I hope you are right, *amie*," Nicole said with sadness. "These pirates look to be much rougher than the boys of our village."

Brianna just smiled.

"Cap'n, that devilish fog is getting worse," Graff said. "I swear I hear singing and ropes creaking in the distance, too."

Bartlett cocked his head to the side and listened. "Aye, Mr. Graff. I hear it, too. It's a woman's voice. There may be another packet approaching. Today is a very good day for us."

He couldn't have been more wrong.

Chapter 14

The *Incubus* had almost finished her Atlantic crossing. Readings showed she had stayed true to course and now sailed just west of the Cape Verde islands. Viktor knew that nearby land meant increased shipping activity and sent Lazarus ahead to scout in his raven form.

He still missed the companionship of his former first mate, Jim Rigger. He viewed the man like a brother since their first encounter as boys. He still felt guilty for making Jim the source of his second blood meal after Mamaan Juma cursed him to vampirism. Mother Celie, Viktor's foster mother, resurrected Jim as a black cat named Lazarus and gave him the ability to turn into a raven. Only a few months ago Viktor learned Lazarus could eat the flesh of another creature to take on their form temporarily; human flesh allowed him to regain his original form, but as a vampire rather than a man.

Of all Lazarus' forms, only the raven allowed Viktor to spy out situations or prizes. In that form, the pirate could see through the raven's eyes.

When Vik started to chuckle in a menacing tone, it piqued Grimm's and Belle's interest.

"Why are you so amused?' the siren asked.

"We're about to feed well, pet," he replied. "Sing us up a fog. The one near the islands has already started to burn off."

Grimm gave him a questioning look. "I know we need to resupply, but you don't use *that* laugh on the mere prospect of a fat prize."

Viktor didn't even bother to hide his fangs as he grinned. "Jimmy Bartlett just took a prize. We're going to take it from him."

Grimm almost felt sorry for the man—almost. He knew there was bad blood between the two pirate captains. "That explains why I haven't heard news of him in a few years. You think he moved his operations over here to avoid you?"

"Possibly, but I'm not the only enemy he's made among the Brethren." Vik shrugged.

"Just the deadliest." Grimm smirked.

"Aye." He grinned again.

Vik walked over to the wheel and took the helm. His sharper senses allowed him to navigate safely through the dense fog. He ordered the riggers to furl the sails enough to let him glide to a near stop alongside their victim.

He had to fight the giggles over the other pirate's reaction, as the fog cleared enough to reveal the *Incubus*. The vampire's craft dwarfed both the pirate and the packet ships. Having all sixty guns on that side unmasked and trained on various portions of his enemy's ship only added to the fun.

As a final touch, he'd instructed some of his crew don their stolen Royal Navy uniforms and run up the Union Jack.

"You're putting on quite a show for someone you intend to kill," Belladonna said through the blood bond that tied her to the vampire.

"You are not the only one who likes to play with their food," he replied.

Bartlett's prisoners had a brief moment of hope at the appearance of the *Incubus*. Although no one knew why a British warship would be in Portuguese waters, they knew it would bode ill for the pirates.

Brianna and Nicole both felt the greatest relief. They would soon be free to continue their journey, they believed.

Bartlett and his crew were forced to make a quick decision. They could either try to fight their way out of this, which meant virtual suicide; surrender and try to blend in with their captives, a doubtful proposition; surrender and try to implicate as many of their captives as possible as fellow pirates, only slightly better; or try to bribe their way out.

Only the last option offered even a dim hope of survival and continued freedom. It all depended on the Navy commander.

"Captain Bartlett of the *Viper*, stand down and prepare to be boarded." The hail came from the *Incubus*.

He wondered how they knew who he was, not that it was important. He nodded to his first mate. "We can't fight our way out of this one, Mr. Graff. Here's hoping the man is greedy."

Viktor stopped short of playing dress-up on his own, nor did he require any of his mates to do so. Only riggers and deck hands boarded the *Viper* and the *Jolene* in uniform. He sent men to both ships because he knew Bartlett wasn't foolish enough to leave his own ship unattended.

After the ships were secure, he had Hezekiah board, acting as captain. He wanted to give his prey a false sense of hope. There wasn't any particular grudge between Grimm and Bartlett.

Bartlett made sure he held onto "Brianna" while the bogus Navy men boarded and surrounded pirates and prisoners alike. He did his best to hide his apprehension. The number of cannon trained on him was the main reason he offered no fight.

He visibly relaxed when he saw the Grimm Reaper striding aboard. He might not be on the best of terms with the other pirate, but he knew the Reaper was someone he could bargain with. He might even be able to keep some of the prize.

Chapter 15

"You had me worried, Reaper." Bartlett's laugh held a nervous quaver.

Grimm kept his face neutral. "What makes you think you shouldn't still be worried, Bartlett?"

The captured pirate's composure faltered for a moment. He was forcibly reminded that, although he hadn't made an enemy of Hezekiah Grimm, they weren't friends, either. The Reaper had a reputation of ruthless efficiency. If he didn't handle this negotiation carefully, he and his crew could still wind up dead. He wasn't so greedy as to try to hold onto any of their take if giving it up would get them out of this alive.

"I wish to *parlez* for safe passage for my crew and myself."

"No!" Brianna protested. She did not realize she was speaking to another pirate rather than a naval officer. "*M'sieur* Reaper, these pirates attacked us unprovoked! They have committed murder and threatened further slaughter as well as rape and holding us for ransom!"

"Shank, if you can't keep that bitch quiet—," Bartlett growled; the threat implied.

The pirate who held her put the edge of his blade against Brianna's throat. She went very still. The danger had not passed, yet. Still, she looked at Grimm with eyes that demanded rather than begged for him to help them.

Grimm gave the girl a calculating once over. She had spirit and fire. He easily discerned she was more angry than afraid. The split and bruising lip did not go unnoticed, either. She'd already given Bartlett some trouble.

He then turned his attention to the girl that the pirate captain held. Physically, there was a strong resemblance between the two, but the similarities only went as far as that. Bartlett's prisoner looked petrified and about ready to faint.

"Very well, what is your proposition?" he asked with a bored tone.

"A percentage of the ransom for this wench."

Grimm raised a dubious eyebrow. "Only a percentage? Who is she, and what makes her so valuable?"

Bartlett thought he had gained the upper hand. He'd seen the scrutiny the notorious pirate gave the troublesome other lass. "*Mademoiselle* Brianna Belmont; she's the intended bride of old Percy Worthing."

Grimm snorted. "He's at that again, is he? What does this make for him now, seven or eight?"

Bartlett shrugged. "It's been a few years since I've been to Virginia. I have no idea. From what I remember, they seem to get younger every time." The fact that Grimm bantered with him put him more at ease. "He's on record as willing to pay a small fortune for this one to be delivered intact."

Grimm gave Nicole a reassessing look. "Really? She's pretty enough, but she seems a bit more timid than he prefers. The other lass would be more to his taste." He hooked a thumb toward Brianna.

"I wouldn't pay for the mouthy, lying slut," Bartlett said with a growl. "She tried to pass herself off as the bride; said she'd changed places with her maid to avoid the marriage."

Hezekiah smiled. He actually found that believable, especially if the intended caught wind of any rumors of her future husband. "How much is she worth?"

"Seven hundred gold."

Grimm gave a whistle. "She must be quite special, or he truly intends to marry her. He didn't leave much margin for profit."

Nicole, in her state of shock, didn't really comprehend what had just been implied. Brianna, on the other hand, caught on quickly. She now realized that this was another pirate rather than their deliverer. She blanched at the realization of the fate her father had unwittingly sold her into, though. If she and Nicole made it out of this alive, she intended to get word back home of the kind of man her betrothed truly was. For now, she would just be happy with survival.

Bartlett started the negotiations. "How does half the ransom sound?"

"I'll take it all."

"Half and the other wench."

Grimm's laugh was sinister. "You don't seem to understand, Mr. Bartlett." He saw that the omission of the title of captain wasn't lost on the man. "This is not a negotiation. My Captain claims both ships and all aboard as prize."

Bartlett looked confused. "Your captain? I don't understand."

Viktor dropped down from the rigging, where he'd hidden to listen in, as agile as a cat. "You always were slow, Jimmy."

Bartlett whirled and clasped Nicole to him like a shield. "Bloody Brandee! I should have known! Hadn't heard that you and the Reaper were working together again."

"Since you've been hiding on this side of the ocean, I imagine there are a lot of things you haven't heard." Vik smiled, tight-lipped. "Be that as it may, you still owe me a little over a thousand that you cheated me out of back in L'Orient."

"I cheated you?" he protested. "I haven't cheated you out of anything, Brandee. I'm not suicidal. I was there when you told me to be. A ship of the line showed up, and my crew and I thought it best not to stick around. I came back later but couldn't find you."

"So, you have the money to give me, then."

"N-no. We hit a dry spell and had to live off of it until we could catch a prize."

"Oh, well then, it is fortuitous that we've met here. Between the girl's ransom and what I can get out of both ships, that should about cover your debt to me." Vik's voice was at its most deadly calm.

What happened next, Viktor had to admit he hadn't anticipated.

Bartlett came to the realization that he was not going to survive this encounter. He knew Brandee intended to kill him. Quickly, he made the decision that his nemesis would not see the full value of this prize.

Before even Viktor could react, he reached up and slit his captive's throat from ear to ear.

"Nicole!" Brianna screamed. In a quick movement, she rammed her elbow back into the stomach of the pirate holding her. At the same, she dug her thumb into his wrist at the pulse point, forcing him to relax his hold on his knife. She took the weapon and rushed at Bartlett.

Thrusting upward, she rammed the knife up under his chin as far as the hilt. One thing that saved her from getting stabbed by her victim was another knife which seemed to have materialized, embedded in his chest.

Chapter 16

Viktor was just there as Bartlett's body collapsed. He pulled Brianna's blade from her grip. Keeping an eye on her as she crouched beside the dying girl, he knelt and retrieved all three knives. He surreptitiously slipped one back into its sheath at the nape of his neck. The other two quietly vanished to other hiding places about his person.

Brianna cradled Nicole's head in her lap, mindless of the blood that soaked into her skirts. She whispered over and over, "I'm sorry."

It took all of Viktor's self-control to keep from attacking and feeding. The aroma of that much blood in one place nearly overwhelmed his senses. As it was, his eyes began to glow with emerald fire as he stared intently at the two women.

Grimm took notice of the impending danger from his Captain. He walked over and pulled Brianna to her feet. He kept his voice uncharacteristically gentle as he spoke to her. "Come along, lass. She's gone. There's nothing more you can do for her."

He turned to Viktor and said, "Captain, I invoke our agreement that I get first choice of the wenches."

The moment he said it, Brianna's temper flared anew. "Let me go! You filthy pirate! You could have saved her! You could have s-saved h-her —." She broke off into hiccoughing sobs as her grief overrode her rage.

Viktor smirked. "You always did love a challenge, Mr. Grimm. I suggest you get her secured before the lads get any ideas. And get her out of that bloody dress."

"No!" she shrieked, under the impression he meant to rape her. She began to struggle in earnest.

If it hadn't been for her escape from Shank, Grimm might have been caught off guard. He'd already seen she knew something about fighting, though, and he knew how to keep his hold on her. He hadn't lived as long as he had as a pirate by underestimating those around him.

"Mr. Jon!" Grimm bellowed.

"Aye!" Jon-Jon made his way over to the first mate and gave the girl an appreciative leer in the process.

"Coordinate the salvage and the sorting of the prisoners. Also, see to it that the lass, there, gets a proper burial at sea." He looked over at Viktor. "Captain, would you ask Belle to leave her?"

"I'll make sure she knows not to touch the body." He nodded.

"What are you talking about? Who is this woman? What would she do to Nicole if not forbidden? Answer me!" Brianna ranted.

Viktor smiled wryly. "She's a vocal one, isn't she? Be interesting to see how she and Belle get along."

Grimm grimaced. "My luck, they'll unite to drive us mad with their harping. Come along, lass. It is not safe for you to wear that blood-soaked garment."

He started to drag her with him. She tugged against him, screaming and protesting. To her credit, she got in a few painful blows. When they got to the gangplank and ladder to get back up to the higher deck of the *Incubus*, he knew she was going to be a problem.

He grasped her arm almost painfully tight and growled. "I don't want to hurt you, lass, but if you do not shut your mouth and quit fighting me, I will throw you to the crew. Trust me, girl, you don't want that. They'll take you right here on the deck one after the other until you are torn, bleeding, and can no longer walk."

The threat proved enough to stun her into temporary silence.

He took advantage and hefted her over his shoulder. They made the crossing from one ship to the other. The sight of the hulls rubbing together, and the dark waters below prompted her to cling to him.

"Don't drop me!" Her voice held a note of panic.

"Quit squirming, then," he replied gruffly.

He had to set her down to finish climbing over the rail. She took advantage of this to try to make a run for it. Grimm sighed, but chuckled when she tripped over a line that suddenly dropped in front of her.

"Thank ye, Sniff." He laughed. "You're on a ship, lass. Where were you planning on running to?"

"I could have found some place to hide," she said petulantly as she tried to get untangled from the heavy line.

"You would be found eventually, especially with that much blood on you." He shook his head. "There are things on this ship that are drawn to blood like steel to a lodestone. That is why you need to change clothes."

"I don't believe you. Aaiee!" she cried in pain. The moment she tried to put weight on her now freed leg, it collapsed under her.

"Don't touch me!" She tried to shy away as Grimm reached to help her up.

A plop of mucous landed beside her hand on the deck. She recoiled from it. Grimm chuckled. "Well, if you won't have me help you, and I really don't want to share you with the rest of the crew, I could just let Sniff have you for a few hours. You can't get away from him like most women can, at least not on that ankle. That should take some of the fight out of you."

"Who or what is this 'Sniff'?"

In answer, the legless, noseless, hairless, one-eyed rigger lowered down to dangle like a leering putrid spider. Most of the sailors she'd encountered so far were a bit ripe, but the odor from this creature proved positively nauseating.

Covering her nose and mouth with her hand, she glared between the two of them. There was a cold fury in her eyes that reminded Grimm of Viktor. Even Sniff backed off a little from that baleful stare.

Clear of the worst of the stench, she took her hand away from her face. In a calm, quiet voice, she addressed the rancid pirate. "If you come near me again, your legs, nose and eye won't be the only parts you'll be missing." She glanced pointedly at his crotch.

Belladonna, who had just returned to the ship from feeding on the slain, walked up at that moment. "Oh, I like her. Can we keep her?"

It stunned Brianna to see a naked woman moving about freely and unmolested on the pirate ship. The siren smiled down at her, but her smile and eyes had not returned to their human guise. Nearly ear-to-ear razor-sharp teeth and amber-gold eyes were not a comforting sight.

"Belle, you didn't eat the woman, did you?" Grimm asked.

"No, Viktor made it clear she was not to be touched," she replied and shrugged. "Human females can be bland, anyway, compared to the flavor of the males."

Sniff took the opportunity to flirt with the siren, who usually avoided him. "I've got enough to take care of both you lovelies, my sweet Belladonna."

Belle extended one hand to a talon and smiled menacingly at him. "Go away, troll, or I'll peel you slowly, starting with your scrotum."

He quickly retreated back up into the rigging, but he hollered back down to the first mate, "She wants me!"

Looking back down at Brianna, she said, "You should change out of those blood-soaked clothes before the Captain returns, and definitely before dark."

"Speaking of clothes, you should go put some on, Belle," Grimm suggested.

She smiled and chuckled seductively as she sashayed away toward her cabin.

Still stunned, Brianna let Grimm help her up and support her weight. "What is she?" she asked in a fearful whisper.

"Belladonna is one of the things I was telling you about." He picked the subdued woman up and carried her. "She is a sea witch and a siren, not to be confused with a mermaid. They are her favorite food, by the way, when she can't get sailors."

"She eats people?!"

"Yes, and it is not pleasant to see."

Once he got her to his cabin, he set her down on the bed, then turned and began to rummage through one of his sea chests. He muttered to himself, as he rifled through the contents.

"No, too big. Gah! Oh, that color will never do." He looked back over his shoulder at her, then returned to digging through the chest. "I know it's still here somewhere."

Brianna's fear of being raped began to ease. Her captor had not even flirted with Belladonna, which went against the lusty nature of pirates that she had always read about. Also, the look he had just given her seemed to have nothing to do with sex.

Grimm finally found what he was looking for. He stood up holding a spring green frock. "This should even fit you comfortably."

He walked over to her and laid the garment beside her. "You can change while I fetch the ship's surgeon to look at that ankle and leg. I'm glad Sniff stopped you before you could get too far, but I hope nothing was broken."

All the same, he locked her in the cabin when he went in search of the doctor.

She still sat on the bed with the fresh dress beside her when he returned.

"Lass, why haven't you changed? Are you deliberately trying to be difficult?" He frowned.

She looked at him with a tear-streaked face. "I can't reach the laces. N-nicole always h-helped m-me —," she broke off into fresh sobs.

The two men stood awkwardly for a moment. Brianna finally composed herself and wiped at her eyes with the back of her hand. "I hate to impose, but do you think *Mademoiselle* Belladonna could help me get out of this?"

Grimm shook his head and smiled wryly. "I'm sorry, *Mademoiselle* Belmont. I'm afraid Belle doesn't have much experience with finer fashion. Getting her to wear clothes at all is a trial sometimes. You will have to settle for my help."

"But you are a man," she said, puzzled. "What do you know of it?"

"I am a pirate. Trust me, lass, I know my way around a corset and how to get a woman out of one." He chuckled. "However, to spare your modesty, let's see to your leg first. I imagine having two men see you undressed would be even more offensive to your sensibilities."

Stitches cleared his throat, looking almost as embarrassed as Brianna. "Erm, yes. Right."

Grimm suddenly remembered his manners. "Oh, forgive me. Dr. Coffin, may I introduce *Mademoiselle* Brianna Belmont? *Mademoiselle*, Doctor Matthew Coffin, affectionately known as Stitches."

Oddly, Coffin's awkwardness seemed to restore some of Brianna's confidence.

"*Ma'm'selle*, can you move the leg at all?" he asked.

"*Oui*," she replied. "It only hurt when I tried to stand on it."

"Forgive my forwardness, but I need to see your ankle." He slipped into his medical mindset and ceased to allow the fact that she was female fluster him. He lifted her foot up onto his knee and pushed her skirt back enough to reveal her calf. "Can you move your foot?"

She rotated her foot around stiffly. The ankle was already swollen.

"Hmm, it may just be sprained. I'll have to see it without the shoe and stocking to know for sure."

"Why?" she asked suspiciously.

He was blunt, since he didn't want this to take longer than necessary. There were wounded prisoners that had been chosen to add to the crew who also needed his attention. "To make sure no bones are poking through the skin. With all this blood on you, I can't tell otherwise."

"Oh."

Grimm kept his face stoic when it looked like she was about to burst into tears again. She lifted her skirt a little higher to unhook the stocking. Then she rolled it down her leg. Dr. Coffin removed her shoe and her stocking, doing his best to cradle her ankle gently.

He prodded and examined her bare ankle and made a final diagnosis with suggested treatment. "It is not broken, but the sprain is very bad, and the skin is feverish. Soak some bandages in salt water and wet wrap it tightly, but not so much that it makes the toes turn dark. Change the wrapping every couple of hours to keep down the swelling and cool the skin. If the pain gets to be too much, put a few drops of laudanum in a good shot of liquor. Also, stay off that foot for at least a week, or it will take longer to heal."

He lowered her foot and stood. "Now, if you will excuse me, I have other patients to attend to."

"Thank you, doctor." She nodded.

After Coffin left, Grimm came and sat beside her on the bed. "It will be dark soon. We really need to get rid of these bloody garments."

Too mentally, physically, and emotionally exhausted, Brianna quit trying to fight. Other than the threats to let the other pirates have at her, the man had been almost kind to her. She was curious, however. "Why is it so important to get rid of the bloody clothes?"

As he unlaced her dress he answered, "Belladonna isn't the only creature aboard this ship that is drawn to human blood. There are six members of the crew who can drink nothing else, and they will be up and about the moment the sun sinks into the sea."

Even though still in shock, Brianna blanched. She had heard tales of such creatures in her childhood. "Vampires?"

"Aye." He confirmed her guess and helped her push the dress down over her hips and to the deck. He then started on the corset. "I'm afraid this will have to go, too. There's too much blood to wash out. You'll be more comfortable without it, anyway."

Her mind was no longer on clothing. "*M'sieur!* I see no garlic or crucifix; how do you keep them out of here?" Her voice neared panic.

Grimm chuckled. "I don't. The Captain does. He made them. They obey him."

"But how? I saw him walking about freely in the daylight."

"Aye, and you'll also see him wearing a crucifix from time to time." He nodded. "The Captain is unique."

He got back up and opened the chest again. He didn't have to dig in it this time. The item he wanted was on top, where he'd left it. "I wasn't sure at first, but it looks like you are going to need this after all."

He handed her an under-shift. Pointing to the one she wore, he said, "That small amount of blood should wash out, but for now it is still too much for safety's sake."

To her amazement, he turned his back to give her some privacy as she changed. As Brianna pulled the soiled shift over her head and donned the clean one, she began to wonder if her captor preferred men. She had heard of such affections manifesting among men who were long at sea with no access to women. With all the other incredible and frightening things that had happened this day, it wouldn't surprise her.

Surreptitiously watching her in the small shaving mirror, Grimm puzzled over his treatment of this woman. He definitely wanted her, yet there was something that held him back from just taking her. She evoked a tenderness that rarely surfaced in him.

He wanted to take his time with her.

Her voice broke his reverie. "Tell me, *m'sieur*, why you believed my claim of being Brianna Belmont?"

The look in his eyes when he turned to face her again made her rethink her opinion of which gender he preferred. There was no mistaking the heat in his gaze. For a moment, she forgot what they were talking about.

"It sounded more plausible. Although I've never met the man, I am acquainted with his taste in — brides. You fit that bill much better than the other girl," he replied. "Then your reaction to her death was too genuine for you to be lying about her name being Nicole. The final proof was your difficulty with your wardrobe. It's rare to encounter a servant whose mistress would help her with her laces."

The mention of Nicole's name was enough to dampen the mood. Once again, Brianna began to cry. Other than the hiccoughing sound of her breathing, however, her sobs were silent.

Grimm realized she must have been closer than usual to her maid and kept his silence. He sat down beside her and folded her to his chest. She continued to shake and sob as he rocked her and stroked her hair.

They stayed like that until she cried herself out and fell into an exhausted sleep.

Grimm situated her into a comfortable position on the bed, then gathered up the bloody garments and took them away for disposal.

Chapter 17

The *Shining Star* put in at Havana. Captain Bainbridge hoped they could get more recent news of Brandee there. The only useful information they gleaned from their encounter with Paella and Dorada was that the Grimm Reaper had joined forces with Brandee, hence the decision to sail to Havana. It was a known haunt of the Reaper.

Samantha, oddly enough, was the one with misgivings about this part of the venture. Hezekiah Grimm's reputation was just as deadly as that of Viktor Brandewyne. She feared it would be difficult to get information from the Cubans about the pirate.

At first, it looked as if she would be right. Very few people would even admit knowing anything about the Reaper. Those that did claim to, for the most part wanted money before they would say anything.

This, of course, raised suspicion to both Bainbridge and Samantha. Most of the ones demanding money looked and smelled like drunkards. Like as not, they were merely looking for their next bottle.

There was one lead, however, that cost them nothing. If Samantha had not been there, Bainbridge might not have gotten that much.

The man, though oily looking, did not appear to be destitute or drunk. Rather, he sized the young woman up with an appreciative leer.

"I hear you've been asking around about the Reaper. If you're looking to sell, she's definitely to his taste; but you won't have much luck," he said.

Bainbridge took the lead and hoped that Sam caught on quick and didn't step out of character. "Why is that, sir? If she's what he likes, why wouldn't he meet the price I'll ask?"

"For one thing, you missed him by over a year. For the other, word has it that the Reaper takes what he wants. He doesn't pay for it. Just ask any of the wenches down at the Crescent Inn."

Bainbridge steered away from the topic before the man could make an offer on Sam. "I've heard scuttlebutt that he sails with Bloody Brandee."

The informant blanched a bit. "Aye, 'tis true," he said. "They have joined forces again. There had been reports of Brandee's death, but he has been seen here with the Reaper since then. You want to steer clear of that one."

"Aye, he is a dangerous one."

"It is more than that." The man shook his head. "The man is fey, not just dangerous. If Hezekiah Grimm is the Grimm Reaper, Bloody Vik Brandee is Death himself. Some say that the reports of his death were true, but that he made a deal with the Devil to come back. I caught a brief glimpse of him with the Reaper the last time they were in port, and I swear his eyes glowed with a green fire. Unholy, it was."

"I will keep that in mind."

After the encounter, Sam and Bainbridge made their way toward the Crescent Inn.

"Captain, we've known quite a while that Brandewyne and Grimm sailed together," she said.

"Aye, but I wanted to know how widespread that knowledge was. Sometimes word travels fast. Sometimes it doesn't," he replied. "After all, when your brothers were taken, most people thought Brandee was dead."

"Oh."

They walked on in silence for a few moments before Sam said, "If this place is a regular haunt of the pirates, do you think they'll willingly tell us anything?"

"I think it will all depend on how we ask."

Several eyes turned toward them as they entered the tavern. Although Sam no longer tried to hide her gender, she continued to wear men's clothing. This, coupled with her blonde hair, which she was growing back out, drew attention. Blonde women were a rarity in the islands.

As the murmur in the room resumed, Bainbridge quietly spoke to her, "We may not have to ask. I see a few faces we encountered earlier today. It's already common knowledge that we seek the Reaper, just not why."

They found a table and sat down. For a while, they thought they would get no service. Several of the girls passed them without a glance. Stubbornly, they remained at the table.

Finally, the tavern keeper came over to them. "*Señor*, I must ask you and the *señorita* to leave."

"Why?" Sam asked bluntly.

He glared at her. "We do not serve your kind here. Pirate hunters are bad for business."

"We aren't pirate hunters," Bainbridge stated.

"Do not insult my intelligence, *señor*. You have been seen around port asking after the Grimm Reaper. I will grant that using such a lovely *señorita* as bait is a trick I haven't seen before, but I know you are no friend or business acquaintance of his."

"The only reason we seek him is that he sails with Viktor Brandewyne. That's who we truly are looking for," Bainbridge tried to explain.

"You do nothing for your case, *señor*." The tavern keeper's tone grew dangerous.

Samantha could see they were making no headway. "Please, sir," she said as she placed her hand on the man's arm. "Captain Bainbridge is telling the truth. We are not pirate hunters. We are looking for Captain Brandewyne because we believe he has my brothers. I want to try to ransom them."

One of the tavern wenches serving a table nearby stopped to listen to the exchange. She paid special attention to Sam. She walked over and said, "They are telling the truth, Manuel. Remember the new navigator?"

Manuel frowned at her. "Luz, your customers are waiting for their food."

She put a fist on her hip and glared at him. "I just gave them their order, you bull-headed oaf. Look at her!" She jutted a finger toward Sam. "You can't tell me they aren't related." She turned to the pair and asked, "What is your name?"

"Samantha Brumble."

"See?" she said archly.

Grudgingly, he really looked at Samantha. He had to admit he saw a strong resemblance to Brandee and Grimm's newest navigator. He snorted in disgust. "I accept your word that you are not pirate hunters; but you are on a fool's errand. I know the men you seek. They will not ransom your brothers if they have not demanded it," he told her. "In truth, it would be best for them if you do not find Brandee and the Reaper."

"Why is that?" Sam asked, flushing red with the beginnings of anger.

Manuel decided to be blunt. "They will either have to stand by while you are raped or get themselves killed trying to protect you, and you would still be raped."

With that, he turned and went back to his bar, muttering at Luz to take their order.

Luz shook her head after him before she turned back to them. "Manuel is rough around the edges, but he has a good heart. The two pirates you are looking for have always been generous customers, but he is right about what would probably happen if you found them."

Sam looked at her and said, "It is not the first time I have been told that. But they are my brothers. I would willingly offer myself to gain their freedom."

Luz shook her head. "I will not try to change your mind, *señorita*. If you would like to order something, I will bring it to you. One of your brothers left a message for you when they passed through a little over a month ago."

That caught Bainbridge's attention. "The man who sent us here said we'd missed them by a year."

"Did he have stringy hair and a gold tooth?"

"Yes."

"Rodrigo Puenterez; his information is out of date. He only returned from St. Augustine last week, so he wasn't here the same time as Captain Brandee. He will not be welcome here if Manuel hears of this."

They placed an order, and Luz left to tell the cook then retrieve the note.

"We've never been this close before," Sam whispered excitedly.

Bainbridge nodded. "Aye, we'll only stay in port a couple of days. The lads need a little spell ashore, and we need to resupply. We still don't have a heading to follow."

She sobered instantly. Just the knowledge that they were maybe only a month behind their quarry had been more than she'd hoped for. The captain was right, however. They still needed an idea of where to go next.

Luz returned with their drinks and a folded and sealed note. Samantha recognized Zachary's mark. He, at least, was still alive. To her consternation, her hands shook too badly to break the seal.

Bainbridge took pity on her and opened it for her. When he tried to hand it back, she shook her head and wiped at her eyes. "I don't think I could see to read it right now. Please, look it over and see if it is safe to read in public."

He glanced at it and said, "I believe it would be best to wait until we are back aboard the *Shining Star*."

"Very well. Thank you, Captain Bainbridge. That should give me time to calm down and regain control of myself." She tried to smile.

It was late that night in her cabin before Sam could bring herself to read the message from Zachary.

Dearest Samantha,

We have just received word that you are hunting for us. I would explain how, but I fear you would think I've gone mad.

The Captain and Mr. Grimm have been fair to me, and I am accepted as part of the crew. But make no mistake; they are ruthless and quite dangerous. They do not hesitate to kill, regardless of age or gender.

Please, Sam, do not try to find us or rescue us. I have accepted my fate, and Thomas is beyond salvation. He belongs to the Captain, body and soul. What he has become could cause him to harm or kill you before he could stop himself.

I do not know when or if this missive will ever find you. I only hope that you heed my warnings. I could not bear to think I had brought you to harm, dear sister.

Zachary

"Oh Zach," she sighed, "what have you and Thom gotten into?" She felt particularly worried about her youngest brother.

They managed to learn that Brandee's next destination had been New Orleans. Sam left a note with Luz for Zach, just in case he passed through before she could find him.

Chapter 18

The lead was old. Carpathia knew this, but she wanted to pursue it anyway. If nothing else, perhaps she could get a better sense of her prey's habits. That alone would help her predict where he was most likely to turn up, even if she didn't learn where he went.

Her informant, a sorry excuse for a slave trader in Port Royal, failed to survive the encounter. Thia, too long without a good feed, drained him along with nearly half of his inventory.

Near sunset, the *Lorelei* approached a small, unassuming island—with enough of a lagoon to provide a natural harbor. Several structures adjoined or stood close to the docks.

A sloop lay at anchor close to a landing platform in the deepest part of the lagoon. Captain Wormsloe blinked in surprise at the pennant it sported.

"This should be interesting," he muttered. "Mr. Borescue, inform milady that there is an emissary of the Church here ahead of us."

"Aye, Captain," the first mate replied. "She's not going to be pleased."

On his way, Borescue snagged a sailor who didn't look busy. Wormsloe understood the precaution. The vampire was apt to lash out over the unpleasant news. The sailor would be easier to replace than the first mate.

The moment the last sliver of sun vanished beneath the waves; Lady Carpathia erupted onto the deck. The very air around her crackled with dark energy. Her eyes glowed with an un-light.

A few moments passed before Mr. Borescue managed to stagger back topside. The grey pallor of his skin made the wash of blood staining his neck and shirt stand out in stark contrast. Wormsloe felt relief she hadn't killed the man, but feared his first mate might not survive the night.

"Mindoe, see that Mr. Borescue gets to the infirmary and send a couple of men down to retrieve Clarkson," he ordered. He carefully avoided looking directly at their deadly passenger until she could compose herself. He had his master's protection, but he didn't trust that protection from half a world away with *her* in a foul mood.

Finally, Carpathia got her temper under control and damped her powers until she once again appeared to be human. She moved to stand close to Wormsloe and gaze across the lagoon at the vessel which was the source of the uproar. To his credit, he didn't flinch at her proximity.

"If you don't mind, I'd like to be able to select a few sailors from that lot to replace the ones we've lost before you feast," he said.

"Careful of your tone, human," she warned. "I am in no mood to tolerate your insolence."

His smile was not friendly. "Just as I am in no mood to lose a good officer and mate to one of your snits, milady. Do not forget that I know how to contain you, or whose protection I am under."

She growled at him but made no move to attack.

Satisfied with his continued safety, Wormsloe made an observation. "The Church generally frowns on slavery, but this is not one of their battle ships come to enforce their will. Although I have never dealt personally with this slaver, Delacroix has a reputation for being a brothel supplier and somewhat deviant in his sexual tastes."

"He prefers men?" Carpathia smirked as she began to see a way to take control of the situation. "That is not so deviant."

"Perhaps not to you, milady, but to ordinary mortals, it is," he replied. "Be that as it may, men are not his particular taste. He prefers children; the younger the better."

"Interesting. You make me wonder about this priest. Perhaps his faith is corrupt," she said.

"We won't know until we get ashore. Delacroix must have at least enough women in stock to keep the sailors occupied. There is no watch aboard that vessel or along the shoreline."

"How careless of them," she purred.

Without warning, she launched into the night sky. Mere moments later, she hovered above the deck of the sloop. She called out, "May I come aboard?"

A cabin boy answered back from a nearby hatchway, "Welcome, madame. My master is not here right now, but he should be back before the night is done." Obviously, he hadn't seen her flight and thought she stood on the deck.

It didn't take her long to go through the vessel and confirm its lack of occupation. The cabin boy and a couple of old tars were the only ones aboard.

She drained the two men in their sleep: their lives the price for not posting a watch. The boy, she carried back to the *Lorelei* for questioning.

Once back aboard, she and Wormsloe took the boy to the captain's cabin. The youngster seemed to be more despondent than afraid, something Wormsloe took immediate notice of.

"What have you done to him, milady? I need him clear-headed if there is any hope of getting reliable information from him."

"He was like this when I found him in the priest's cabin," she replied. "I have not clouded his mind, nor did he witness my two kills."

At that statement, the boy showed a glimmer of hope. "Are you here to kill me?"

"Why do you ask that with such hope, child?" Thia found it unusual. Normally, humans begged for their lives.

"If I am dead, he can't hurt me anymore. I will be free," the boy answered. "It is damnation to commit suicide, but not to be killed." He grasped her skirts, tears of desperation in his eyes. "Are you the angel of death? You are as beautiful as an angel. You said you killed Garmin and Fitch. Please, please kill me, too."

She reached down and caressed his face with a gentle smile. "Poor sweet child, if you answer Captain Wormsloe's questions, I will grant you the eternal peace you crave."

The boy looked over at the captain. "What do you want to know?"

Delacroix and Father Jerome shared a cask of wine while the father looked over the children the slave trader held in stock. Though the practice of selling children to craft masters as apprentices or planters looking for laborers was growing less socially acceptable, it still went on quietly and brought good profits to the traders that dealt in them. A variety of races were represented, mostly boys, with only four girls in the lot.

One could easily tell which ones had been in Delacroix's possession the longest. They showed a world-weary resignation to their fate as slaves about them. The newer ones seemed to have more of a mix of shock and fear.

"I am not interested in the girls, Delacroix. They cannot be easily explained away like the boys can. The Church frowns on slavery. Oh, I want some of the native stock this time, as well."

"Very well." Del snapped his fingers. One of his men separated three boys from the group and moved them forward for inspection. "Just out of curiosity, why only the native stock?"

"The bishop has been dogging me to increase the converts in my congregation," he answered as he looked the boys over. "A couple of native altar boys should satisfy him. These two should do nicely. The other one looks like you've already broken his spirit, Del."

"Some of my clients prefer them that way. They're more obedient and less likely to run away. The two you've chosen aren't from the same tribe, you know. They aren't even from your vicinity."

"Doesn't matter." Father Jerome smirked. "The old fool doesn't know one breed from another. He just sees bronze skin and black hair and sees ignorant heathens in need of salvation."

Del chuckled. "You white men never cease to amuse me. All right, now that you've made your selection, let us discuss price."

Before the negotiations could go any further, the door opened, and the cabin boy walked in. The priest frowned at him. "Patrick, I told you to stay with the ship. Why are you here?"

"Please come in, milady," the boy said in response.

"Milady? What are you talking about?"

Del noticed the boy looked unusually pale, and he bore two angry wounds on his neck. Carpathia swept into the room before Del could voice a warning. The invitation gave her access. She moved so fast she seemed to materialize beside Patrick. She smiled and placed a hand on the boy's shoulder.

"Thank you for inviting me, Patrick. Now I will fulfill my promise to you." Before anyone could stop her, she lifted the boy in her arms and buried her fangs in his throat. He died in mere minutes. She ripped his head from his body as if she were tearing a piece of cloth.

Throughout this, everyone in the room remained too stunned to react. As soon as the beheaded body hit the floor, and the vampire raised her blood-soaked face, chaos erupted.

The children cowered against the wall; their guards drew what weapons they had but were plainly terrified. Father Jerome stood agape at the horror before him, still in shock. Only the slaver kept his head. He recognized exactly what they were dealing with.

He grabbed the priest by the arm, shook him, and yelled, "Use your rosary, man! She can't defy anything holy!"

Carpathia snarled at Del, angry that her attack might be thwarted.

Jerome fished inside his cassock and pulled out a golden rosary. With a shaking hand, he thrust it toward her. "Begone, foul servant of the Devil!" His voice quavered with fear.

For a brief moment, she flinched; then she blinked at him. Finally, she began to laugh.

"It's not working!" he cried desperately at Del.

Carpathia stood at his side in a heartbeat. "Of course not, silly man." She laughed as she tore his arm off, then flung it, the hand still clutching the rosary, out the door behind her. She clasped the bleeding priest to her and said, "Your faith is corrupt, and your God has turned His back on you. And now, I shall usher you into Hell." She bit into his upper shoulder and tore it wide.

He didn't scream for long.

Delacroix's men made a run for the door. She let them leave. The children remained huddled in a corner.

Seeing that his men made it out, Del tried to escape as well. Carpathia appeared directly in front of him just as he reached the door. As he stumbled back, she stalked toward him.

"Leaving so soon? I have business with you, Delacroix." She tsked and wagged a finger at him.

He kept backing away from her until he tripped over Patrick's body. He crabbed backwards into the wall, kicking the boy's dismembered head in the process. It rolled to rest facing him, with a bloodless, peaceful expression.

Del heard someone screaming. It took him a few moments to realize that it was him. In that time, the vampire moved to stand over him and grasped his chin.

This forced the slaver to meet her gaze. "You are going to tell me everything you know about the pirate, Viktor Brandewyne."

Chapter 19

"I know that I want to kill that son-of-a-bitch," Del snarled, instantly angry. That his anger was strong enough to afford him partial protection from her power said something.

"Interesting; why is that? I thought he occasionally sold to you," she said.

"His prices are exorbitant. He demands full market value, which makes it nearly impossible to make a profit." He stopped and glanced at the vampire. "And he seems to attract murderous bitches. You are the second woman who has come to me wanting information about Vik Brandee."

"Really?" She tilted her head. "What kind of woman was the first one?" Thia remembered Critchfield also mentioning she was the second female seeking Brandee. She thought perhaps her master sent another hunter as backup. If so, it complicated her plans.

"I've sent out scouts to find out about her. Samantha Brumble is the only daughter of Tobias Brumble, proprietor of the Brumble & Sons Trading Company of Boston. Apparently, Brandee took her brothers, and she wants them back. The crusading bitch stole my inventory and almost castrated me. If I ever get my hands on her, I will use her body in every way known to man while her father is forced to watch; then gut her in front of him."

"So, you really don't like her." Thia smirked. "You show potential, Delacroix; but I don't have time to train you properly. I could teach you how to make her death last weeks." She shook her head and got back on course. "What else can you tell me about Brandee?" She put the full force of her will behind the question.

Del's face went slack as his will and anger evaporated before her power. "His ship is almost a dreadnaught and is called the *Incubus*. His first mate is Hezekiah Grimm, the Grimm Reaper. There is a woman on his crew, a redhead. The Reaper told me she is a siren. The last time he was here was well over two years ago. Very few crewmen were allowed ashore. Scuttlebutt was they were heading to Islas de la Roques."

"What about ports he is known to frequent?" She knew chances were that Brandee was nowhere near the named islands by now. She needed a better grasp on his habits and haunts. There had to be a good place to intercept him.

"Vik Brandee is hard to predict. There are some that say Savannah is his home port, but he has been seen in just about every major port in the Caribbean, as well as up the Atlantic coast. The Reaper, on the other hand, seems particularly fond of Havana and New Orleans."

Carpathia smiled. "You have been very informative and helpful, Delacroix."

He grinned at her approval. Her pleasure with him filled him with pure joy. He was still grinning when she tore his head from his shoulders.

The entire time, the children huddled in the corner had not moved. They were frozen with both fear and fascination. She saw the hobbles on their ankles and realized those probably played a part in it, as well. A chain ran through the hobbles and connected to a ring in the floor.

She strode over to the ring and ripped it from its mooring in one swift pull. She looked at the children with no expression on her face and said, "Come."

They obeyed. Even the ones who had not been in Delacroix's possession very long had been prisoners long enough to know that they would just be dragged by their hobbles if they resisted.

One of the older children asked, "Why didn't you eat him like you did the other two?"

Carpathia stopped and peered at the child. "You do not fear me, even after all you have seen. Why?"

He looked back at the pale-skinned woman who held his chain. She was monstrously beautiful; standing there soaked from chin to knee in the blood of her victims. He shrugged and said, "At worst, you will kill me. After what that bastard put me through, death would be a blessed rest."

"Only if it is the true death," she amended with a cryptic qualifier. "I did not feed on the slave trader because I did not want to take the chance of him becoming what I am. He did not deserve that kind of power."

She started to lead them again. They passed the organized chaos of the raid on the slaver's camp. Wormsloe's men had been swift and silent. Only a few of Del's men and sailors from the priest's ship had been killed.

Carpathia found the captain and stopped him for a moment. "Once you've selected the men you need, place the rest of them in one of the holds; that includes the slaves."

"You're lucky we have the room for them, milady." He put no respect into the title. Then he sighed. "I shouldn't complain, I guess. It will keep you from decimating my crew again."

"Yes, it will." Her tone sounded surprisingly amiable. "I have fed well tonight. These will suffice for tomorrow night. Young blood is more nourishing."

She turned to lead her captives back to the docks, but then turned back and smiled. "If you like, Captain Wormsloe, I will save the females for last. I imagine your men would appreciate some sport."

He blinked in surprise. He had not expected such generosity. "Thank you, milady. I will let the lads know."

Once she and her captives were out of sight, he caught the attention of his second mate. "Mr. Mindoe, inform the lads to round up all the prisoners and find room for them in the main hold."

"Aye, Captain. She wants them for her larder?"

"Yes, but she is saving the women for last. She's offered them to the crew for sport until she's ready for them."

It was Mindoe's turn to be surprised. "That's very unlike her."

"Don't question it, man. Just be glad she's feeling generous. Her mood can change without notice."

"Aye, that it can."

The crew of the *Lorelei* stripped the island and Father Jerome's ship of anything of value or use. They left nothing behind.

As they sailed off, the glow of burning huts, piers and the stripped ship gave the illusion of dawn.

Chapter 20

The *Incubus* put in at La Laguna on Tenerife; not so much to resupply as to get information. The port was the last stop before crossing the Atlantic for many ships sailing from western Africa or the Mediterranean. Viktor wagered that La Forte probably used it as a supply point in his slave trade route. If so, someone there might be able to give them an idea of where to look for the man.

It also served to give the crew some sporting time. Vik and Grimm both decided years before that it best served morale to let their men have time to enjoy the shares they got from any prize taken. Where some pirates would hoard their wealth and were stingy with their crew, Brandee and the Reaper had never been that way. Having all the treasure in the world meant nothing if you were never allowed to enjoy it.

The cadre took the night watch on board, which freed the rest of the crew to go ashore. Grimm opted to stay aboard, as well.

Viktor figured he was going to set to taming Brianna. He knew his first mate hadn't bedded the girl yet. His heightened senses would've let him know if Hezekiah had. As it was, her scent was barely discernible any distance from the cabin his first mate kept her in.

Amazingly, for such an important port, they found only two taverns owned by brothers who tailored their individual businesses to specific clientele. The Drunken Goat, close to the docks, catered to the working classes on the island and the crews of any ships in port. The Singing Mermaid, further into town, catered more to the tastes of the ships' officers and the wealthy landowners.

The crew of the *Incubus* descended on both taverns like locusts. It was one of the benefits of being pirates. They couldn't care less about class divisions. Of course, they also found it fun to go in and take over an establishment where they obviously weren't welcome, but no one dared to throw them out.

Viktor and Belladonna headed to the Mermaid. Jon-Jon went to the Goat. The latter stood a better chance of getting information at the dockside tavern than his captain did. In a port that made such a fuss about class distinction, a ship's captain would be viewed with distrust by the Goat's regulars.

The rest of the crew split fairly evenly between the two taverns.

The packet and pirate they recently took left them flush with gold. Viktor decided he would try a business approach to getting information before resorting to force. He could spare the gold, but the time a fight and its aftermath would cost was something he didn't want to spend.

Since about half of the crew joined him in the tavern, as well, he didn't bother trying to get Belladonna to wear a dress. He just felt grateful she no longer fought him about wearing clothes at all.

Although the locals were distracted by the influx of pirates, all eyes turned to the vampire and the siren when they entered the Singing Mermaid. Belladonna's blood-red hair and curvaceous figure clad in a loose shirt and form-fitting leather breeches drew the gaze of every male in the room, save for the pirates.

The women there with their husbands might have been jealous had they not been so taken with Viktor's tall, raven-haired form. His emerald eyes already glowed faintly from the scent of several women's arousal at one time.

He picked a table near a wall and sat down. He smirked and Belle sneered at the sight of the two serving wenches nearly racing each other to come take their order. Both women arrived at the table about the same time.

"Welcome to the Singing Mermaid," the first one said. "My name is Clara. May I get you something to eat or drink?"

Before Vik could reply, the other one said, "Hello, sir, madam. I'm Janine. Is there anything I can do for you, anything at all?" Clara spared her a quick frown before she turned back to smile at the handsome pirate.

Belladonna sat back and gave an amused snort. She began to enjoy the rivalry between the two human females.

Viktor made a point of raking his gaze over both of them. "Oh, I can think of several things you could both do for me." He chuckled. "However, for now I'll take two bottles of your best rum, Clara. Janine, pet, you can have a seat and keep me company for a while."

Clara instantly bristled. "Janine, no! With Sharon too sick to work, I can't do all the serving by myself!"

Viktor grasped her jaw and forced her to look at him. His eyes flared, and his voice breathed power. "Bring me what I asked for, pet. You'll have your turn with me later."

Obediently, Clara's smile returned as if she'd never been angry. "I will be right back with your rum, sir. Will there be anything else?"

"Not right now, pet. I'll let you know."

She left to fill the order, totally oblivious to the absence of Janine's help. Viktor turned his attention to Janine.

"Have a seat, pet." He indicated an empty seat.

The serving wench looked at the siren. "Is that all right with you, miss?"

Belle blinked in surprise at the courtesy. This proved to definitely be a higher class of establishment than the pirates usually frequented. She smiled and replied, "I've a feeling it is necessary."

Reassured, Janine sat down. No sooner had she settled than the vampire leaned over and kissed her passionately. In the midst of it, he nicked his tongue with a fang and passed the blood on to his victim. Janine's will instantly succumbed to his.

In a low voice, so as not to draw unwanted attention, he began to fire questions at her.

"Does Quentin La Forte use this port?"

"Yes."

"Do you know how frequently?"

"Maybe once or twice a year."

Viktor frowned. It meant he might have missed La Forte by months. "When was the last time he was in this port?"

"Seven months ago."

"Can you tell me anything about him? Does he come to this tavern?"

Janine bit her lip in thought. Finally, she answered, "He has been in here a few times. Clara dealt with him more than I did. He felt like an evil man the one time I served him. He tried to assign me, but I refused him. Clara took him on, instead."

"Hm, thank you for your help, pet." He handed her a small bag with some gold coins in it.

"Ah, Clara, pet!"

The woman smiled at his greeting as she set down the tray with two bottles and three glasses. At his unspoken command, she took the seat Janine had just vacated. He lifted one of the bottles and uncorked it. After he poured a small amount in one of the glasses, he tasted it. Both his eyebrows raised in approval of the flavor.

"Not bad at all. A few Jamaican rums are just as rich, but this still has something unique in the flavor. It's almost smoky. Is it local?"

"Yes, sir," Clara answered. "My employer distills it himself. He keeps the source of his molasses a closely guarded secret."

"I cannot fault him for that." Viktor smirked and filled his glass, then poured some into the other two glasses. "I doubt he lets you have any very often. You can have some, too, Belle."

"No, he doesn't." Clara quickly grabbed the glass as if afraid someone would take it away from her. She began to drink it, obviously forcing herself to sip rather than downing it rapidly.

Belladonna sniffed experimentally at the rum. She drew back and looked at it sideways before sniffing it again. Viktor smiled wryly at her approach.

"What's the matter, pet?"

"It smells like a cross between Jon-Jon and Sniff," she stated. "And I've never had drink before."

"Oh, this should be interesting." He chuckled.

She took a small sip and swished the liquid around in her mouth. She swallowed it. Her pupils dilated and she gave the glass of rum a strange smile.

"That is good!" The siren quickly downed the rum and held out her glass for more.

Viktor chuckled and poured her a second glass. "Easy, pet. This tastes strong. It may hit you hard and fast."

She giggled. "It burns, but it makes me feel tingly inside, too."

The liquor had another effect on the siren, one that Viktor did not care for. As she drank the second glass, he could feel the bond between them grow fuzzy. It did not dissolve, but he sensed a partial barrier and lag to the connection. Given that he was still unsure of how far Venoma's influence stretched, he definitely did not like this turn of events.

"I think we should get back to the ship, pet," he said as he corked the bottle. "Clara, join us. I need to ask you a few things, but this is no longer a safe place to do so."

The serving wench stood and followed them out the door.

The tavern keeper didn't see them leave and had no idea what had happened to Clara. Janine didn't even have a memory of Clara being there for work that day. She wouldn't have remembered Viktor, if it hadn't been for the coins he'd given her. She carefully kept those a secret.

Back aboard the *Incubus*, Vik locked Clara in his cabin before escorting Belladonna to her own cabin. She started shedding clothes on the short distance between cabins.

"Pet, stop that."

"But it is so hot, and these things are so binding," she whined. As she dropped the last garment she stretched, sighed, and then laughed. "Much better!"

"Belle, are you well?" Her behavior reminded him of how she'd been when they first met.

In answer, she hopped up and wrapped herself around him. She then kissed him soundly. When she pulled back, she said, "You tell me, Vikkie."

"Don't call me that. I think you are drunk." He then set about disengaging her from him.

Jon-Jon picked that moment to come looking for the captain. "Oh, sorry, Cap'n. Didn't mean to interrupt," he said as soon as he saw them. He turned to give them some privacy.

Belle unexpectedly released the vampire and pounced on the second mate, knocking him to the deck. Jon-Jon managed to at least get face up, only to find the naked siren straddling him.

"So, tell me, Mr. Jon," she purred as she rubbed herself against him, "why do they call you Big Jon?"

Before he could think clearly enough to respond, Vik grasped Belle around the waist and lifted her off of him.

"That is enough!" he bellowed. "Mr. Jon, I suggest you go topside — now!"

As Jon-Jon scrambled backward in his haste to escape his captain's ire, Grimm emerged from his own cabin.

"Captain? Is something wrong?" he asked.

The siren locked on him immediately. "Grimmy!" she squealed and beamed at him. She made no real effort to get away from Viktor, though.

"Keep your distance, Hezekiah. She's a bit out of control," Vik said. He hefted her from behind and moved her toward her cabin. Grimm took in the sight of his captain, who looked a little frazzled, holding onto the naked siren, who behaved downright bubbly. His mouth quirked up in an amused smirk, but he avoided laughing.

Vik managed to get to her cabin door. As he tried to get her into the cabin, she extended her talons and dug into the door jamb. She left furrows in the wood as he forcibly pulled her in. He then turned her so she was facing him. On a gamble, he kissed her passionately.

The gamble paid off. It distracted the siren long enough for him to use his supernatural speed to push her away, get out the door and shut it, before she could grab him back.

"Vikkie, come back!" she whined through the door. The wooden door started to rattle. Before long, the sounds of scratching on wood could be heard.

Grimm wisely refrained from commenting on the pet name. She had called him "Grimmy," after all. Instead, he said, "If we don't give her someone, she's going to claw her way through the door or the bulkhead."

"Aye, and heaven help the first man she catches." Vik nodded. Silently, he summoned the one crew member he believed she wouldn't kill. "Mr. Brumble should be here soon."

"Can we afford to lose him?"

"Not really, but I don't think he'll be in any real danger. She seems to think of him as a pet."

"Ah." He tried to keep quiet about the situation, but his curiosity got the better of him. "Any idea why she is like this today?"

Viktor actually looked embarrassed. "I made the mistake of giving her rum."

"Let's not ever do that again."

"Believe me, I won't. Ah, good of you to join us, Mr. Brumble," Vik said as Zach joined them.

"You sent for me, Captain?"

"Aye, Belladonna is not well and is in need of someone to tend to her."

Zach noticed the banging and scratching at the cabin door, as well as a pleading, whining sound. "Why is she locked in?"

"Safety of the crew."

Before he could ask anything else, Vik unlocked the door and pushed him toward it. Belladonna squealed and snatched him into the cabin so fast it was a wonder she didn't snap his neck.

"Right," Grimm said after a minute. "Well, if I'm not needed for anything right now —."

"Go on, Hezekiah." Vik shook his head. "I need to find Jon-Jon and let him know he is not in trouble. I can smell his fear from here."

Clara recovered from the vampire's enchantment shortly after he locked her in his cabin. She remained unaware that he had manipulated her, however. She knew her employer would be angry with her for leaving him short-handed just before the busiest time of day, so she began to snoop around for something valuable enough to mollify him.

She'd done this before, to their mutual profit.

It didn't take her long to locate the small casket that contained a beautiful gold cross. The icon was encrusted with emeralds, several of good size. Their color was a vibrant green, much like the eyes of the man who had brought her there.

She'd just managed to slip it into her pocket when Viktor came back to the cabin. It surprised her to hear a key turn in the lock. She'd been unaware he had locked her in.

☠

Viktor caught the scent of her surprise as he entered and shut the door behind him. He also detected a touch of guilt. She had been doing something just before he came in. Looking around, he saw a couple of things slightly out of place. He did his inspection so rapidly she didn't even notice.

He smiled and approached her. She smiled back. He could see she thought he had no clue she had stolen something. He allowed her to continue in her delusion. He wanted information about La Forte first.

"Clara, pet, what can you tell me about Quentin La Forte?"

The question caught her off guard. "What? I thought you brought me here for sport."

"Oh, no fear there, pet. All in due time, but I must attend to this first. I have business with Mr. La Forte, and I need to know where to find him and what kind of man he is. You will be well compensated."

Still not realizing she was not in control of the situation; she treated it like the business transaction it was. "He is a dangerous man. How much will you pay?"

Viktor suddenly stood right in front of her, startling her. With lightning speed, one hand was at her throat and the other on her wrist. He forced her hand out of her pocket, the emerald cross still clutched in it.

"I won't kill you for trying to steal from me. Is that payment enough, pet?" he asked with a deadly purr.

"Y-y-yes," she stammered when she caught sight of his fangs. He made no attempt to hide them.

"Good, now tell me what you know about Quentin La Forte."

The next day, Vik sent Jon-Jon to round up the crew; then he met Grimm at the helm.

"I see you finally decided to come out of your cabin," Vik said to his first mate.

"I'm taking my time with this one." Grimm nodded. "May keep her a while."

"She's not being cooperative; is she?" He made it more of a statement than a question. "I've a dress you can give her that should be about her size. That tavern wench won't need it anymore, and there's no sense in giving it to Belle."

"Aye, that one positively hates wearing dresses. I'll get it later this evening. Did you kill her to keep her quiet?"

"I didn't kill her." When he saw the skeptical look Grimm gave him, he said, "You know I don't break my word, Hezekiah. I told her I wouldn't kill her for trying to steal from me if she gave me information about La Forte. She delivered what information she had; then I gave her to the cadre. They haven't had a woman in a very long time, so I'm afraid she didn't survive the experience."

"Ah. Well then, what is our heading?"

"Abidjan. Jon-Jon found out more valuable news at the Drunken Goat. Clara couldn't tell me where he sails from, only the kind of man he is."

Zach finally put in an appearance a couple of days into the voyage. He looked wan and gaunt, as if he'd been deathly ill. It reminded Viktor of how René Thibideaux had looked after Gloribeau finished with him.

He sent the navigator to the galley with instructions to help himself to triple portions for the rest of the week. As far as Vik was concerned, the man had earned it.

Belladonna sang up favorable winds for them. They reached Abidjan in a few days rather than the nearly two weeks it would have taken under normal conditions.

A few inquiries at the docks let them know that La Forte was currently in the port town, although his ship lay at anchor further down the coast. Apparently, he kept a loading site near the mouth of a local waterway.

The harbor master directed them to the slave market not far from the docks. When they finally found the man, he was in the process of putting his own hobbles on a young woman he'd just purchased. The local traders preferred to keep their hardware rather than let it go with the merchandise.

The woman was not being very cooperative. This led Viktor and Grimm to believe she was a fresh capture and had not been broken yet. Grimm found the fact that La Forte was mullato to be a surprise. Viktor had neglected to share that bit of information with him. If his captain was equally surprised, he didn't let it show.

Without warning, the slave bolted. Her hands were tied behind her back, but she was only half-hobbled. La Forte had removed the trader's set but had only gotten his on one of her ankles when she made a run for it.

By chance, she headed straight for the two pirates. Just as she reached them, she tripped over the loose hobble. Grimm, being closest, caught her before she could fall.

"Easy lass," he said out of reflex. She immediately began struggling violently in response. This provided just enough of a distraction for them to take their attention off La Forte briefly.

Viktor only glanced at them, but when he turned his attention back to La Forte, the man was no longer there.

Chapter 21

"Take her back to the ship," he growled to his first mate. Without further notice, he launched into the air.

Grimm slugged the struggling woman and knocked her unconscious. He lowered her to the ground and finished securing the hobbles. With a grunt, he hefted her up over his shoulder to carry her.

One of the slave market workers spotted him and yelled, "Hie you! You didn't pay for that!"

Grimm responded by pulling one of his pistols and aiming it toward the man's forehead. The slave wrangler threw up his hands and backed away.

"Take her, then," he said. "One unbroken bitch isn't worth it. Watch her, though. That one bites."

"Noted. Go away."

The wrangler obediently turned and made a hasty retreat. Grimm shoved the gun back in his belt and adjusted his grip on the unconscious woman before he headed back to the docks.

Search as he might, Viktor could find no trace of La Forte. The man had simply vanished. The only thing he could detect was a slight sensation like insects crawling all over him when he stood on the spot he'd last seen the slaver at. He couldn't even detect a scent to pick up.

Thoroughly disgusted, he flew back to the *Incubus*.

As he headed in search of Grimm and their latest captive, Belladonna intercepted him.

"Be careful, Viktor. That woman is more than she appears to be. Do not trust her."

"What is she? You are talking about the slave Grimm brought back?"

She nodded. "Yes, her. I am not sure what she is, but she is not fully human. There is a strange magic around her. Now, if you will excuse me, I need to go hunt."

"Of course, pet. I will be wary," he assured her. "Feed well."

He found Grimm's cabin door locked. Knocking brought a feminine yelp from the other side.

"Hezekiah?"

"*M'sieur* Grimm is not here," the female voice answered.

"*Mademoiselle* Belmont, do you know where my first mate is?"

"I heard him say something about *m'sieur* Jon's cabin. I also heard a woman whimpering."

"Thank you, *mademoiselle*." He smiled to himself as he headed toward the second mate's cabin. He'd almost swear he detected a note of jealousy in Brianna's voice.

Grimm and the slave occupied Jon-Jon's cabin. Even though unconscious, she remained hobbled. They had placed her in a chair and tied her in an upright position.

Viktor walked around her and did a visual inspection. "Has she awakened since you first knocked her out?" he asked as he lifted her lip to inspect her teeth and gums. The teeth looked human and relatively healthy. Her gums had a blue-black tint to them.

"No," Grimm replied. "She's made some noise, but she hasn't come to yet. One of the wranglers, who thought he'd try to stop me until I convinced him otherwise, warned me that she bites."

Viktor stepped back so his first mate could see the woman's gum and smirked. "It was a fair warning, Hezekiah. Mother Celie once told me that blue-gums were poisonous. It may just be an old wives' tale, but why take the chance?"

"Aye."

"Mr. Jon, bring that bottle of rot-gut gin you have hidden behind that lose plank in the back of your cabinet," Vik ordered.

"How did you—?" Jon-Jon thought it a perfect secret hiding place until that moment.

"My ship, Mr. Jon; I know everything."

The second mate obeyed and fetched the bottle he used to keep his flask full. Viktor took it from him, uncorked it, and held it under the bound woman's nose. She woke coughing and sputtering.

Once she was able to breathe again, she pled in perfect English, "Get that away from me!" That raised a few eyebrows.

Viktor re-corked the bottle and handed it back to Jon-Jon. "You speak English; good. That will make this easier."

She eyed the bottle and asked, "What was that?"

"For all intents and purposes, turpentine, but he calls it gin and drinks it," Vik replied with a grin and hooked a thumb toward Jon-Jon.

Her eyes grew wide at the flash of his fangs. "What are you?" Her voice held a tremor of fear.

He smiled at the phrasing she used. "I have been told I could ask you the same question. I am many things. For now, all you need to know is that I am the one to ask questions. You are the one to provide what answers you can."

She nodded her understanding; obviously aware he was a dangerous predator. "What do you want to know?"

"Do you know the man who was trying to hobble you?"

"Yes."

"Who is he and how do you know him?" Her scent told him she was hiding something. Belle's prior warning also put him on guard for any use of magic, something he usually ignored. The woman radiated a low level of power of the kind used to cloud perceptions.

"Quentin La Forte is the bastard who sired me," she replied with some venom. "He calls himself my master."

He blinked at this revelation. It verified the slaver's reputation. Many fathers would virtually sell their daughters, usually to a husband to cement some contract, but very few would be bastard enough to sell a daughter openly into slavery.

"Do you know how he disappeared or where to?"

"He practices black magic. If you free me, I will lead you to where he is going."

"Tell me where he is going, and I will decide if it is worth your freedom," he countered.

"He has gone on a raiding expedition."

"A raiding expedition *where*?"

She remained stubbornly silent.

Viktor exchanged a silent look with his mates then turned his attention back to their captive. He loomed over her, a hand on either arm of the chair she sat tied to. He sighed and smiled.

"As much as I would enjoy making you tell me what I want to know —," he paused and straightened, "I don't have the time. I will grant you your freedom in exchange for your guidance to La Forte."

At a nod from his captain, Jon-Jon removed her hobbles and untied her. She rubbed her wrist then ankles as she watched the three men warily. The bindings had bitten into her flesh enough to leave indentations.

Grimm noted her eye movements and body language. It told him she contemplated running. He said, "I wouldn't if I were you, lass. You'd never make it to the door."

She glared at him, confirming she'd been hoping to escape.

Viktor drew her attention. "Earlier, you asked what I am, pet. Pray you never have to learn. However, I will tell you *who* I am in exchange for your name, of course."

"My name is Nahila."

"I am Viktor Brandewyne," he said and watched for her reaction. She almost fainted. "I see you have heard of me; good. You will then know I mean what I say. After you have led me to La Forte, I will ensure your freedom. If you try to run away or lead me into an ambush, your freedom will be forfeit. I do not tolerate betrayal."

Chapter 22

Nahila directed them to sail about a day's travel down the coast to the mouth of a river. She claimed that her father used it to get at the tribes of the interior. The story raised suspicions to him.

"By the accounts I've gathered, the *Black Scorpion* has too deep a draft to sail up that waterway. Where is the ship, Nahila?"

"Further down the coast to resupply. There are some villages he uses," she replied.

"Mr. Grimm, stay with the ship and keep a watch posted. I don't want the *Scorpion* damaging my ship."

"Aye, Captain."

"Mr. Jon, Mr. Brumble, you're with me. Inform Mr. Bland to ready the launch and select a crew for it," Viktor ordered. "I want it ready within the hour."

A chorus of "Aye, Captain" answered him.

He looked over at the siren and said, "As much as I would appreciate your help when we catch up with the bastard, I don't think it wise for you to go. There's no telling how far upriver we'll have to go."

"Thank you. I will hunt while you are gone. There is abundant prey in these waters."

"Very good, then. Mr. Grimm, you might want to set a detail to fishing."

Grimm smiled. "I'll do that. Always wise to add to the stores whenever we can. Belle, would you be so kind as to herd a good-sized school our way?"

"Of course, just give me a couple of hours." She walked over to the railing, disrobed and plunged over the side. All of the men gave an appreciative stare just before she vanished overboard.

"Right." Vik clapped his hands to break the spell. "Let's get our gear together."

The men in question immediately headed to their cabins to pack.

It didn't take long to finish the preparations. Not even an hour after they dropped anchor, Viktor, his mates, Nahila, and a rowing crew headed upriver.

They pulled to shore at a natural landing not far from the river mouth. A small campsite lay clearly visible from the river. He wanted to investigate it.

The campsite consisted of two large holding cages and a makeshift shelter for use of the slave wranglers. The pirates found a cache of supplies secured above the tide line as well as a storage bin inside the shelter. This contained several sets of wooden hobbles, locks, and lengths of chain.

Zach had never encountered a slaving processing point before. Although he found it disgusting, it also piqued his curiosity more than a little.

"Why are there two cages? Do they really take that many slaves at one time?" he asked.

Jon-Jon answered, "They segregate the wenches from the bucks."

"Oh."

Something troubled Viktor about the campsite. "Why did he not leave a guard?"

"Given the man's reputation, I'd imagine no one would want to steal from him," Zach said.

Viktor shook his head. "No, that might be true for his slaving hardware, since it bears his mark, but there's nothing to keep someone from taking the food stores or other supplies."

He stopped, sniffing the air a moment, his eyes slightly unfocused. He started to head back to the boat. Nahila crouched over the camp's food supplies and reached for a flask. In a heartbeat, Vik loomed over her and grasped her wrist. She gave a small scream.

"You don't want that, pet. I can smell the poison in it." He smiled grimly. He then spoke to his men. "Leave the food stuffs and drink. We've enough of our own, and this has been poisoned. We're heading on upriver. Keep a sharp eye. This camp was used not long ago."

As they returned to the boat, Nahila asked him, "How do you know my father has been here recently?"

"The reek of his magic is fresh and heavy. It almost masked the scent of the poison."

As the pirates rowed upstream away from the slaving camp, dark eyes watched from the shadows.

Quentin La Forte felt puzzled by this man hunting him. That he could smell poison, let alone magic, was very curious. He remembered the dream which warned him about this pirate.

Venoma said her Sisters thought this man was "the One." He wished he'd paid more attention all those years ago, when she'd babbled something about "the One" and some prophecy during their lovemaking.

He decided to shadow them for a while to see what he could learn. He would exercise caution, however. He didn't want to be found out before he was ready.

Nahila knew her father watched them. She also knew about the poison in the supplies he left behind. It was a practice of his to prevent theft and save having to leave a guard behind. He gave all of his people the antidote on a regular basis to protect them.

What she didn't know was what this man who held her captive was. Plainly he was more than human. His unnaturally long and sharp canines, his ability to detect both the poison and the magic that masked its presence, his blinding speed, and the fact that he never seemed to sleep or appear tired all pointed to him being at least some kind of sorcerer. She had a feeling he was even more than that, though.

He bore an aura that seemed to call to her, but it also made her feel like helpless prey, marking him definitely as a predator of some sort. Something told her he might prove just as dangerous as her father.

With her captor's vigilance, there would be no safe means to communicate with her father. It would probably mean her death, if she were caught. Still, she knew the plan.

La Forte utilized a network of informants that covered almost all the way around the perimeter of the Atlantic. He'd established it to aide in his slave trading, but it also kept him aware of anyone looking for him. Word would reach him amazingly fast. He'd made several enemies over the years and didn't want anyone to catch him unawares.

The ruse Nahila aided him in was one they had used several times before. She would distract and lead hunters astray, until one of them could learn who the hunter was and why they were after him.

She had no real reason to think it wouldn't work this time.

Chapter 23

La Forte grew frustrated after four days of following them. He couldn't get close enough to them to overhear anything without risking exposing himself; and it seemed impossible for Nahila to sneak away to confer with him. As it stood, he had no way of knowing who this man or his crew was.

He would just have to assume that they were enemies.

That wasn't really a dilemma to him. A couple more days upriver, he had an ambush waiting for them. His men knew to kill all but his daughter if they didn't get word from him to stand down. He had no intention of giving that word.

Instead, he would return to his base camp and spy out the hunter's ship. Getting a new ship was one of the potential perks of this plan. He held no qualms about committing a bit of piracy.

He also wanted to see if he could find and subvert the siren from this much closer proximity. He'd faintly sensed her presence when the hunter first presented himself. La Forte almost believed he'd killed her in his attack from a few weeks ago when her presence went dead to him.

He reached the camp within an hour. A shaman from his mother's people once taught him how to use the spirit world to transport from one place to another. In exchange, he had not taken the old man as a slave. Instead, he'd slit the old man's throat, giving him a quick death.

The spell allowed him to transport short distances at a time. His transport range only extended as far as he could see. The old man had warned him not to try further than that. He'd said the spell could take him beyond his line of sight, but there was the danger of finding himself in a rock, tree, animal, or person upon exiting the spirit world. At the least, that would maim him. More likely, it could prove fatal.

He used it to get himself out of scrapes but found himself only able to use it three times in a row before it wore out. If he used it a fourth time, it left him weak and nearly unconscious for over an hour.

That changed, however, when he seduced that witch in the jungles of the New World. Not only did he gain the ability to use his transport spell without limitation, but he also "borrowed" an amulet from her; one which held a small portion of her power. She gave it to him, but he escaped before she could extract her price for it. It gave him sway over all poisonous creatures as well as immunity to any poison.

That power sang out to him shortly after he made the camp. Something very large and very poisonous was near the shore. He thought it could just be a school of jellyfish blown in by a sea storm, but he wanted to investigate anyway.

As he neared the source, a brief fear that the old witch had traveled with the hunter and come to reclaim her amulet washed over him. A very strong aura of magic associated with the poison.

Then he saw what it really was.

He heard a woman singing just before a large wave came ashore. When the water receded, a sea creature lay on the beach. It appeared to be half human and half shark, but the human features appeared to be off just a bit. She, it was definitely female, had beautiful blood-red hair, but her eyes were amber-gold. Her mouth stretched almost ear-to-ear and looked to be filled with needle-like teeth, and her hands had elongated fingers that terminated in razor-sharp talons.

La Forte had never seen anything like her before, and he thought she was magnificent. So, this was the siren he'd seen in the dream.

Before his eyes, she began to change. Her shark tail shrank and grew lighter to a flesh tone from its greenish black and silver. It then split and reformed as legs. Her fingers and mouth shrank to a more human size and shape. Even her teeth squared out to look human. Lastly, her eyes changed from gold to a shifting shade of sea grey.

As a human, she was stunning and voluptuous enough to lure any man to her deadly embrace. La Forte found that even he wasn't totally immune to her raw sexual magnetism.

Belladonna was well aware that human eyes watched her as she changed form. She took no heed of the scent of magic. The breeze came from land, and she assumed it was the scent of the slaver's camp blowing to her. She hadn't been with Viktor and Grimm when they'd seen La Forte, so she didn't know what he looked like.

All she saw was a potential meal that was well-formed enough to warrant playing with it first. After all, the vampire wasn't there to stop her, and this man wasn't part of the crew.

With a smile, she stood and strode toward him. Too late, she realized her mistake.

La Forte was aware of the exact moment she tried to fight his power. Her power almost proved enough to break her free before he could get a good hold. He had to concentrate to force her to continue to him until she got close enough to physically touch.

Belle tried to fight him. If she could just get back to the water, she could escape. Struggle as she might, it was no use. The second he touched her skin, she was trapped. She couldn't even scream.

"Oh, you are magnificent!" he gloated, admiring how her eyes reverted to gold in her struggle against him. She obviously put escape at a higher priority than glamour in the use of her magic. When her needle teeth reappeared, he tsked and shook a finger at her. "Now, now, none of that, my lovely."

At his will, her teeth returned to human. "You are Quentin La Forte?" she asked, eyeing him warily.

He walked around her and inspected her in much the same way he would a slave he was considering buying. "You seem to have me at a disadvantage, my dear. You know who I am, but I do not know who you are, although I was warned this latest hunter had enslaved a siren. You are she; I assume."

When she didn't volunteer the information, he tightened his magical grip and completely stifled her will. She could feel the connection she shared with Viktor, but she could not access it.

"I am Belladonna."

"Intriguing; I have heard of your breed of merfolk, but I have never encountered one before. How did this man snare you?"

"Fuck you."

"Obstinate female," he growled. "I have been gentle thus far. I can make this much more unpleasant." To prove his point, he used his powers to force her to produce toxins but not release them. He kept this up until her fingertips began to swell with poison.

"So that is the source." He chuckled and "drew" more on the poison. Her fingers soon swelled to match the tips and began to darken.

"I know this hurts. I can see it in your eyes. I will allow you to discharge and ease your pain if you give me your full cooperation, my lovely."

To keep hold of her sanity, she nodded her acquiescence. With her true master not near enough to help her, she would soon lose herself beyond recovery to this tormentor if she continued to fight. She felt it better to appear to give in and hope for a lapse in his attention. If she could lull him, perhaps she could contact Viktor and warn him.

"I will not fight you anymore."

"Good." He nodded. "Is the one who is hunting me your master, or are you a different siren?"

"Yes, he is." She wondered how he'd know about her. Had someone raced ahead of them from Tenerife to warn him? How had they known what she was?

"Who is the hunter, and what does he want with me?"

"Viktor Brandewyne was sent to retrieve an amulet that *Mere* Venoma Noir claims you stole."

It mildly surprised La Forte that the old witch managed to get the most notorious pirate of this age to do her bidding. She'd said she'd sent a pirate, but he found the fact she'd sent Bloody Vik Brandee impressive. He knew she wanted the trinket back, but he'd figured he was relatively safe from her influence, regardless of the warning dream she'd sent him. After all, holding part of her power both rendered him immune to it and weakened her.

"Hmm, this may prove more than my men can handle by themselves," he mused aloud. "Still, I've time to give them better instructions. Now, tell me everything you can about Bloody Vik Brandee, his ship, and his crew."

Chapter 24

Belladonna told him everything about the ship, from its draft, to the number of guns, to all of its special features. He found the harpoon swivel guns and collapsible masts particularly interesting. The *Incubus* had been designed to be a pirate hunter. The ship's specifications pleased La Forte very much. He thought it would make an excellent slave ship.

The news that the Grimm Reaper was first mate and still aboard did not make him quite so happy. The Reaper had quite the reputation as a battle commander. La Forte wanted the ship, but he didn't want to damage it in the process of taking it. He decided on treachery as the best way to gain possession.

"So, you say you share a mental bond with Brandee," he said.

"Yes, although you have managed to block me from using it," she replied. Though she told him about how powerful Viktor's magic was, she managed to keep a few things secret without him sensing it. La Forte didn't know about Viktor's vampirism or about his cadre of six vampires still aboard the *Incubus*.

Still, just knowledge of Viktor's magic proved enough to make him completely rethink his plans. If Brandee were any other pirate, La Forte would go through with the regular ambush; but adding in magic powerful enough to ensnare a siren made it too risky.

"Belladonna, do you wish for your freedom?"

She nodded to avoid qualifying that she wanted free of the slaver not Viktor. She'd had a chance at freedom from the pirate and had chosen to forfeit it. Only one thing could free her from Viktor now, and she didn't want him dead.

"I have to go retrieve my men. While I am gone, return to the *Incubus*. Let no one know that you have seen me or that anything is amiss. Tonight, kill the crew, starting with Hezekiah Grimm," he ordered.

The power of his hold on her was such that she had no choice but to obey.

Against her will, Belladonna reached out through the link she shared with Viktor. La Forte's spell only allowed her access long enough to send the message, *"Come back."*

She found herself unable to even put any kind of warning tone into the thought. Silently, she vowed to never complain about being bound to the vampire again, provided they all survived this. La Forte proved to be a merciless master.

He brought out a small silver vial, much like the one Viktor wore to collect magic from the Sisters; he only allowed her to release the venom from one finger at a time and only into the vial. The process felt excruciatingly painful. She hoped he would get a little on his skin.

If only something would've distracted him enough for her to strike out at him. Luck refused to favor her that much, though. At least she'd been able to resist enough to protect the secret of Viktor's true nature.

She sensed that he heard her and ordered his crew to turn about, but it would take him a few days to make the return trip. For now, the siren worked under the compulsion to return to the ship to fulfill the next step in La Forte's plan.

"Stop the boat," Viktor ordered suddenly. "Turn 'er about."

"Aye, Cap'n."

Nahila nearly flew into a panic. "What? Why? I thought you were trying to catch my father."

"I don't explain myself to you," was the only response he gave her.

Ignoring the woman's sputtering, Viktor pondered what could have happened. After the initial request from the siren to return, he found himself unable to get a response from her. He could still sense her, but he could not hear her; and apparently, she could not hear him, either.

He suspected Uncle Zeke had a hand in this. That Viktor knew of, only he could block the vampire and the siren from each other. It irritated him to be called back this close to his prey, but he suspected the old wizard had a good reason for it.

It did surprise him about Nahila's reaction. He wondered if she feared he was reneging on his agreement to free her, or if a more sinister reason lay behind it. He already held doubts about her really leading them to La Forte. Not only did he put stock in Belle's warning not to trust this woman, but he also caught a faint whiff of the common magic most witches used to hide a lie or outright deception.

Whatever the reasons behind Belladonna's call and Nahila's panic, he would learn it in a few days. There hadn't been a tone of urgency from the siren, so he didn't feel rushed.

☠

As quickly as he could, La Forte transported back to his men. They were used to his mysterious coming and going, so no one was startled when he appeared among them.

"Change in plans, men," he announced. "Our prey is a little too big to take on here. We are going to take his ship and be waiting for him when he returns."

"If he's too strong to take from here, how are we supposed to take out the crew of a ship and then our target?" one of the men asked.

In a blink, La Forte transported to just behind the man and clapped him on the shoulder. The man's body went rigid then started to spasm. Before long he foamed at the mouth. When La Forte released his hold on his victim, the man collapsed to the ground.

He continued to foam, but his body grew rigid with paralysis. His face began to darken as he suffocated, unable to draw breath. Finally, the life faded from his eyes as his heart seized up.

La Forte wore a strange smile on his face. His new toy pleased him very much. As the remaining men looked on, not daring to say anything for fear of being the next victim, he held up the specialized ring he kept poison in. It utilized a retractable barb for delivering the poison.

"I think I'm going to like this siren's venom." He grinned. "He was aware right up to the end. Gentlemen, our prey has brought his downfall with him. I have taken a siren from him, and she is going to kill his crew for us. You've seen what her poison can do."

"We are ready to go."

Chapter 25

Belladonna went straight to her cabin upon her return to the *Incubus*. La Forte's instructions had been to strike at night, when most of the crew would be asleep. No one thought anything of the fact she spoke to no one on board. Most either paid no attention or figured she was just in one of her moods.

She did not emerge from her cabin until about an hour past nightfall. Grimm's cabin lay only a short walk from hers. As per the slaver's orders, he would have to be the first to die. He posed the greatest risk.

She used an ability she hadn't had much occasion to since joining up with Viktor when she reached the cabin door. She held her hand over the door latch and emitted a short ultra-sonic burst. The resulting echo/vibration told her it was locked, as she had expected.

There had hardly been any sign of the Belmont woman since the first mate claimed her as part of his share. Either he worried about a potential escape, or he just didn't trust the crew, or both.

Belle extended the talon form of just one pinkie and used the tapered point to pick the lock. A simple spell prevented anyone from hearing the tumblers fall into place. The same spell allowed her to slip silently into the cabin.

Both occupants slept. The siren started to move toward the bed. As first mate, Grimm rated better accommodations than the rope hammocks used by the crew. Grimm wasn't in the bed, though, only the woman.

This surprised the siren. She really didn't pay that much attention to the humans when she wasn't interacting with them. Although she liked to play with her food, she didn't like to get to know her potential prey. As far as she was concerned, all of the human crew members were potential prey. Viktor might give them to her either as punishment or as the sacrifice needed for one of her visions.

She wondered where the first mate was. She knew why she and Viktor hadn't shared a bed yet, but she didn't understand why Grimm wasn't with his woman. He'd never been shy about sporting with tavern wenches and whores, nor with the occasional female found aboard ships the pirates had taken. Why was this woman different?

She shook her head to clear it. Why was not important. She had to find and kill Hezekiah Grimm. The sleeping human female could wait. The first mate had to be the first to die. La Forte had been very clear on that point.

Looking about, she finally spotted him. He dozed in an armchair that had been nailed in place to keep the rolling of the ship from tossing it about the cabin.

She moved to loom over him and extended the talons on one hand. He had been decent to her. She would make his death swift and as painless as possible. She owed him that much.

Something made Grimm start from the doze he had finally fallen into. The chair was comfortable, but it was not well-suited to sleeping. Even though he was a light sleeper, he hadn't had a good night's rest since bringing Brianna to his cabin. He'd made a point of giving her the bed and not trying to violate her.

He wasn't sure why, but he sensed something special about this girl that set her apart from women he'd known in the past. When he did finally bed her, he wanted it to be at her invitation. He even contemplated making her his wife, something he'd never felt an urge to do before.

The cabin was darker than usual. There had been clouds moving in since that afternoon. Very little light came in through the cabin window as a result.

When his eyes adjusted, he could make out a female form standing by the bed. At first, he thought it was Brianna just getting up to use the chamber pot, but the silhouette was wrong. This woman was fuller figured at breast and hip, and nude.

He realized it was Belladonna, when she turned to face him. Although she appeared as little more than a shadow in the darkness, he could make out the fact she had her talons out. She was here to kill.

He wondered if he'd be able to reach his knife in time to defend himself. As she moved toward him, her walk seemed almost to be forced. It was as if someone or something else controlled her. It gave him the time he needed, but it also made him hesitate to strike first.

He waited for her to come to him, his eyes no more than slits. He didn't want her to know he was awake until the last minute. Very gently, he eased one of his knives out of its sheath.

Belle stood over him. Only one hand bore talons. She drew it back across her body as if to backhand him. He realized she was going for a slit throat or a beheading.

Faster than even he thought possible, he surged up. He grabbed her wrist, put a foot behind her legs and swept them out from under her, and crouched down on top of her using a knee to pin her other arm down. With his free hand he held the knife to her throat.

"If you have hurt her, I will gut you," he hissed angrily.

Belladonna came to herself the second Grimm touched her. The sudden release from La Forte's spell shocked her but not as much as the revelation it gave her about the first mate.

"You carry the Elder's magic," she whispered, retracting her talons and looking up at him in awe.

Grimm refused to be distracted. "What's wrong with you? How dare you come in here and try to kill us!"

"I was compelled," she answered. "Your lady was not harmed. My orders were to kill you before anyone else on board. The spell is broken now."

"Hezekiah?" A sleepy voice spoke from the bed. The sound of a striker and a lantern shade sliding into place presaged the return of light of the cabin.

Brianna's eyes adjusted quickly, as did Grimm's and Belle's. She took in the sight before her. Grimm still sat astraddle of the naked siren but had already put his knife away. He knew Belle was not given to lying about magic and was no longer a threat; or so it seemed.

"Mr. Grimm, how could you?" The iciness of Brianna's tone cut him deeper than the siren's talons ever could. Her face filled with a mixture of rage and pain.

Belladonna responded before he could as he got off of her. "He was protecting you from me."

That threw her into total confusion. "Protecting me from you? What do you mean? Are you a lover of women?"

Belladonna smirked. "I have dabbled in the past. I like to play with my food, but tonight I was here to kill."

"But you are unarmed," Brianna pointed out.

"Oh, I wouldn't say that." The siren gave a sinister laugh. She extended her talons and revealed her true teeth in an ear-to-ear smile. The woman gasped sharply and stumbled back on the edge of the bed.

Grimm moved with lightning speed to grab the siren by the hair from behind and held his knife to her throat. "I don't care how angry Vik gets, I will not let you hurt her," he growled in her ear.

Belle returned to her full human guise. "I already told you the spell compelling me has been broken, Mr. Grimm," she sighed. "Your lady is in no danger from me. I am curious as to how you came to wield some of Zeke's magic."

"I don't know what you're talking about," he mumbled, releasing her and putting his knife away again.

She turned to face him, crossed her arms and gave him a disbelieving look. "Oh really? I think you do, and you've been carrying it since we went looking for Dorada. I didn't recognize it then, but only Zeke's power could break La Forte's spell. He is tapping into the amulet from Venoma."

"Is that how he got control of you?"

"Yes," she answered but refused to be put off. "Does Viktor know about you?"

He saw he was going to have to deal with this. "No. I don't like keeping it secret from him, but Zeke warned me to keep quiet about it."

"Why would he share power with you?"

"Because he didn't trust you. Keep in mind that this happened before you bound yourself to Vik," he replied.

She frowned. "It was a wise precaution at the time. Vik will not take it well when he learns of it, however."

"I know." He sighed and scratched his neck. "To be honest, I'm surprised I've been able to keep it from him this long. He'll want to know how you broke free of La Forte."

She nodded. "And I won't be able to lie to him."

"Well, we'll worry about that when he gets back. For now, we have other things to take care of."

"Yes, we do. I am going to return to my cabin and get dressed. You need to deal with your lady."

"Are you sure that is the safe thing to do? I don't know how far this power's range is," he asked, a note of worry in his voice.

The siren nodded her reassurance. "La Forte is not as powerful as Venoma. The spell has been broken. He would have to get almost close enough to touch me to reinstate it. Calm her down and I will meet you in the captain's study to fill you in on what I know of our enemy and his plans."

Grimm stood pinching the bridge of his nose as he tried to decide the best course to follow with Brianna. If he said or did the wrong thing it would destroy all the groundwork he'd laid with her.

"You've either been with her before or you want her," she stated, her voice shaking him from his thoughts.

"What? No, she belongs to the Captain."

Brianna gave him a skeptical look. "You haven't been with her, then; but you cannot deny that you want her. With that body, what man wouldn't?"

His smile matched his name. "One that knows what she is and values keeping all of his parts intact."

"Oh." He saw that she remembered the nightmare image the siren had shown her moments ago.

He walked to her and gently brushed a tendril of hair behind her ear. "You are right, though, *ma'm'selle*. Belladonna is very hard to resist, especially when she weaves her spells. I have seen men in the grip of blind lust go eagerly to her and their death, even when she was completely in her true form."

He leaned down and gave her a chaste kiss on the forehead. "Stay here and stay safe," he told her.

He then turned and left the cabin, locking the door behind him.

Brianna stared at the locked door, both irritated and touched by his protectiveness.

Chapter 26

As promised, Belladonna awaited Grimm, fully dressed, in the captain's study. She visibly relaxed when she saw the first mate.

"Something amiss, lass?" he asked as he noticed the change in her stance.

"I almost underestimated the bastard again; that or he's closer than I expected."

"What do you mean?"

"I can hear him faintly in my head." She didn't try to hide her fear. "Thankfully, he is not concentrating on me; but I would have thought he would be getting further away."

"Why do you say that?" he asked.

"His plan, as I understand it, is for me to slaughter the crew while he fetches his men to return and take the ship. Let me try something." She paused as an idea struck her. She concentrated and gently reached out along the connection to La Forte but made sure to stand close enough to Grimm to stay anchored.

The first mate steadied her when her body stiffened at the returned contact. The physical proximity to the portion of Zeke's power he carried gave her the freedom to deceive the usurper.

"What is it, my curious siren?" La Forte asked her mentally. By touching the siren, Grimm found himself included in the loop but hidden from their enemy. The novelty of "hearing" their thoughts made him feel slightly drunk.

"I wanted to know how long it would be before you returned," she answered truthfully.

"I will be there with my men by morning. You will have the ship ready for me?"

"Yes, I have already begun. I just wanted to know how much time I had left to finish the job. It is a large crew."

"Then get to it." La Forte abruptly broke the contact.

Belle stumbled a bit and asked, "Did you get any of that?"

"Aye," Grimm replied. "We don't have much time. I saw how he's travelling so quickly, as well."

"You did? I couldn't tell how." She sounded surprised.

"It must be one of Zeke's abilities." He shrugged. "La Forte is using a simple transporting spell. Venoma's power is allowing him to use it without limit, but he can only take one man with him at a time. That's why he isn't here already. He has about twenty men with him. If we can get things in place in time, we should have no problem defeating them."

"Actually, we might. Before he gave me orders, he forced me to produce my most concentrated dose of venom; then he collected it. That strength is enough for a few drops to kill a man rather than just burn him. Be wary of any weapons he has."

"Duly noted. Since you're worried about the bastard gaining control over you, I would say to stick close to me. Zeke's power should keep you safe from La Forte." He stood up. "We need to wake Dr. Coffin. He can help us make the crew look like you did what you were told."

"What about the cadre?" she asked. "I know my blood is deadly to them, but my venom is useless against a vampire."

He thought about it. "That would definitely give us an edge if you can get La Forte to board near or at dark."

"Or just get him and his men to go below decks," she suggested.

"Aye." Grimm smiled, liking the plan more and more. "Can you safely get a message to Viktor?"

She nodded. "Yes, but I will have to touch your skin to make sure La Forte does not pick up on it."

"Do it."

She laid her hand on his bare neck then reached out along her bond with the vampire.

Viktor stiffened at the sensation of the siren opening their link. Something felt different. He sensed another presence there. *"What is it, pet? Who is there with you?"*

Grimm winced. As with La Forte, he found he could listen in on the siren's mental conversation. It was a testament to how much deeper the bond was between Belle and Vik that his captain could sense his presence where the slaver had not.

"Hezekiah is helping me protect myself from La Forte," Belle answered. *"The slaver is using the power of Venoma's amulet. He's after the ship. The bitch was leading you into an ambush. You would have been safe, but your crewmen wouldn't have been. La Forte uses poison. He forced me to give him some of my most concentrated venom. It's strong enough to kill within minutes."*

"But my cadre is immune," Viktor picked the thought from her mind. *"Good thinking. I trust Hezekiah has already devised a plan?"*

"Yes. We are going to have Dr. Coffin help stage the crew to look like I followed the order to slaughter them."

"Good. Go with that. It will take at least another day for the boat crew to get back. After this is over, however, I will want a word with Mr. Grimm." He cut the connection.

Belladonna blinked at the abruptness, then shook her head. "Well," she sighed, "that went well."

"Oh, you think so?" Grimm asked sardonically.

"It did for me. I'm not the one he's upset with."

"Let's go wake Stitches," he growled in reply.

"Mr. Jon," Vik barked.

"Aye, Cap'n."

"Get this boat back to the ship as quickly as possible."

"Aye, Cap'n."

"Mr. Brumble, secure our guest. If she gives any trouble, gag her."

"Aye, Captain."

"I have something to attend to. I will meet you back at the ship." Without further notice, he launched into the night sky.

Chapter 27

A couple of hours before sunrise, La Forte contacted Belladonna. He finished returning his men all to the base camp near the river mouth. Now he wanted to know if she'd finished the task he'd given her.

"Everything is ready for you," she replied. She told him the truth but not in the way he thought.

The crew of the *Incubus* managed to stage the scene remarkably quickly. It didn't require any more effort than what they went through when they used their "wounded duck" ruse.

In fact, it proved easier. They only needed to make it look like they'd been slaughtered. The pirate ruse required also staging the ship to look disabled. That meant setting out smudge pots, lowering the hinged masts, furling the good sails, and unfurling the torn and ragged ones in their place.

One by one, La Forte transported his men to the quarterdeck of the *Incubus*. Belle leaned against the hatch that led to the officers' quarters and watched. Just behind the door Grimm waited. It allowed him to stay close enough to keep her free from the slaver's influence but kept him out of sight.

Once all his men were aboard, La Forte approached the siren. Some instinct warned him not to get too close to her. She stood naked and bathed in blood. She radiated magic far stronger than when he'd first encountered her. He started to wonder if it had been a mistake to use her.

"You seem much stronger," he stated from what he thought was a safe distance. He had no idea of her speed.

"I have fed well tonight." She smiled and showed her true teeth. The blood-coated needle teeth proved a disturbing sight in such a delicate face.

Once again, she spoke the truth, even though it was not the one the slaver thought it was. Four of the remaining prisoners in the larder hold fell prey to the siren prior to this moment. Grimm and Coffin needed enough blood to make the "slaughter" look real. Belladonna disposed of the bodies after bleeding them out.

La Forte accepted her explanation. "Are they all dead?"

"No."

"No? You said everything was ready for me." His temper flared.

"It is. There are a small handful of prisoners from the last prize that I did not kill. You said to kill the crew."

From the shadows in the rigging Viktor admired Belladonna's ability to deceive while speaking strictly the truth. Her careful omission of important details led La Forte to believe exactly what he wanted to believe. It also reminded the vampire that the siren could not be fully trusted.

No one could. Secrets had been kept. They would deal with this interloper, but it would take time to transport the amulet back to Venoma. There would be plenty of time for Viktor to have a reckoning with the siren and with his first mate.

"Where are these prisoners?" La Forte demanded. He wasn't happy that she'd left men alive, but he hadn't considered that the pirate might be holding hostages. He saw he would have to pick his words carefully when giving the siren orders in the future.

"They are in one of the holds below. It's on the lowest deck at mid-ship. If you don't mind, I'd like to return to my cabin and clean up." She waved a hand at the blood coating her skin. It already had begun to dry and grow tacky and itchy.

"Very well, I'm sure we can find them on our own." He nodded permission. Once again, that instinct of self-preservation told him he did not want to be in an enclosed space with her until this power rush ebbed.

Belle slipped through the door behind her, relieved to put some distance between her and the slaver. She wanted to run to her cabin but stopped herself short. She knew Viktor was aboard. She sensed him when he arrived at the ship shortly before La Forte brought his men aboard. The problem was he wasn't close enough for the Elder's stone to protect her. Only Grimm was, and Viktor wasn't happy with him right at the moment.

La Forte caught just a hint of the siren's relief as she left him. It restored his confidence somewhat. She feared him to some degree.

He turned and motioned for his men to follow him below. Passing through the gun decks, they witnessed enough carnage to convince him she had indeed slaughtered the entire crew. Many of the pirates still lay in their hammocks. The overpowering stench of blood and offal almost drove them back topside.

Moving on, they made their way to the hold the siren had indicated. It was barred and locked from the outside. A ring of keys hung on a nearby peg.

La Forte knocked at the door. "Is anyone in there?"

From the other side came the sound of whispering and shuffling about, but no other answer.

He knocked harder. "The pirates are defeated. It is safe to answer."

"Liar!" said a voice from within. "They can't be defeated. There was no sound of battle."

"I don't have time to argue with these fools," he muttered. "Be prepared for them to resist. I'm not really interested in saving their sorry hides anyway." He took the key ring off the hook and tried each key until he found the one for that lock. He stood back and two of his men removed the bar that still blocked the door.

The door opened onto pitch blackness. Nothing inside made any movement. From out of nowhere, a large black cat darted into the darkness.

Growing even more impatient, La Forte motioned for four of his men to go in. "Looks like we're going to have to drag them out."

Obediently, the men went in. The darkness soon engulfed them. After a few moments, screams then growling and disturbing sucking sounds emanated from the hold.

La Forte started to call out to his men when their bodies were flung out of the hold. The corpses were pale and bloodless; their throats had been ripped as if by the jaws of some beast.

It didn't take him long to realize the siren had betrayed him. In rage, he lashed out with his power at her only to find the way blocked. That, more than anything else, unnerved him.

"Who are you? Show yourself!" he demanded of the dark hold.

Behind him spoke a darkly amused voice. "Lazarus, come forth."

La Forte whirled to see a tall, black-haired man with gleaming emerald eyes standing a few feet behind his group. At the same time, the cat emerged from the darkness. It sauntered over to one of the corpses and commenced to gnaw at the torn flesh.

"Lazarus, old friend, you are a greedy thing." Viktor laughed. "Aren't you satisfied yet?"

In answer, the cat looked up at his master, made a *meh* sound, and seemed to stick his tongue out at him before returning to his meal. Viktor laughed harder, not bothering to hide his fangs.

"Who are you?" the startled slaver asked. He wondered what he'd gotten himself into.

"Viktor Brandewyne, at your service." Vik gave a mock bow. "And you would be Quentin La Forte."

"What's your game? You don't expect me to believe that a cat did this to my men."

"Of course not. Lazarus has a rapacious appetite, but four men would be a bit much for him to drain that fast in his current form."

La Forte had no idea what he meant by that last remark.

"Lads, show yourselves." Viktor summoned, and the cadre of six vampires emerged from the dark hold, fangs gleaming and blood dripping from their chins. "You might as well surrender now, La Forte."

"Never!" La Forte flipped a trigger on his ring and slapped the nearest vampire on the neck, injecting pure siren's venom into him.

"Ow," Thomas Brumble stated calmly, as if it had merely been a mosquito bite. Other than that, the venom had no effect. Only siren's blood would have been deadly to the vampires.

At a silent command from his captain, Thomas stripped La Forte of the ring.

The slaver had only one thought: escape. "Make for the deck!" He had to get somewhere with long distance visibility. His transport spell did him no good in the narrow confines of the ship.

The battle commenced immediately. The humans quickly learned they were no match for the speed or strength of the vampires. The battle turned into a route. La Forte's men stopped trying to fight and merely tried to get away.

A small handful did manage to get past them and back up to the gun decks. There a nasty surprise awaited them. All of the "dead" pirates stood waiting with weapons drawn, grinning like mad men.

The slaver's men dropped their weapons in surrender.

La Forte was not one of the ones who made it out of the hold deck. Not wanting to take the chance the man didn't have more poisoned weapons, Viktor cold-cocked him. Satisfied the man was unconscious, he thoroughly searched him, stripping him of anything that might possibly be used as a weapon.

The cadre treated their surviving prisoners similarly. About ten of the slaver's men survived the battle only to be captured. Their fate would be no better than that of their companions, however. The cadre had to have blood.

A brief surge of power was the only warning Viktor had before Lazarus transformed from cat to vampire. Jim Rigger stripped the pants off the corpse he'd been feeding on and slipped into them.

"Jim, it's good to see you." Viktor smiled, genuinely pleased. He and his former first mate had been like brothers since their teens.

"Cap'n." Jim gave his customary cocky smile. "You'll want to blindfold that one." He nodded at La Forte.

"Why is that?"

"To keep him from escaping. When you sent me to watch him, I noticed he talks to himself when he uses certain spells. He's got a transport spell that lets him travel as far as he can see," Rigger replied. "It'd be best for him to be either blindfolded or kept in a small dark place."

"Duly noted, Mr. Rigger. That explains how he disappeared so easily back in port." He stood up after tying his prisoner. "Brumble, Corning, see to it that Mr. La Forte is properly housed and hooded."

"Aye, Cap'n," the two vampires answered.

"Mr. Rigger, can you hold this form for a while?"

"I'll probably be this way for the next few hours. I ate quite a bit plus had a good blood feed."

Viktor nodded to himself. He sent a mental message to Belladonna to close the shutters in her cabin. Then he returned his attention to his erstwhile first mate.

"Come with me, Jim. I must have a word with Mr. Grimm and Belladonna."

Chapter 28

Grimm and Belle waited in the siren's cabin for the arrival of the two vampires. She passed the message to the first mate that Viktor wanted to meet with them there and that he was perturbed.

As a result, Grimm deliberately removed his weapons and locked them up in his sea chest. He told Brianna to stay put but neglected to lock the cabin door. The outcome of this encounter concerned him more than he cared to admit.

The sight of Jim Rigger coming in behind Viktor did nothing to calm Grimm. In fact, it set him even more on guard. At least the Captain wasn't smiling. That would have been a sure sign of impending doom.

"You have been keeping secrets, Mr. Grimm," Viktor stated flatly.

"Not by choice, Captain."

"Explain yourself."

Grimm took a deep breath and sighed. "Zeke summoned me to Hell's Breath. He used his magic to force me to drink a couple of drops of his blood."

"Why?"

"Because he wanted me to be able to watch your back, and he didn't trust Belle," he answered.

"You've always been able to watch my back, Mr. Grimm, and I have trusted you to do so many times in the past. As for Belle, she is mine and poses no threat to me," Viktor countered. His tone made it plain he didn't quite accept the explanation.

"I wasn't yours when Zeke did that to him," Belle pointed out.

He turned on her. "That reminds me, how long have you known about this? And what do you mean you weren't mine at the time? How long ago did this happen?"

Rigger had been tense to the point of motionlessness. He visibly relaxed as Viktor's voice rose. If the Captain was letting his temper show, chances were he wasn't going to kill anyone. Viktor was at his deadliest when he appeared calm and pleasant.

Belle and Grimm both started to talk then both stopped, unsure of who should talk first. Growling irritably, Vik pointed at the siren. "Go on. I'll deal with Mr. Grimm in a moment."

"I have only known since today. I've known since we've been on this ship that he held some kind of vaguely familiar magic, but I didn't recognize it at the time or give it much thought. I've never seen him behave in any way that was dangerous to you or counter to your quest. I first sensed the Elder's power in him back on the Isle of Youth."

"Before you took a chunk out of my shoulder," Vik said. He turned to stare at Grimm. Tension rose in the cabin as the vampire grew deadly calm. His expression betrayed no emotion at all.

To his credit, Grimm didn't flinch, nor did he start trying to talk his way out of this.

Finally, Viktor spoke. "You kept this secret for over three years. How am I supposed to trust you?"

"I can't make you trust me; I can only ask you to. I don't believe I've given you any reason not to trust me," he answered simply.

In a heartbeat, Vik had him pinned by the throat to the cabin wall. "You keep a secret like this from me for this long, and you say you don't think you've given me reason to distrust you?" Raw pain filled his voice.

"Leave him alone! It's not his fault!" an unexpected female voice cried.

A brief flicker of terror crossed Grimm's face as he recognized its source. "I knew I should have locked that door. Brianna, get out of here," he ordered. "You don't need to see this."

"Jim." Viktor spoke only one word. Obediently, Rigger grasped the young woman from behind and pinned her arms to her sides.

"*Batárde!* Let me go!" she yelled. Struggle as she might, the vampire's grip was unbreakable.

Jim grinned over her shoulder at his Captain and the first mate. "You've got a feisty one here, Hezekiah." He laughed then grunted as she stomped his bare foot as hard as she could and managed to shove an elbow into his gut. "Oof! She's a scrapper, too. That's enough of that," he added good-naturedly and tightened his grip a little, making it hard for her to breathe.

"Don't hurt her, Jim," Grimm managed to rasp past the weight of Viktor's hand on his throat.

Something caused Viktor to relax his grasp a little. He still didn't release his first mate, but he brought his emotions under control.

Meanwhile, Rigger caught an unmistakable scent. It brought a smile of amazement to his face. "My God, man, she's still a virgin!"

Brianna blushed brightly. She let out a shriek that impressed even the siren and launched into a rapid-fire string of expletives in French and a few other languages.

Viktor couldn't keep the half-smile from quirking at his lips. He released Grimm and started to chuckle at the irate young woman's reaction. "Sounds like she's not too happy about it either, eh, Hezekiah."

Grimm swallowed a few times and rubbed his throat before he answered. "She is too special for me to just take her. I don't want it forced."

Vik blinked in surprise at that. Silently, he warned Jim and Belle not to joke about it. He wanted to keep the situation under control, and there was something he wanted to ask *mademoiselle* Belmont.

"You said it was not his fault, pet. What did you mean by that, and how would you know?"

Her color still high from her outburst, Brianna looked at the vampire. She made the mistake of looking him in the eye and instantly fell to his power. Automatically, she stilled, and her expression went slack.

"He talks in his sleep," she answered, her own voice sounding sleepy. "Often, I have heard him argue with someone he calls Old Man or Zeke. He wants to tell you some secret that weighs heavily on him but finds he is forbidden."

"I see. Thank you, *ma'm'selle*." He released her from his thrall. If Jim had not been holding her, she would have fallen.

It didn't take her long to recover. Once again, she struggled to get loose. This time, Jim let her. Immediately, she ran to Grimm and clung to him, her face buried in his chest.

His tender, wonder-filled smile spoke volumes to his shipmates. Gently, he stroked her hair and whispered, "Thank you for my life."

She looked up at him, and he leaned down to kiss her forehead. In response, she scowled up at him.

"What kind of a thank you was that? You will thank me properly, Mr. Grimm," she growled then pulled him down into a passionate kiss.

With a wry smile, Vik declared, "I believe the lady has earned her prize. Jim, Belle, let's give them a little privacy."

"It's my cabin," the siren protested.

He glanced at her and saw she was still nude and covered in dry, crusty blood. "You can clean up in my cabin, pet. Come."

Without a further word, he turned and left the cabin. They followed obediently, closing the door on Grimm and Brianna.

By the following evening, Jon-Jon and his boat crew returned to the *Incubus*. Nahila lay in the boat hobbled and hog-tied. They had also gagged her.

"Problems?" Vik asked as they hauled her aboard.

"Bitch wouldn't shut up," Jon-Jon told him. "She also tried to tip the boat three times."

"Ah."

Zach added, "Had trouble with snakes, too. We had to beat them away from the sides most of the trip back after you left."

"Interesting. I wonder if that was La Forte's doing or if she shares some of her father's power," Vik mused. "Anvil!"

"Aye, Cap'n?" the dark giant of a smith replied.

"Fetch our guest from the hold and keep that hood on him."

"Aye."

Before long, a bound and hooded La Forte was brought topside. Viktor ordered Nahila ungagged but didn't have her untied. She tried to talk, but her effort turned into a violent coughing fit.

"Give her something to drink," Vik ordered.

Jon-Jon gave her a swallow from his flask. This resulted in more coughing. Viktor pinched the bridge of his nose.

"Perhaps I should have been more specific. Give her some water. Mr. Grimm informed me we took on several barrels here," he amended.

"Water?" Jon-Jon made a face but brought a dipper of the liquid to the choking prisoner.

Finally, her coughing subsided. "Thank you," she rasped to the burly second mate. Then she glared at the captain. "You broke faith with me! I demand you release me at once!"

Viktor gave her a look of mock offense. "I beg to differ. You broke faith with me. You were, after all, leading me to an ambush."

"But you turned around!" she protested. "You went into no ambush. You came back to your ship! You didn't let me finish leading you to my father. If you didn't let me finish, how can you say I broke faith?"

He gave a harsh bark of laughter. "How can you say you were leading me to your father, when I found him trying to steal my ship?"

"What?" She hadn't known her father had already made a move on the pirate ship. Would he have truly abandoned her?

"Anvil."

The ship's smith brought the prisoner forward to where Nahila could see him. At a silent command from the vampire, he pulled the hood off La Forte's hood and forced the man's gaze toward his daughter. After a moment, he shrouded him again, not giving him the opportunity to use his transport spell.

"Father! Help me!" she cried.

"Why should I help you? You betrayed me!" La Forte's snarled, his voice muffled by the hood.

"No! I did not! I was leading him upriver like you wanted me to."

"You helped him!" he shouted back. "How else would the siren be able to escape my thrall? You had to have helped him block me from her."

"What siren? What are you talking about?"

La Forte turned a deaf ear to her. Instead, he called out to his captor. "Captain Brandewyne, do with that faithless child as you will. I disown her. What I want to know is what ransom you demand for me."

"What gave you the idea I planned to ransom you?" Viktor laughed, mildly amused.

"You have neither released me nor killed me. Why else keep me prisoner if not for a ransom?"

"Sound enough reasoning. There is something I want from you, but do not consider it a ransom."

"What?" His voice sounded cautiously eager.

"Some years ago, you borrowed an amulet from an old witch in the jungles along the Spanish main. She wants it back," Viktor told him.

Chapter 29

La Forte managed to make his voice sound incredulous, even though Viktor knew the siren already gave him this information when he ensorcelled her. "You mean you sailed all the way to this coast based on the lies of some old hag?" He laughed. "There is no amulet. You are free to search me if you don't believe me."

Viktor smiled, and it wasn't a friendly smile, regardless of the fact that the man could not see it. "Oh, do not doubt I will do so. In fact, I'm going to search both of you. Venoma Noir is not the first Sister of Power I've dealt with, Captain La Forte. They may misdirect or make deliberate omissions, but they do not tell outright lies, at least not without detection."

At a nod from the captain, a handful of pirates set about stripping the two prisoners. The men went through the garments methodically. The results were just as La Forte had predicted. No amulet was found.

Frowning, Viktor summoned Belladonna. To say she came unwillingly would have been an understatement. She didn't want to be anywhere near La Forte. That the slaver seemed to sense her presence didn't help.

"I know you're there, siren," he said through the hood. "You can't hide from me. You will do my bidding."

"The hell she will." Viktor walloped La Forte on the back of the head and knocked him out. He sensed her distress at the slaver's words. He also didn't share, and Belle was his.

With La Forte unconscious, the power he had exuded dropped off markedly. Belladonna breathed a sigh of relief.

"Thank you. He is really annoying," she said. "Now, what did you need?"

He hooked a thumb at the prisoners and said, "I was hoping you could pinpoint Venoma's amulet. He claimed she lied about its existence. We couldn't find the thing on either one of them."

"I'm glad you knocked him out," she replied. "I don't think I could do this if he was conscious."

She held her hands toward the prisoners, palms flat and fingers splayed. She half-closed her eyes in concentration. For a moment, she moved closer to Nahila; she frowned and stepped back. She looked over to Viktor and said, "She holds some of the power, but she does not possess the amulet nor, it would seem, the ability to wield the power. It's more like she is a vessel and an amplifier."

"Amplifier, like a witch's familiar?" he asked.

"Similar." She wobbled her hand. "I would take her with us. I have not had a vision to confirm it, but I believe she is a crucial piece in your quest. However," she cautioned, "you should keep her as far away from him as possible, or he could use her to cause trouble."

"Noted. Continue, please."

The "please" earned him a faint smile from the siren, as she turned her attention back to the unconscious man. After a while, she cocked her head to the side. She looked confused then her eyes grew wide.

"What?" Viktor could tell she was shocked.

She backed away and said, "For all intents and purposes, he *is* the amulet. He must have ingested it or something, but the power courses through his body. Do not feed on him. His blood is toxic, and Venoma would view it as an attempt to steal her power.”

“Joy,” Vik grumbled. “I can see this is going to make for a pleasant voyage. Mr. Jon!”

“Aye, Cap’n.”

“Find a place for Mr. La Forte in one of the forward holds,” he ordered. Turning to Belladonna, he added, “Gather your things and bring them to my cabin, pet. You’ll be safe from that bastard only around Mr. Grimm or me. I seriously doubt Miss Belmont would appreciate you bunking with them.”

“Probably not.” She smirked. “You trust me to share your bed?”

“No, but the alternative is far more dangerous.”

A few days later aboard the *Black Scorpion*, the captain’s cabin boy ran to find the first mate. The lad was in a cold sweat of panic.

Following him back to the captain’s cabin, the man saw why.

Spiders. Everywhere.

The room teemed with the creatures. Cobwebs stretched from floor to ceiling and wall to wall. The eerie thing was the message woven into the strands of spider silk.

Prisoner aboard Incubus. Making for Spanish Main. Come.

Sharing a cabin proved a difficult adjustment for the vampire and the siren. Both soon began to feel like prisoners.

Belladonna couldn’t hunt during the voyage. She didn’t dare get that far away from the influence of the Elder’s Stone. Only old

Zeke's power protected her from the portion of Venoma's power that La Forte carried.

Since she couldn't hunt, it meant she needed more sleep, and that Viktor was going to have to give up some of his men to keep her fed. Maintaining a human form took energy.

The loss of crewmen was an obvious drawback. Not so obvious was that either Viktor or Grimm had to stay with her while she slept. It proved a major inconvenience to both men.

Viktor didn't sleep. Staying with a sleeping siren kept him from other activities. For Grimm, who did require sleep, it was extremely awkward, given his mistrust of the siren and the fact he now had a "pirate's bride." Brianna would have been a harpy to Viktor over the situation if Grimm hadn't made her understand how dangerous that would have been.

About halfway through the crossing, things came to a head between Vik and Belle. She wanted to feed, and he was unwilling to give her a victim so soon after the last one. He believed she'd eat her way through the entire crew if he let her. He

also worried that La Forte was still influencing her.

"Dammit Viktor, I'm hungry!"

"Bilge! I've seen you go for over a week without feeding, and that was on a diet of sharks," he countered. "I know for a fact you get more from feeding on humans. You just had a couple of the prisoners yesterday.

"But I'm hungry!" Her voice took on a whiney tone. It only served to irritate him more.

"I said no!" His tone brooked no argument.

She snarled at him, her true needle-teeth showing. "I am going to feed, Viktor. You can't stop me." She started toward the door.

He blocked her. "I don't think so, pet."

She levelled a deadly gaze at him. "Feed me or get out of my way."

"No. La Forte's magic is influencing you; I believe. You can't be that hungry."

Rather than reply, she used her siren's strength to try to shove him aside. If she'd had better leverage, she would have succeeded. Viktor grabbed her by both arms and tossed her back across the cabin. Colliding with the table, she caught herself and got her feet back under her.

A quick cut of her eyes gave him the only warning. It took all of his speed to cut her off before she could dive through the window.

She growled in frustration and swung on him, landing a good solid blow that knocked the wind out of him. Still struggling to catch his breath, he managed to trip her up as she made for the door again.

He grabbed her ankle and yanked her back down when she tried to get up. He found he had to crawl up her body to keep her from escaping. She managed to wriggle around to face him as he pinned her beneath his weight.

The sensations of it gave him an idea, but he knew he'd have to act fast. He could see she was preparing to cut loose with a scream. Her screams could destroy the minds of any humans within hearing range.

Viktor did the one thing he knew would silence it. He kissed her.

Belladonna's scream died in her throat. Her madness died with it. She'd been prepared for him to strike her. Instead, the tenderness and passion of his kiss completely disarmed her with its unexpectedness.

Sensing her calm return, he pulled back enough to see her face. "There are other ways for you to feed, pet," he said with his most sultry smile.

The heat in her smile grew to match his as she realized what he meant.

Grimm worried for a while about the sounds coming from the captain's cabin. He heard the shouting and the thump of something being thrown or perhaps broken.

When everything grew quiet, his concern intensified a notch or two. Then entirely different sounds started to drift through the door.

A wry smile crossed his face, and he chuckled to himself as he returned to his own cabin.

"It's about damn time."

The next day, Grimm noticed that the ship seemed to be slowing. He found the phenomenon puzzling. The sails billowed, full and straining against the spars and lines. Yet, he could swear the ship was losing momentum.

The timbers creaked with the strain the wind put on the sails, but no one could see what slowed them down. At first, he thought they'd run into a flotilla of sea grass, but no vegetation could be seen over the side.

Instead, the water seemed to have a milky gelatinous appearance. It also looked like it pulsated in a disturbingly nauseating manner.

It took the first mate a while to realize they were stuck in the largest swarm of jellyfish he'd ever seen.

Belladonna woke first. Stretching, she was momentarily startled by the heavy warm body wrapped around hers. Then, she remembered.

She smiled and turned to look at Viktor as he slept. The significance of that fact was not lost on her. Since he'd become a vampire, Viktor had not slept nor had any need for sleep.

She had to suppress a giggle when he snored lightly. She noticed that he looked about ten years younger when he was asleep.

Gently, she brushed a strand of hair away from his face. In a heartbeat, he was awake and grasping her wrist, his eyes alight with emerald fire.

"Sexual vampire," she stated simply.

"I thought you already knew that, pet."

"No." She laughed. "I promised I would tell you what incubus meant when you gave me what I wanted."

"Oh."

"I didn't know you snored." She smiled mischievously.

He lowered both eyebrows and released her wrist. "Did Hezekiah tell you that?"

"No." she shook her head, and her smile widened to a grin. "You were snoring right before I woke you up."

"Woke me up? I don't sleep anymore."

"Oh, you were asleep. You looked almost innocent. You were even drooling just a little bit," she teased.

He raised his hand to his face and was astonished to find some moisture in his beard. "I really was asleep?"

"M-hm." She nodded. "Don't worry; I won't tell anyone." When she saw the look of relief on his face, she continued, "There's something else you might be interested to know."

His eyes grew guarded. "What?"

"Don't worry." She laughed again to his consternation. "This is a good thing. It seems you've been wearing the Elder's stone so long that you've absorbed some of its power. Now, you've passed a portion of that power on to me."

"And why, pray tell, is this considered good?"

All teasing left her face. She told him, "You were correct. I was being influenced by La Forte's magic, probably because of the proximity of his daughter. I doubt she's even aware he's using her in this instance. I can still sense his magic, but I am now insulated against it."

"So, you no longer require my constant presence to protect you?"

"I do not." She carefully kept her tone neutral, unsure of how he would react to this revelation.

He sighed. "Well, that's good. I know you hated being cooped up."

"Yes. Cooped up." She wouldn't meet his gaze. She felt awkward, a sensation she was unfamiliar with.

It was obvious that he felt the same way. Both of them had chafed from the forced proximity, but now that it was no longer necessary, neither seemed willing to end it right away.

Lazarus's appearance on the shelf above the bed interrupted the moment. He let out a clarion call just a moment before a knock came at the door.

Chapter 30

Scent told them it was Grimm. Knowing his first mate would not interrupt without a damn good reason, Viktor untangled himself from the siren.

"What now?" he growled. "Enter!"

Obediently, Grimm entered the cabin and closed the door behind him. He ignored the occupants' state of undress. "We've got problems."

"Obviously," Vik stated, pulling on a pair of pants, "else you wouldn't be in here right now. What is it?"

"The ship is stuck and unable to maneuver, and a ship has just topped the horizon aft of us. I could just make out the name through the glass. It's the *Black Scorpion*," he reported.

Belladonna held no inclination to get dressed. The first part of the report puzzled her. "Stuck, not run aground, but stuck? What do you mean?"

"Stuck. We're in a swarm of jellies so thick we can't move. Had to have the lads furl and reef the sails. Wind was so strong it threatened to snap the spars," he replied.

Viktor and Belle reached the same conclusion at the same time.

"La Forte."

"That explains why I can still sense his magic," Belle said. "I could tell it wasn't directed at me anymore, but I didn't know what he was up to."

"Can you fix this?" Viktor asked.

"Oh, yes. I just need to know if you want to outrun our pursuer or face her in battle."

"I think we should deal with the *Scorpion*. La Forte owes me replacements for the prisoners and crew you've eaten. Put some clothes on before you come on deck."

He finished dressing, while the siren went to the chest that held her clothes. Once he made sure his favorite weapons were in place, he headed for the door. "Mr. Grimm, with me."

"Don't I need to stay with her?" Grimm asked in confusion.

"There was a slight power shift last night. Our Belladonna no longer has any reason to fear Quentin La forte. That," he paused for emphasis, "does not leave this cabin."

"Understood."

By the time they reached the bridge, the *Black Scorpion* was just out of range of the *Incubus'* guns. Viktor doubted their pursuer could match their range, and he knew they couldn't match the firepower of his ship. It amazed him that La Forte's crew still entertained the idea of attacking after seeing what they were up against. After all, the *Incubus* started life as the *HMS War God*, the ultimate pirate hunter — until she encountered Belladonna on her maiden voyage. The ship survived that incident without a scratch. The original crew was never seen again.

"Lazarus, come forth."

Black Venom

At the command, the demon cat materialized. Viktor smiled grimly. "Go take a look at our opponent, old friend."

The cat's form grew amorphous and rematerialized as a raven. With a harsh caw, he launched from the railing, headed for the *Scorpion*.

While Lazarus scouted the enemy ship, Grimm ordered the riggers aloft to await his signal to unfurl the sails.

Belladonna emerged on deck and scaled the main mast with inhuman speed. Once she reached the crows' nest, which the lookout vacated for one of the spars, she started to sing. As she wove her weather spell, the wind gradually died down, slowing the pursuing ship, and giving the crew of the *Incubus* more time to prepare.

She changed a few notes and the sea currents swirled around the ship. She had to grasp the edge of the crows' nest to steady herself as La Forte's spell clashed with hers. The melodic changes came quicker as she fought to maintain control.

With one final, dissonant chord Belladonna collapsed, falling from her high perch. Viktor flew up and caught her just before she would have hit one of the spars. She recovered shortly after he landed them safely on deck.

"Did it work?" she managed to ask; her voice raspy from the magical battle.

"Aye, pet," he confirmed. "The current swept the jellies away and turned us to better greet the *Scorpion*."

"Hmm," she hummed a single note, releasing the wind and currents. She passed out.

Viktor sensed through their bond that she merely experienced exhaustion which posed no real danger to her. He kissed her forehead gently. "Rest, pet. You shall feed well tonight," he said. "Mr. Jon, take her to my cabin and report back on deck."

"Aye, Cap'n," the second mate replied and took the unconscious siren from his arms.

Viktor turned and bellowed to the crew, "I want as many taken alive as possible!" He then returned to the bridge.

"What tactic do you want to use, Captain?" Grimm asked.

"Have the lads ready the buffers and the harpoons. We'll pull the bitch to us."

"Haven't used that one in a while." Grimm grinned. "Might I also suggest having someone render the girl and the father unconscious?"

Vik nodded. "That would keep the bastard from being a nuisance. Do it but be careful not to spill blood or accidentally kill either of them."

"Aye." Grimm left to take care of it. He sent Dr. Coffin to give Nahila a dose of laudanum, while he took a cudgel, and went to pay La Forte a visit.

The battle proved surprisingly short. By the time the counterweights attached to the harpoon lines pulled the *Black Scorpion* to the *Incubus*, over half the slaver's crew desperately wanted to surrender. The rest were either dead or had jumped overboard.

With La Forte unconscious and Nahila drugged, the man's control over the host of venomous spiders aboard had been shattered. Once they had the survivors aboard and disarmed, Viktor ordered his men to cut the *Scorpion* free and set it afire. He then set a special detail with torches to make sure no unwanted passengers made it aboard. Only as an afterthought, Viktor asked if they'd had any live cargo. The prisoners assured him they left without taking any slaves on.

It wasn't so much that the vampire cared; he just hated the thought of having to waste blood stock.

True to his word, he made sure Belladonna fed well that night.

The next day, she was back to her old self. Noticing Viktor's gaze following her, she walked over to him, smiled, and said, "You know the other night doesn't change anything. I was just using you to control my magic."

"Oh, of course, pet." His smile matched hers. "I hadn't had a woman in a while, and you fulfilled the need."

"Just as long as we know where we stand."

"We do."

Venoma felt a tug on her web of power. She stilled her mind and quieted her pets; she then concentrated and "listened."

She felt it again, and it was familiar. Sending out a wispy strand of magic, she touched the source of the disturbance. Once again, she "listened."

She detected four distinct flavors of magic: the siren and the vampire, both of which seemed to be mingled with that of the Elder's Stone; and her amulet sang out to her. That had been what had initially caught her attention.

All of them sat just at the edge of her perception, but the missing portion of her power had flared, grown quiet long enough for her to wonder if she'd really sensed it at all, then flared again a bit weaker than before.

She could only come to one conclusion to explain this new turn. Viktor Brandewyne had not only found the amulet, he was trying to use it.

"How dare him?" she snarled to herself. "I have not given him any of my power. He has no right to try to wield it. Very well, you presumptuous upstart who dares pretend to be the One; I shall prepare a reception for you the likes of which you have never encountered before."

She summoned her creatures and was soon engulfed in a living cocoon of snakes, frogs, spiders, and various other poisonous creatures. The deadly living ball then began to undulate through the jungle headed toward the shore.

An estimated three days from their destination, Dr. Coffin knocked at Grimm's cabin door. "A word with you in private, Mr. Grimm?" he asked.

"Of course." Grimm nodded when he saw the look of worry on the doctor's face. He stepped out of the cabin, shut the door, and asked, "What is it, Matthew?"

"It's the girl, Nahila. I can't keep dosing her with laudanum. It could easily kill her at this point," he explained. "Besides which, I'm almost out. We'll need to find an apothecary to restock from."

"You do keep it locked away when not administering it."

"Aye, sir. I always check how much is there before I put it away and make sure it matches when needed again. I've seen how easily some men can come to crave it without a true medical need for it," Coffin assured him. "I keep the location of where I store it secret, as well."

"That is wise, doctor. Very well, I'll inform the Captain," Grimm said. "We'll just have to let her wake up. It shouldn't be much longer until we make shore, anyway."

La Forte grew aware of the moment his daughter came out of her opium-induced coma. The range of his power surged. Since the drugging of Nahila and the shielding of the siren from him, his magic still felt weak. He could not sense any viable sea life for him to use, either. Apparently, the siren had used her magic to drive off any poisonous sea creatures. It left him with very little to draw from.

Then he felt *her*, Venoma Noir, and she was angry.

His first instinct was to panic, but he fought that down. He knew they were on the fringes of her web. Struggling would draw more of her attention, and he knew she could strike with her power from afar.

However, he couldn't just meekly let this pirate take him back to her. The spider always devoured her mate afterward, unless he proved fast enough and lucky enough to elude her. Quentin La Forte had been that lucky, once, but that luck threatened to run out soon. He desperately needed to build his power back up.

Reaching out to Nahila first, he gently spread the tendrils of his magic. His daughter helped amplify it, but he had to be careful. He didn't want the siren to sense the activity until he found some weak spot in her defenses which would let him in.

Unable to find an opening after a day of searching, he realized he had no choice but to make an all-out assault. He could not let them take him back to Venoma.

Belladonna felt the attack immediately. It didn't take her off guard, however. She felt the magical probing since it started. La Forte wasn't nearly as clever as he fancied himself to be. She had allowed him to think she was unaware.

The siren felt gratitude for the newfound protection Viktor had given her. That small portion of the Elder's Stone's power gave her the ability to resist the magical influence of all the Sisters, even though Venoma and Gloribeau were the only ones they encountered so far who posed a problem to her.

Belle felt no need to challenge Gloribeau; but defending herself against Venoma was vital not only to her freedom but to Viktor's quest. She knew the old witch didn't want to control the One. She wanted him dead.

Well-fed from the taking of La Forte's ship, Belle's power was near its peak. Smiling maliciously, she sent a spike of magic back at the slaver, metaphysically slapping him down. She was not about to feed his power.

As she prepared her deadly reception, Venoma sensed the clash of power. She mistook it for a clash between the siren and Viktor, thinking he was using or trying to use her amulet. That the siren's power seemed stronger amused her.

"Ha! You fool!" She laughed. "Now you begin to learn what happens when you try to use magic that doesn't belong to you."

Chapter 31

The ship lay at anchor. As the selected boat crew made preparations, Belle pulled Viktor aside.

"What is it, pet? You should be getting ready."

"Oh, my trousseau and bearers have been ready for hours." She snorted sarcastically. "In all seriousness, though, there is something I need to do before we leave."

"What?"

"I am going to sing up a spell of protection around the ship. She knows we're here, and she's going to make this delivery as difficult as possible; especially since we made such good time. I fully expect her to launch an attack against the ship as soon as the protection offered by the Elder's Stone is away from it."

"I could have Mr. Grimm stay with the ship," he said.

Belladonna shook her head. "I have a feeling you're going to need him with you. Besides, it's better if she doesn't know he carries some of Zeke's power. The taste of it that I got from you will be sufficient to reinforce my spell. The way it works, only I can open a portal through it, however. None of her creatures will be able to breach it, but anyone still aboard will be trapped here until I lift it."

He thought about it for a moment then said, "Do it."

Venoma watched from the shore as a lone boat left the pirate vessel. She bided her time until it was halfway to shore to launch her attack. She knew she couldn't target Brandewyne directly. He enjoyed protection from her power; but his ship was a different story.

She shrieked in frustration when the swarm she'd sent at the *Incubus* seemed to bounce off some invisible barrier. Worse, unlike the bubble of protection the pirate used before their first encounter, which would have turned into a death trap, powerful winds scattered her swarm. That detail smacked of the siren's magic.

This confused her. She had clearly felt the siren's victory over the weak use of her amulet. Why would the sea witch aid the pirate now? Unless—, perhaps she merely protected her food supply? She sensed that the spell kept things in just as well as keeping them out.

Finally, the boat reached the shore. The passengers got out and pulled it up on the beach. Brandewyne, the siren, a handful of pirates, and two prisoners strode toward the old witch.

Venoma paid little attention to the female prisoner; but when she recognized Quentin La Forte as the other, she grew livid. Her horde of venomous creatures writhed about her, unable to breach the protection afforded to Viktor's party.

"This was not our agreement! You have failed." She spat at Viktor. "I told you to bring me the amulet not the thief!"

"I have brought you your amulet," he replied calmly.

"Then show it to me."

He shoved the bound slaver toward her. She glared at Viktor and growled, "Perhaps you didn't hear me before. You were supposed to kill him and retrieve the amulet."

"I heard you perfectly. Quentin La Forte *is* the amulet. If there ever was a physical amulet, he has absorbed it into his body. If I had spilled his blood, some of the magic might have been lost."

She walked toward the prisoner, who tried to flinch away from her. She sniffed the air around him and said, "You speak truth, Viktor Brandewyne. He has become the amulet. Why is he blindfolded?"

"To prevent his escape," Belladonna spoke up. "He uses a transport spell in tandem with the amulet's power which can instantly move him from his present spot to as far away as he can see."

"Interesting; I wonder, Quentin, was that how you escaped my web the first time?"

"Yes." He kept his voice to a mere whisper.

Venoma circled him for a few minutes to study the situation. Even though blindfolded, he flinched every time she got close. Her expression gave nothing of her thoughts away.

Finally, she stopped in front of him. She kept her gaze on La Forte but spoke to Viktor. "As long as he is alive, my amulet's power cannot be returned to me. Until it is, I cannot give you what you seek."

"That's remedied easily enough." Viktor began to reach for the dagger he kept sheathed at the nape of his neck.

She held up a hand to stop him. "Not so fast, Viktor Brandewyne; this power must be won, not taken. You will remove his blindfold, and then the two of you shall fight to the death.

"If I remove his blindfold, he will use his transport spell to escape."

She gave him an evil smile. A ripple of magic resonated through the jungle. In minutes, spiders wove a dense, opaque web around a clearing just past the beach. The area soon was completely enclosed save for a few small openings at the top to allow light in and a tunnel-like entrance.

"There will be no escape from my arena until one of you lies dead. Before your duel begins, however, here are some rules and stipulations I will place on you both," she said. "You cannot take the Elder's Stone in with you. Its power would collapse the webs prematurely and give you unfair protection."

"Very well," Viktor agreed. He took the milky crystal and its silver chain off and handed it to Grimm. This took Venoma by surprise.

"You trust this man with such power?"

"I trust Mr. Grimm with my life."

Belladonna and Grimm exchanged a look at that statement. Ever since he'd learned of the secret Grimm had kept from him, there had been tension between the captain and the first mate. This was the first sign that Viktor might be forgiving about the whole situation. Forgiveness was usually an alien characteristic to the vampire.

Unaware of the full importance of Viktor's words, Venoma Noir continued, "If either of you try to cut your way out, the duel is forfeit. You, Captain Brandewyne, will be free to go your way, having failed in your quest to gain my magical aid. You, Quentin La Forte, will end your days with me. Your limbs will be amputated, and your eyes gouged out to prevent any escape attempts. I will leave your manhood intact, of course. I may have some use for it, after all."

"Will you be coming in to watch?" Viktor asked.

"That will not be necessary. When the battle is over, and one lies dead, the web will dissolve. If you still stand, I will reclaim my stolen magic from my former lover's body, then grant you the portion you seek."

La Forte spoke up. "If I defeat Brandee, will I gain my freedom?"

She laughed. "You would think so, but no. There is always a price for power, thief; whether you earn it, buy it, or steal it. Regardless of the outcome of this battle, the time for you to pay for what you stole has come, and that price is high. You will remain here with me until your dying day."

"So, you want to teach the slave trader what it is like to be a slave." He smirked. "You forget, witch, that I started my life as a slave. Just go ahead and kill me now."

"No. You know the rules of magic are capricious, Quentin." She shook her head. "I cannot kill you. To do so would make the power you stole forever lost to me. You must die by the hand of another or by natural cause, and I must be present to reclaim what is mine. That is why I cannot allow you to leave."

"Then I will just let Brandee kill me and be done with it."

"You will not!" she snarled. She walked up to him and placed a hand on his shoulder, holding it there for a while. He screamed in agony. "You will fight for your life. I will it so."

La Forte growled at her but had no choice except to submit. Her power was stronger.

"Yes mistress," he hissed between clenched teeth. He sweated from the struggle to fight her will.

"Mr. Grimm, cut his bonds and give him your blade," Viktor said. "He'll need to be able to defend himself."

"Aye, Captain." Grimm guided La Forte to the entrance of the webbed arena, cut the wrist ropes and hobbles loose, and handed the prisoner his sword.

Quicker than expected, La Forte whirled around with the blindfold still in place. If Grimm hadn't been nearly as fast as Viktor, he would have received a crippling if not fatal wound.

Viktor's sword was there like a thought before La Forte could get another swing in. The slaver reached up to remove the blindfold. Before he could get it off, however, Viktor grabbed him by the arm and half-flew, half-dragged him into the web arena with him.

Within seconds, spiders closed the entrance to the arena. It only took a few minutes for the new section of webbing to reach the same thickness and opacity as the rest of the arena.

All anyone left outside could do was to wait for the outcome.

Chapter 32

Once they were both inside the silken chamber, Viktor distanced himself from La Forte and gave the man a chance to finish removing his blindfold.

"Your quarrel is not with my first mate. I protect what is mine."

"You bastard!" La Forte spat. "That was my one chance at escape! I'd rather be castrated than be trapped with that bitch for the rest of my life."

Viktor smiled at him. "Well then, I'll just have to make sure you don't live that long." Without further warning, he launched his attack.

La Forte was not so easily defeated, however. He transported to stand behind his foe before the pirate's blade could strike. He then began to bring his borrowed blade down.

Viktor anticipated this move. He'd seen the slaver's eyes glance past him a split second before the transportation. He brought his blade up to parry. Eyes and fangs flashing, he grinned. "Oh good; I was hoping you'd make this interesting. It is so hard to find a good challenge these days."

From there, the battle raged on in earnest. La Forte proved to be an impressively skilled swordsman. All magic aside, they were almost evenly matched in form and strategy.

After a while, Viktor noticed an odd feature of the chamber. The entrance was no longer detectable, and it seemed as if they had less space to battle in.

"The room is getting smaller," La Forte commented.

"Oh, you noticed that, too?" Viktor asked between the clatter and clang of their swords. "I imagine the bitch is giving us a time limit in which to kill one another or trying to force us to cut our way out. Nothing is ever easy with a Sister of Power, even if they like you." He ducked a blow. "If you or I cut our way out, or if you kill me, I lose. I have to kill you to get what I need from her; and you want to die rather than accept the fate she has in store for you."

"I am doomed either way; and she made sure I couldn't just surrender." La Forte grunted as he blocked a jab at his gut. "If these walls keep closing in, we'll both be encased and only Venoma will win."

Belladonna frowned and moved closer to Grimm. Something wasn't right. The Sister's power flared high. Belle felt safer being closer to the first mate, since he held the Elder's stone as well as carried a portion of old Zeke's power.

"Hezekiah," she whispered, "I suspect treachery on Venoma's part. Her power is surging."

"What say we even the playing field, lass?" he murmured back. He moved to stand just behind the witch.

Venoma frowned, puzzled for a moment, not immediately sensing the presence behind her. When she did, she whirled angrily on the pirate. "What do you think you are doing?"

Grimm's smile matched his name. "Keeping you from meddling," he replied. "The battle is between them."

Both combatants became aware of the moment Venoma's interference stopped. La Forte took advantage of the distraction to summon some of the witch's creatures to attack his foe. Scorpions and spiders swarmed Viktor's legs to the knees.

The venom of the stings and bites had no effect on the vampire, but the placement of them caused reflexive muscle spasms. It threw him off balance and gave La Forte an opening.

The slaver swung his blade down in what he meant to be a killing stroke. If Viktor had still been human, it would have been. The borrowed sword bit deep into his shoulder close to his neck. Blood gushed from the wound as bone, tendons, muscles, and arteries were severed.

Viktor's head lolled to the side, no longer supported by that shoulder. The arm hung limp, and his hand dropped his sword. His torn shirt was soaked in blood. Yet, he still lived.

La Forte raised the blade again to finish the job. He aimed for the other shoulder and, hopefully, decapitation.

Acting on instinct, Viktor grabbed his sword with his good hand. With vampiric speed, he thrust upward into La Forte's belly at an angle. He gave the blade a twist and savaged the man's heart and lungs.

Blood bubbled from La Forte's mouth. The light faded from his eyes, and he collapsed on top of his opponent, dead.

Belle staggered and stumbled to her hands and knees when she felt La Forte's last blow to Viktor. The vampire drew sharply on her life force to contain the damage. She didn't know what the damage was, but she knew it had to be bad for him to use their link in such a manner.

"Viktor!" she cried out before she could stop herself.

Venoma grinned in victory. The siren's distress could only mean La Forte had been victorious. She could not sense the duel's outcome one way or the other with the Elder's Stone blocking her magic.

Spiders scattered away from the web chamber, retreating to the forest, their task complete. Slowly, the web began to fray and break down, seeming to dissolve.

The witch's grin grew wider. Two bodies lay on the ground, both soaked in blood. The wound in Viktor's shoulder had yet to heal, but it no longer bled. The tip of his blade protruded from La Forte's back, plainly visible.

Venoma's cackle was interrupted by a growl from the siren.

"If Viktor is dead, consequences be damned, I'll have your head!"

"Ha! You would have to answer to the Elder for such a disruption of the balance of power," Venoma scoffed.

Belladonna stood and gave her a deadly smile. "If you think that frightens me, you are sorely mistaken. Zeke is not my master." She turned and started toward the fallen men. The scent of fresh blood and meat and the drain Viktor had put on her raised her hunger.

Black Venom

Before she could reach them, Nahila rushed past her. The young woman had not been hobbled; she had still been lethargic from spending days drugged with laudanum.

"Father!" she screamed, pulling at La Forte's body. "No!"

As Nahila held the corpse of her father, Belladonna pulled Viktor from under him, taking care not to get debris in the slowly healing wound. She carefully lined up tissue, bone and tendons. The wound needed to heal correctly. At the sacrifice of the control of some of her glamour, she concentrated on speeding the healing.

Seeing the siren show her amber eyes and needle teeth, Venoma said, "You are wasting your magic sea witch. He cannot survive such a wound."

Not even looking up, she replied, "I've seen him pull out a sword that was piercing his heart and bitch about it ruining his shirt."

Venoma snorted in either disbelief or disinterest and turned to Grimm. "You need to get that thing away from me. Whether your captain lives or dies, I still have to restore my amulet to its true form and reclaim it. If Quentin's blood cools, I will not be able to do so."

Without a word, Grimm nodded and stepped back. Not turning his back on the witch, however, he said, "Jon-Jon, get the girl off La Forte so *Mere* Venoma can do what needs to be done."

"Aye, Mr. Grimm," Jon-Jon answered. He pulled Nahila up as gently as he could. "Easy, lass, easy." He tried to soothe her. She turned and sobbed into his chest as he patted her hair awkwardly.

Venoma stood over La Forte's body. Free from the damping influence of the Elder's stone, she exerted her power and called her stolen magic back to her. The spilled blood flowed into a single pool, even the spatter gathered from where it had sprayed. As the witch chanted, the blood condensed, took on a blackish hue, and tried to solidify. It seemed to be trying to take on a shape, but it remained amorphous. La Forte's body lay as pale as a vampire's kill.

"Thank you, pet." Vik smiled up at Belladonna, his wound fully healed. As he rotated his arm around to make sure everything knitted back to its proper place, he added, "When we return to the ship, we'll both feed. We'll just have to take another prize to replenish our larder."

"You have failed, Viktor Brandewyne," Venoma stated. Surprisingly, she didn't sound that happy about it.

"Failed how? I brought you La Forte, who was in essence your amulet." He stood and faced her.

She indicated the blackened blood that stubbornly remained a shapeless blob and said, "Some of the magic is missing. I don't know how, but he must have lost it somewhere over the years."

Viktor puzzled for a moment; then a thought occurred to him. "Could he have passed some magic on to another, say a lover or a child?"

The look on Venoma's face showed she hadn't considered that. She turned her gaze to the weeping woman.

"What is your name, child?"

Nahila did not answer, continuing to sob. "Her name is Nahila," Jon-Jon answered for her.

"Nahila." Venoma kept her tone gentle, but with power behind it. The young woman turned her tear-streaked face to the witch. "Child, step forward, please."

"Why?"

The slightest hint of irritation flickered in Venoma's eyes, but she quickly masked it. "I may be able to reunite you with your father's spirit. I need to see if you carry a certain gift."

"Are you going to have me killed, too?" Nahila asked fearfully.

"What? No! No, child. You will not be harmed; I swear it."

Trembling, Nahila stepped away from the large pirate and toward the witch. Venoma held her hands out at her, palms toward her, and closed her eyes. After a few moments, she opened her eyes with a wondrous smile and held her arms open to the girl.

"Daughter! Come to me."

"You are not my mother," Nahila stated in confusion and fear.

"In body, no," Venoma confirmed. "You were born of the magic your father stole from me, however. I can bind his spirit to you and give you power to protect yourself from your enemies."

"You can do that?"

"Yes."

Nahila went to the witch. Her eyes still held fear, but they also held hope. Venoma embraced her and led her to stand beside the body of her father. The witch stepped back from them and muttered a few unintelligible words.

Nahila gave a startled yelp when the bloody blob suddenly attached itself to her leg. Quickly, the viscous fluid flowed up her body. She made protesting sounds, and she tried in vain to push it back down. When it sped up her torso and arms, she screamed, until it finally engulfed her completely.

"You swore she wouldn't be harmed." Jon-Jon scowled at the witch.

"She has not been. What you hear is just fear. Physically, she is experiencing no pain."

Before their eyes, the blood-covered woman writhed and seemed to shrink in on herself. In moments, a nearly foot-long, glossy black scorpion scuttled where Nahila once stood.

Venoma smiled. "She was the vessel. Where once I had a tiny amulet that was stolen, I now have a living amulet and familiar. Come to me, child."

Obediently, the scorpion crawled to her hand. Turning, it rested on her forearm. Venoma gazed at Viktor. "Do you have a vessel for what I am honor-bound to grant you?"

He nodded and took off the silver vial and chain and handed it to Jon-Jon.

"Why do you give it to that one to bring to me?"

Belle answered, "Mr. Jon is magically null. He cannot contaminate the exchange."

"A wise move."

Jon-Jon handed her the vial. She opened it and held the mouth of it to the tip of the scorpion's tail. A single drop of venom glistened on the barb for a moment before dropping into the vial to mingle with the other contents. She replaced the cap and hasp pin and held it out for Jon-Jon to take.

The moment he took the vial in his hand, Venoma grasped his wrist. Before anyone could stop it, the scorpion stung him. He screamed as pain washed over him. Almost immediately, the sting site turned black. The blackness rapidly spread to cover his whole hand and began to send deadly lines up his veins.

Viktor caught him just before he fell.

"You have what you came for, Viktor Brandewyne. Take it and be gone. I hope your quest fails. I still do not believe you are the One."

Viktor ignored her. He took the vial from Jon-Jon's hand. He used the chain to make a tourniquet, stopping the poison from spreading any closer to the man's heart. Grimm came over, handed him back the Elder's Stone and helped hold pressure on the tourniquet. He knew that if he let up for even a moment, the second mate would have a swift but agonizing death.

Viktor retrieved his sword from La Forte's body and raised it to amputate the putrid limb.

Grimm saw the black lines retreat from Jon-Jon's hand and cried out, "Vik! Wait! Use your dagger."

"Dagger would take too long and wouldn't cut through the bone," he argued.

"No, I mean use it to cut the sting open enough to force the crystal into it. The Elder's power trumps all of the Sisters, remember," Grimm explained.

"Oh."

Just as he'd expected, the experiment worked. As quickly as it had blackened, Jon-Jon's arm returned to a natural, healthy hue; at least what was visible under the tattoos. When Viktor removed the glowing milky crystal, even the cut he had made sealed itself.

"Get out! Go!" Venoma screamed impotently at them.

Viktor gave her a mock bow. "As you wish; it has been an extreme displeasure." He smiled cordially, which elicited another shriek from the witch.

Just before they reached the boat, the scorpion that had been Nahila stung itself.

"No!" Venoma cried as it dropped from her arm and curled up. It transformed back into the young woman.

Her skin already blackened from the poison. She wore a bitter smile on her lips. "You lied," she gasped out. "You said it didn't hurt. You said you would bond my father's spirit to me. Truly, I am glad the last was a lie. I was foolish in my grief. He was the only family I ever knew, but all he ever did was use me. All you did was use me."

A coughing fit took her. It took a few minutes to pass. When it did, her voice was almost too weak to hear. "You cannot use me anymore. I — am — free."

Venoma shrieked in anger and frustration as the venom reached Nahila's heart. The girl's body contorted in one final convulsion then lay still.

"No, no, no-no-no-no," the witch moaned. "Now that power is forever lost to me."

Viktor and his crewmates pushed their boat off the sand, got in, and started rowing back to the *Incubus*. They almost reached the perimeter of the protection spell, when the vengeful Sister hurled a swarm of bees and wasps at them.

Belladonna stood in the middle of the boat, a crackling of static the only warning before she sang a single note. A gust of wind thrust the swarm back to shore, and a bolt of lightning struck the beach. It instantly fused the sand under Venoma's feet into glass, cooking the soles of her feet into it in the process.

"I'll have to answer to Zeke for that, but it was worth it," she said.

Commodore Critchfield sat brooding in his cabin. The *Quicksilver* had been back in Nassau for two weeks. He gathered numerous stories and complaints about pirate activity since his return, but no word could be found of Viktor Brandewyne or his ship.

He fumed over his errand to Amherst costing him precious time and allowing the trail to grow cold. He hoped the passenger he'd brought back would prove worth the effort. The idea that he'd crossed an ocean to fetch a vampire expert to help him catch a pirate sounded almost insane to him now.

THE END

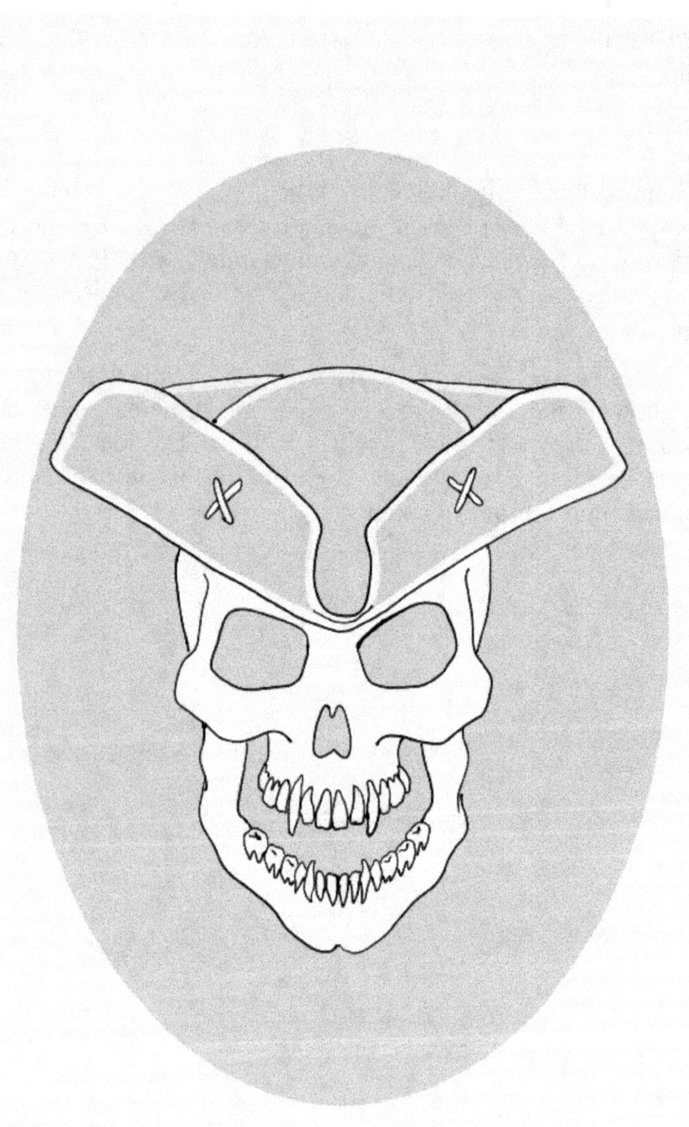

Here Be Spoilers

Blood Curse

After being shipwrecked by a British Navy ship and a killer hurricane, Bloody Vik Brandee and the survivors of his crew make shore in the fishing village of Terra Beau on the north coast of Hispañola. While waiting for a suitable ship to steal, he kills a local boy over a tavern wench, incurring the wrath of Mamaan Juma.

Juma sends her zombies to fetch the pirate. She curses him to become a living vampire. The tavern wench, Carmella, becomes his first victim.

Vik returns to his home port, Savannah, and learns from his foster mother Celie, aka the Thunderbolt Witch, just what has happened to him and how to break the curse before it destroys him. While there, Jim Rigger, his first mate, becomes his second victim. Celie resurrects Jim as a black cat which can take the form of a raven.

Celie sets Vik to find the seven Sisters of Power and sends hum to Hell's Breath Island to Uncle Zeke, an ancient wizard of sorts. Zeke sends the siren/sea witch Belladonna with him to locate the Sisters using her visions.

She pinpoints Madre Dorada on the Isle of Youth. En route, Vik learns an old friend, Hezekiah Grimm aka the Grimm Reaper, has been taken by pirate hunters in Havana. He detours to rescue Grimm despite warnings from Zeke and Belladonna not to stray from his course.

Manages to find and rescue Grimm but arrives at the Isle of Youth only to find Dorada fled. With the aid of Paella, a local girl, he manages to track the Sister down and brokers a deal with her: one of her golden tears in exchange for an opal pendant called the Mermaid's Tear.

After some misunderstanding of what the Tear actually is, he finds it, helps Dorada regain her magic, and makes the exchange.

Demon Bayou

Viktor tracks the next Sister, Granny Glory, to the bayous north of New Orleans. When he finds her, she sets him to capture the demon Tulimanchulo, who possesses the body of a white alligator. He finds and captures the beast with a magic cast-net but is wounded in the process.

Glory slaughters the demon gator, collects its blood in a cauldron, and has Viktor remove all its teeth. She throws them in the blood and pulls them out as a necklace. Viktor must take it to Zeke. She warns him not to wear it at any time. She then has him toss her into the boiling blood. The hag emerges as a beautiful woman.

On Hell's Breath, Zeke burns the alligator teeth, releasing the demon's spirit. He fishes out a coal from his fire and puts it in a conch shell for Vik to return it to Glory with instructions no one else is to touch it and not to let it extinguish.

Vik returns to New Orleans and discovers a storm has altered the paths through the bayous.

While waiting for a guide back to Glory, he encounters true vampires for the first time. He ends up tangled in the local vampire politics because of attacks on two of his favorite brothels, one by agents of the Church, and the other by vampires curious about him.

Black Venom

To get out of this predicament, he must kidnap the daughter of the Lord Mayor and make her vampire. This gives Jeorge, king of the local vampires, a means to spy on him.

On his final return to Glory, Belladonna begins to grow weak as the Sister's black water magic wars with the siren's salt water magic. She falls unconscious into the swamp but does not change into her true form. Vik must remove the coal and place it in his mouth to protect it before he can dive in after Belladonna. He knows she'll drown if she remains in human form. When he surfaces with her, the boat with his other companions is no longer in the area. He climbs out onto a hammock of land and Glory appears to him. He passes the coal to her via a kiss, returning the powers the demon stole from her ages earlier. She adds her spit to the golden tear of Dorada in the silver vial Vik carries for that purpose.

He returns Belladonna to the sea and sacrifices several of his crew to her appetite to restore her. He then abducts a couple of unwary sailors from port to swap for Grimm and Jon-Jon, rescuing them from Glory's amorous clutches, as he's learned she now has the nature of a succubus.

Silent Fathoms

The search for the third Sister, Tia Rosalia, takes Viktor to Mexico. He lands on the Gulf coast and must travel over the central mountains to the Pacific coast to reach her. She first tries to deceive and enslave him. Her spell manages to control his crewmen traveling with him, but his power proves stronger at the cost of one pirate's life. The Elder's Stone proves to her he is the One, and she gives him the quest of procuring Devil's Hoof, a key ingredient in her spells. She deliberately doesn't tell him where to look or what it actually is.

He follows rumors of a cave in the mountains where the Devil is said to live. Instead, he finds an old brujo (male witch) who was once Rosalia's lover. He tells him Devil's Hoof is an extremely hot pepper said to cause hallucinations with its spiciness. The pirates return to the ship. Navigator Zach Brumble tells Vik about such a pepper his father once dabbled in trading found in the northern part of the Bay of Bengal.

When he tries to contact Belladonna to sing up favorable winds to speed the voyage halfway around the world, he cannot reach her or even sense her presence. Unbeknownst to him, Zeke and Hell's Breath Island have sent her to hunt down the mermaid Alyssa, whom Viktor impregnated while seeking for the Mermaid's Tear. He'd also fed on the creature, and she began to turn while still alive. Belle must kill the mermaid but return the child to the island and Zeke's care. To prevent Viktor's interference, Zeke blocks them from any mental contact until her task is done.

The siren is finally able to rejoin Viktor as the ship is caught in the doldrums near the middle of the Indian Ocean. They make their way to a Bengali village near the Sundarbans, a salt swamp jungle. After warnings from a local elder not to anger the jungle goddess, Bonobibi, or the tiger god, Daskin Rey, they enter the swamps to find the pepper (known locally as the naga pepper). They must also harvest honey to safely transport the peppers in. One of their guides harvests more honey than they need, hoping to profit enough to laze away the wet season. This leads to an encounter with the local deities and the man's death.

With Devil's Hoof acquired, Viktor opts to cross the Pacific directly to Rosalia's home port.

Once back in Mexico, she tries her best to enslave him using fresh ingredients for her spell. He proves his power is stronger than hers, and she begrudgingly agrees to give him the portion of her magic he requires for his quest to break his curse.

Black Venom

After he returns to his ship, Hell's Breath manifests. Zeke introduces him to his son by Alyssa and orders him to get the child off the island. When the island vanishes again, Viktor finds the ship has been transported back to the Caribbean.

About the Author

Tamara A. Lowery, who once considered herself close to becoming a Crazy Cat Lady is now down to three cats. She lives with them and her husband in Tennessee and builds cars to pay the bills when not writing. She's been writing since the early 1980s but only published since 2011.

In addition to the Waves of Darkness series, she is the author of a steampunk episodic serial, The Adventures of Pigg & Woolfe.

She hopes to release a short story collection sometime in the near future, as well.

Website: talowery.wordpress.com

Facebook: facebook.com/Waves.of.Darkness

Instagram: Instagram.com/talowery_author

Plurk: plurk.com/Viksbelle

Smashwords author Page:
smashwords.com/profile/view/Viksbelle

YouTube: youtube.com/user/Viksbelle

Tamara A. Lowery

Waves of Darkness

Sisters of Power arc

Blood Curse

Demon Bayou

Silent Fathoms

Black Venom

Hell's Dodo *November 2023*

The Daedalus Enigma *May 2024*

Maelstrom of Fate *November 2024*

Daughters of the Dragon arc

Hunting the Dragon *May 2025*

The Adventures of Pigg & Woolfe

Season 1

The Girl Who Fell from the Sky (S.1 omnibus)

Episodes

A Chance Encounter

The Truce

In the Woolfe's Den

Chase the Lightning

Black Venom

Peril in the Philippines

Rendezvous in Hong Kong

Double Jeopardy

Chance and Fortune

The Italian Connection

Rescue at Sea

Ghost Riders in the Sky

Castle in the Clouds

Season 2

Turmoil in Tunilia (S.2 Omnibus)

Episodes

Airborne Alliance

Under the Mountain

Reversal of Fortune

Frustrations

Going Underground

Evade and Elude

Escape

Sanctuary

Message in a Bottle

Strange Bedfellows

Family Reunion

Berthing Assignments

Season 3 2023

S.3 Omnibus (Title TBD) *Coming January 2024*

Episodes

The Canary Has Flown

Truth and Consequences

Detective Work

Family Secrets

Organizing a Fox Hunt

Divided Forces Part I *June 2023*

Divided Forces Part II *July 2023*

Queen of the Nile *August 2023*

Foiled Again *September 2023*

Doom in Khartoum *October 2023*

Fly Me Away *November 2023*

The Fall of Tunilia *December 2023*

Season 4 *2024*